RUSH TO JUDGMENT

BOOKS BY DAVID CAMPBELL

FLOOD TIMES IN TAWAKANI

THE QUARRY

A FOUL WIND BLOWS

DEAD MAN'S TALE
(First book of The Silent Witness Series)

RUSH TO JUDGMENT

A Silent Witness Mystery

DAVID
CAMPBELL

Archway Publishing books may be ordered through booksellers or by contacting:

Archway Publishing
1663 Liberty Drive
Bloomington, IN 47403
www.archwaypublishing.com
1 (888) 242-5904

ISBN: 978-1-4808-5309-6 (sc)
ISBN: 978-1-4808-5308-9 (e)

Library of Congress Control Number: 2017915743

Print information available on the last page.

Archway Publishing rev. date: 10/18/2017

ACKNOWLEDGMENTS

One of the hardest things an author must control is humility. In this book, I found it very difficult to maintain both my humbleness and anger as I rewrote several large sections of this book after they were stolen by Ransomware. I owe what control I had to my wife, Becky, who did not lose control and assisted me in restoring this work. I believe the rewrite is better than the original. It humbles me to realize that this work of fiction can be restored with tears and effort, while files on my computer which were valuable only to me are gone forever. Thankfully, Becky could temper how I felt toward those violating my privacy and turn that anger into something better.

CHAPTER 1

The deceased was a heavyset man, maybe five eleven, 220 pounds. Conservatively dressed in a deep-blue leisure suit, he appeared to have been dragged or crawled across the floor into the aisle near the cash register. To Reese Barrett, it had always seemed death had a way of diminishing an individual in both size and significance. In brief minutes, the victim had gone from a vibrant, living being to a discarded mass of lifeless flesh.

Homicide Detective Barrett of the Dallas Police Department could draw no definite conclusions as to what might have occurred. Smeared blood trails extended out behind the body, radiating like a fan from his elbows and knees. From the amount of blood the victim had lost, Barrett calculated death had not visited the victim quickly, possibly occurring over several agonizing minutes as he slowly bled out.

A quick survey of the store indicated only one shot had been fired, so it was likely that he had reached this position after the shooter had fled. He must have lost consciousness briefly. Nearly any movement by the victim after the first shot would bring a second shot. Killers normally did not like to leave live witnesses. Reese's dilemma centered on the problem that apparently this killer *did* leave a witness: the store clerk.

The smeared blood trail extended about five feet from where

the victim must have originally fallen. Overhead florescent tubes cast a sparse light onto the floor around the body. Reese speculated that the dead man must have been coming out of the shadows when he was shot. He thought the victim was not the original target.

Reese's partner, Homicide Detective Charlie Dent, standing over the victim, flipped his notepad open with an ink pen before looking up from the body. He stared at the sober-faced patrolman who had been the first officer to arrive on the scene. The officer looked hardly old enough to be in the police force, and from the sickly expression he was extruding, Reese deduced he hadn't seen very many dead bodies.

"Did anyone move the body?" Charlie asked in his gruff manner.

"He was DOA when we arrived," said a uniformed officer named Jameis, who wore badge number 8173 on his shield. "I checked for a pulse, but other than securing the premises, I called homicide immediately and attempted to keep the storekeeper from cleaning up. No one else has been near the victim."

"Who made the original emergency call?"

The pale patrolman stammered, "Store clerk said he did. The 911 operator hadn't specified the caller ID and was unable to gather any information other than that someone needed the police."

"Did they keep the clerk on the phone?"

"No, just relayed the information that a robbery attempt had been made at this location."

"What time was the call?"

"We got it at 2:17 a.m., and we arrived at 2:43 a.m."

Reese calculated the time in his head. "Twenty-six minutes doesn't sound like a very good response time," he said.

"We get maybe a dozen calls every shift. We got it as a priority two call."

Reese was well aware of the infamous priority two designations.

Priority two calls were supposed to be relegated to responses where there was no immediate threat to persons or property.

Charlie noted the times on his pad, but the senior detective continued to gaze at the young officer. Reese Barrett had seen that gaze before. When you were in its glare, you had the overpowering urge to check your pants zipper. Since when did a crime victim dying on a shop floor drop to a priority two? Even if the operator was unaware of what happened, a 911 call from a mom-and-pop grocery at this hour should have triggered a few random brain cells in someone's head. This late in the night, convenience stores were prime targets for crime.

The officer pointed over his shoulder toward the entrance to the small convenience store. "My backup is checking nearby businesses to see if anyone might have seen or heard anything."

"I wish him good luck with that," Charlie said. "This is the type of neighborhood where nobody ever hears anything or sees anything, nor would they admit it if they did. This time of night, people are so accustomed to hearing gunshots that they don't even bother to check."

"Who's the clerk, and where is he?" asked Reese as he looked around the small store. Other than the patrolman, they appeared to be alone. This was certainly not the response he expected from a robbery-murder call.

The officer glanced nervously at his own notes as if unsure. "The clerk on duty is also the owner, Mr. Duc Tran, and right now, he's tossing his cookies in the restroom. He's really scared." He offered a smile that had a sickly edge.

Charlie launched an angry question toward the policeman. "Hasn't anyone ever taught you that you never leave a witness alone until after they have been interviewed?" He made an expression that reflected disgust with the officer's attitude. "Get him back in here immediately," he commanded. "Given enough time to think about what happened, the memory starts playing games with you. I've seen witnesses go suicidal or toss other things besides their cookies in the toilet. Get him now!"

The young patrolman had just been introduced to Dent's Law 101, and Reese didn't feel the least bit of compassion for him. He screwed up, and the best thing he could do was just take his medicine and swear to never let his emotions take the place of common sense again. Although Reese was not a betting man, except for an occasional football game, he expected if he was ever called to another murder case where Jameis was the responding officer, he would find him stuck to the witness with superglue.

Nodding, now with the grin missing, Jameis turned and headed for the rear of the store.

The small grocery store was located in a converted corner gas station in East Dallas, within a mile of Fair Park, where the Texas State Fair would be kicking off in a little over a month. Although the fuel pumps from the former station had been removed, the center island and signage remained. At one time, the station had been part of a national chain, but it had been abandoned maybe fifteen years earlier, going through a succession of increasingly shabby failing businesses and underfunded startups. The windows were papered over with posters advertising, "Lotto tickets sold here," and prices for cigarettes by the carton, colas, beer, and hot dogs. Inside the store were three aisles between shelves covered with chips, cookies, dish soap, small jars of mayo, mustard, soups, canned meats, bread, and other convenience items. Most didn't appear to be fast movers, and the shelves were covered with products declining in quality, appearance, and usefulness. The rear of the store was lined with glass-doored freezers for milk, juices, and beer, and the worn floor indicated most of the traffic in the store flowed to the large selection of beer. Other than the beer, the cigarettes, which were kept in a locked cabinet behind the cash register, and the lotto tickets, there was little else of any real value.

Reese was aware that the shock of a violent crime brought differing reactions from witnesses, but cleaning up seemed to be an odd behavior from the shopkeeper after a murder right in front of him. Looking around, the young detective decided that the accumulation of dust would indicate the store hadn't been swept or cleaned in several years.

The store was situated on a rather dark street a few blocks south of Interstate 30, which offered any lawbreaker quick access to a getaway route. It had been thirty-seven minutes since the first 911 call came in, and, because the first officers on the scene had not issued any bulletins, the shooter had plenty of time to get miles away.

Why was the store open at this hour? Reese speculated that because this was a high crime area, most nearby stores closed much earlier. Business couldn't have been great this time of day, but many of these little stores counted on quick-stop shoppers needing a cold drink, cigarettes, or candy bars on their way home. Apparently, however, no one had stopped in the last hour and a half. The store seemed rather dismal and forgotten. Being less popular probably made it an easier target. Only a few gawkers had gathered outside on the fringes of the parking lot, curious about the spectacle of flashing police cars.

"We need to get a statement from the shopkeeper and an all-points bulletin out on the shooter as quickly as possible," Charlie said.

Reese knew the patrolman had screwed up twice already, first, in not questioning the coding of the 911 call, resulting in an unforgivably slow response time, and, secondly, by allowing the victim out of his sight before his statement had been taken. The response time would officially be charged to the dispatcher, but Charlie, at least, would place the blame on the officers. His opinion was that since the patrolmen should be familiar with the area and the types of crime prevalent in the area, they should have placed a priority one on the call and responded immediately.

Gathering information quickly was something the patrolman would have to learn from experience. The first few minutes were critical because immediately after a shooting incident, the witnesses' endorphins were on full alert and the mind was at its sharpest. That sudden burst of adrenaline usually faded very rapidly once the sense of danger passed. Charlie had taught him that, and while Reese had questioned his senior partner about many things, questioning his methods of interrogation was not one of them. That was one of those rookie things you only did once in a lifetime, with the chaffing response usually in the form of a loud and long lecture burning that fact into a new officer's psyche.

The officer had speculated, probably correctly, that the dead victim had been a customer who had had the misfortune of coming from the rear of the store during the robbery. He had called it unfortunate that the victim had stepped out of the aisle, apparently surprising the robber, who had fired a single shot, and then fled. The cursory survey by the detectives had revealed nothing which contradicted that assessment.

"First I need an ID on the gunshot victim," the older detective said. "Reese, help me roll this body over slightly so I can reach his wallet."

Reese stepped over the body and lifted the victim's shoulder, carefully avoiding contact with the blood which had pooled on the floor. The body had already begun to cool. Again, Reese was reminded that the amount of blood indicated the victim had not died instantly, but had bled out. He wondered how long it had taken the shopkeeper to settle down enough to call 911.

"Can you get it from this angle?" Reese asked.

"I think so," said Charlie, slipping a plastic gloved hand

underneath the partially raised body, then inside the victim's suit coat. After a couple of seconds, the senior detective pulled a black blood-covered case from a breast pocket.

"You got it?" his younger partner asked.

Charlie grunted and struggled to upright his position. Once he gained his footing, he avoided the blood and flipped open the case.

"Hell fire, I didn't see this coming," he said, eyebrow raised, face dead serious. Charlie's face hardened like quick drying cement. "Help me turn him over so I can see his face."

"Someone you know?"

"I'll know in a second."

With the two of them working together, the task of turning the body was easier.

Charlie directed a flashlight on the face of the victim.

"Yeah, I know him. It's Richard Carver, a burglary detective working out of the East Dallas station." He flipped the black case toward Reese so he could see the gold badge. "Our robber just killed a cop."

The senior detective reached for his cell phone and made a call which was going to bring a much faster response time than the original call. There would be no danger of anyone miscoding this call.

Seconds later, the store manager shuffled from the rear of the store, escorted by the patrolman. The clerk was a small Vietnamese man of undeterminable age. Dallas had been one of the major areas where refugees from South Vietnam settled following the war which had ended over forty years earlier. Most of the Vietnamese refugees had been assimilated into the American melting pot, but some had held onto their cultural differences. From first appearances Reese pegged the owner as one of those who had not readily adapted to the American culture.

Reese nodded to the older man, "I am Reese Barrett. I am a Dallas Police Detective. What is your name, Sir?"

"I tell the officer," the elderly Vietnamese storekeeper said. "I am Duc Tran."

Duc Tran looked to be an original evacuee from the Vietnam War. Charlie guessed him to be over seventy. He was about four foot ten, still with dark hair, although liberally salted with gray, cut very close to the scalp. The ageless skin looked the same for all the Vietnamese with which the detective had come into contact, from their early twenties until old age. Duc Tran was not an imposing figure, but like many of the refugees, his face was a map of a harsh life. He had a defeatist air about him, like so many others who lost everything in that worthless war. Reese wondered if Duc Tran had been one of those who abandoned his family to make his escape during the final days in 1975.

"This place is going to be overrun in about fifteen minutes by every cop in the Dallas Metro area," Reese said. "We need some type of description of the suspect and some idea of the direction he took when he left the store."

The little Vietnamese clerk looked at him with priggish eyes.

"You had to have seen him, Mr. Tran, what are we looking for?"

Duc Tran appeared to be confused and afraid. In the background, the sound of patrol cars could be heard coming in from every direction.

Reese felt like he was talking to himself. When he asked a question, the little man nodded that he understood, but except for his name, thus far, Duc Tran hadn't spoken a word. His gaze kept diverting to the slain man on the floor.

Finally, Charlie stepped in. "Let's take him outside. Obviously, there is too much distraction for him in here."

Reese followed Charlie and the storekeeper outside to the sidewalk and somewhat to the side of the entrance where there was a pile of packaged firewood and an ice storage bin. The lock on the bin was broken and the latch was covered with years of rust. It had not been used in a long time. The woodpile also had the appearance of abandonment. Reese surmised that there was little demand for firewood in Dallas during August. Actually, the demand for firewood was never high in Dallas, Texas. Even though it was the coolest part of the day, the temperature felt like it was in the upper eighties.

An overhead florescent light flickered, emitting a high frequency buzz, which made Reese grit his teeth.

Charlie rested a fatherly hand on the shoulder of the storekeeper, even though the old man was probably ten years older than the detective. The small man reacted to Charlie's touch like he had been shot. The senior detective withdrew his hand and motioned for the clerk to sit on the woodpile.

"Did you get a good look at the guy that tried to rob you?" he asked in a quiet gentle tone. The senior detective had to be playing a role because Reese knew Charlie was not in the habit of treating witnesses with such gentility.

The short man immediately took advantage of Charlie's demeanor. "He had gun. Don't like gun—tried to hide."

"Can you give us a description of the man who shot our officer?"

Duc Tran nodded. "Black man. B-b-big g-gun. Going to shoot Duc Tran. I hide." He nodded enthusiastically. "Why would he want to rob Duc Tran?" The little man stared defiantly. "I have nothing."

"I'll be sure to ask him, when we catch him," Charlie said, apparently trying not to be sarcastic, but unsure of how to respond. "Can you give us a better description? How tall was he? How old, maybe? How about facial hair, was he clean shaved or did he have, you know, a mustache or beard? Scraggly hair or what?"

"He always coming in store. Read newspaper. I tell him go away," Duc Tran said, bobbing his head up and down. "He no pay to read."

"Does your security camera work?" Reese asked, pointing at a small camera overlooking the parking lot, which appeared to have been vandalized. He pointed at the door, indicating inside the store. "Either outside here, or inside over the cash register?"

Duc Tran glanced up, then shook his head. "No work, long time. Cost much money."

Reese doubted expense of operating the recording system had been a major factor. Probably the old man had just skipped resetting the system for so long that it had been all but forgotten. It wasn't a dead-end issue, however. It had probably been used at one time and Duc Tran didn't seem the type to erase old tapes or throw the records away.

"Do you think you may have recorded the shooter at some time, I mean back when the camera worked?" Reese asked.

Duc Tran shrugged. "He come to store back long time. Don't know."

"We are going to need those tapes and we need you to come down to the station to help us identify the man who shot the police officer," Charlie said.

"Dead man, he was policeman?" He turned his head to look back inside the store toward the fallen cop. Charlie had stated that the dead man was a detective in Duc Tran's hearing, but the old storekeeper had made no sign at that time that he had heard him.

"I did not know he was policeman," the old man lifted his head and stared at the senior detective, but refused to make eye contact. Reese noticed that once he was away from the crime, Tran's speech improved and he appeared to be more comfortable with English. His eyes were still watery and he continued to cower like someone was about to hit him.

"So sorry," Tran said. "I will try to help."

"I'll get the tapes," Reese said. He turned and moved toward the back of the store.

"When you find them, we'll take Mr. Tran downtown," Charlie

said to the retreating junior detective. "It doesn't look like he is going to be able to help us immediately. Maybe his memory will improve if we find the shooter on the tapes."

Duc Tran spoke up in protest. "I cannot leave my store." He appeared to be genuinely concerned.

"Nothing is going to happen to your store," Charlie said. "Mr. Tran, this is now a crime scene. Policemen are going to be all over this store for several hours and you may not be able to go back inside for at least a week. Nothing is going to happen to your store."

Except the police will take it apart looking for evidence in the murder, Reese thought.

Charlie continued. "A police officer was murdered here in cold blood. Things are going to be different for a while."

The clerk deflected the rebuke, dismissing it as he continued to plea for his store.

Reese walked away on the rant issuing from the scared storekeeper, for once grateful Charlie was handling that situation. When a law enforcement officer is killed, the department would move heaven and earth to bring a suspect to justice. Until the dead man's identity was ascertained, Reese and Charlie would have conducted the investigation themselves. However, as soon as the two detectives discovered that the dead man was a Dallas Police Detective, the control of the investigation moved to their lieutenant. Charlie and Reese had no way of knowing how the investigation would go now. The entire department would utilize unlimited manpower to conduct a comprehensive manhunt for the suspect until he was apprehended or killed. Things were moving very quickly out of the control of the detective team. Everything had just moved to fast track.

Reese found the tapes scattered haphazardly on a shelf in the backroom office. The tapes were old, covered with dust, and some of them looked like they had been used for coffee cup coasters. He gathered them up and stuffed them in a cardboard box he found in the office. Like the store, the office had a feel of depression and defeat about it. Chilled by what he had seen tonight, Reese felt like the walls were closing in around him. Shivering, he wasted little time getting out of the cramped office and back out of the store as quickly as possible.

When he came back out the front door of the store, Reese's partner was still trying to convince Duc Tran of the need to go downtown tonight to view the tapes. The senior detective looked exasperated by the argument the little old shop owner was putting up.

"No, you are not under arrest, we just need you to come down where we have the equipment to view those files, and then, hopefully, you can give us a face for our suspect. The sooner you do that, the quicker we can get you back here," he said. Charlie rolled his eyes at Reese as he approached.

Reese gave him a supportive smile. But, he avoided stepping into the conversation. The tapes he carried were not catalogued in any perceivable order and he estimated their chances of getting a photo ID of the suspect from the recorded mess before two thousand angry policemen hit the streets in a few hours were slim to none. It was going to be a long night. As he listened to the shopkeeper drone on, he knew Charlie was going to have a headache. Reese tiptoed around the two men very gingerly.

Several police cars swerved into the parking lot kicking up dust on the broken concrete slab. Lieutenant Mattie Reynolds, head of the Dallas Police Department Homicide Division, climbed out of the passenger seat of the closest police unit.

"I don't appreciate being dragged out of bed at three in the morning, gentlemen," said their supervisor. "What do you have for me?"

Mattie Reynolds was a thin Black woman whose presence bore

a much more powerful mantle than her slight frame would indicate. A second-generation Police detective, she had risen through the ranks on her own merits, eclipsing the stellar career of her father. At sixty, she was approaching retirement, but she was the type who would have to be carried out fighting and screaming. She had already stated that she was not going to show up at her retirement party. She intended to be too busy on a murder case. If she didn't have a case working, Reese speculated she just might kill someone just so she would have a case to solve. It went without question that she was very good at her job.

"Murder victim is a police detective out of robbery," Charlie indicated. "I know it's a cliché, but he was just in the wrong place at the wrong time. I don't think he even saw what was coming."

"I know most of those guys," the lieutenant said. "Who was it?"

"Detective Richard Carver; works out of Eastside. Took a slug through the chest and probably died before he could reach his weapon to defend himself. His police issue .38 was still in his shoulder holster and it looked like he never tried to draw it."

Mattie nodded. "Good man. Haven't worked with him for a few years, but I understand he was an upright cop." She motioned toward the Vietnamese storekeeper. "Was he able to give you an ID on the robber?"

"No luck there, so far," Charlie said. "We think he might be able to pick him out of some old security tapes, so we are going to take him down to the station. The security system was not turned on tonight. He did indicate the man had been in the store several times in the past, though, so we're hoping the tapes will put a face on our shooter."

Mattie sighed as she looked back toward the store. "I'll stay with the crime scene team." She pointed a finger toward the storekeeper. "Take him and let me know the second you get a face. Every cop out there is going to be as jittery as a deer in hunting season, if you know what I mean. I want a face on this man out before morning roll call." Mattie stopped them one last time while they were loading Mr. Tran into the back seat of their unmarked police car. "I'll call the chief and the police chaplain as soon as we have confirmed the ID of the victim. Drop any investigations you two are working on right now and concentrate on catching this killer. It's your case. I'll clear it with the chief, but I can guarantee you are going to have a lot of unofficial help. Every cop in the city will want in on bringing this killer down."

CHAPTER 2

To call Duc Tran's security tapes VCR tapes would have been a mistake. The box of tapes Reese and Charlie brought back to the police station gave the appearance that Mr. Tran had raided a Radio Shack shortly before the archaic Betamax recorders gave up the ghost and disappeared from the marketplace. Tran must have purchased their entire stock. Apparently, he never erased anything, either through lack of desire or lack of knowledge of how to over-write the tapes. When he had them all full, he deserted the system rather than continue.

The detectives' problem was finding a system which could read the old tapes. A call down to their crime lab produced Walter Oglesby, a movie buff, who had an old Betamax machine gathering dust.

"We get maybe two or three requests a year for this system," Oglesby said. "It's not the best system for security, but it was one of the first. Updating can be expensive, so a lot of people hang on to the *'dinosaurs'* to save a few bucks."

Dressed in a blue-jump suit, unshaven, with a wild thatch of thinning hair, Oglesby looked more like a night janitor than one of the Police Department's top experts on Audio and Visual Media. However, if it was possible to retrieve anything from the tapes, Oglesby was the one likely to be able to do so.

Oglesby arrived in the squad room pushing a cart loaded with the Betamax, a box of electronic cables, and connectors for the various hook-ups he needed.

"I can tell you right now, that most of those tapes are worthless," he said, flipping his head in the direction of Reese who was sorting through the security tapes. "They have not been well maintained."

Reese was inclined to agree. In the better light of the squad room, a large segment of the tapes appeared to have been damaged beyond recovery. He was separating the least damaged and hopefully newer tapes, from the others. Odds were that the older the recording the less relevance it would have to the investigation into Detective Carver's murder. From the scant information that Reese and Charlie had managed to extract from the shopkeeper on the way back to the station, the detectives both had doubts Duc Tran would retain his memories of the face for very long.

Reese had found dates on a couple of the newer looking tapes which indicated they were four years old. Even if by accident they could find a photo of the suspect, he would have aged and might not be recognizable. They were placing a lot of faith in an old man's memories.

"Okay, I got it," Oglesby said, after several seconds of searching. He held a piece of cable aloft. "Let's get this show on the road."

He screwed the connector into the back of the Betamax player and extended it to another cable leading to a computer set up on Charlie's desk. "I got the recorder hooked up to the printer so you will be able to print out any image you want. I must warn you that they are not going to have the best quality of reproduction."

"Anything we get will be better than what we have now," Reese said. "Charlie has our witness in an interrogation room. So far we haven't even been able to determine anything about the suspect except that he was a black man."

"Bummer. Well, good luck," Oglesby said. He had finished

with the cable work and flicked a switch which lit up a TV screen. Another switch lit up the front of the Betamax. "This machine works a whole lot like a VCR. You have your fast-forward button, pause, stop, reverse, even a slow motion. I hope you are not interested in sound; I mean it's available, but I think it will sound pretty much like hen scratching; but if you think you want to try it, I can see what I can do with it," he said pointing out the features as if Reese had never seen one before, which he hadn't, but would never have admitted.

Reese went down the hall to the interrogation room and signaled Charlie that they were ready. Charlie and Mr. Tran arrived about the time he returned, so he slipped the first tape into the recorder. The image which came up on the screen was dark with barely enough light to record an image.

Indicating there was nothing more he could do to the Beta Max to improve the image, Oglesby manipulated the screen brightness on the TV, which provided a few more details, but made the view grainier.

"We might be able to put this on computer and clean it up a little bit, but you will never be able to use it in court," Oglesby said.

"Court is not our concern right now," Charlie interjected. "By roll call this morning we are going to have a couple thousand police officers hitting the streets to find a cop killer and we need to get them a face."

Reese admired his partner's control, because they were both feeling the same burning anger. It was the general opinion among law enforcement that anyone who would kill a cop would not hesitate to kill anyone else that got in their way. The shooter was viewed as a monster that had to be stopped at all costs. As a result, murdering a cop would be a very scary proposition; the percentage of unsolved cop murders has always been very low.

Charlie seated Duc Tran in front of the screen, then he grabbed a chair and seated himself on the shopkeeper's right. Reese pulled up a chair on the left, and Oglesby stood beside the machine and manipulated the Betamax. The senior detective signaled for Oglesby to start the first tape. It was a nighttime scene, displaying the front counter beside the cash register. Evidentially last night's slow business cycle was no fluke. Large gaps in the grainy film showed few customers or any other activity. Most of the scenes were of the back of Mr. Tran's head, occasionally a customer could be seen roaming about the store or paying at the front counter. The camera was stationary, mounted about seven feet above the counter, behind the cash register, pointing down at an angle. This gave a very distorted view of the customers. All a suspect had to do to defeat the camera was keep his head turned down, which would reveal only the top of the customer's heads. Even with the camera only a few feet away, unless the person looked up for some reason, faces would be distorted, making identification a difficult task, although not totally impossible.

"Fast forward the tape. Stop only on facial shots," Charlie said to Oglesby. "Right now, we are not interested in anything other than the faces."

It took about fifteen minutes to view the first tape. After the first tape, Charlie turned his attention to the little shopkeeper.

"Do you only record the store at night?" he asked.

The old Vietnamese man looked up at Charlie and nodded enthusiastically.

"Only nights. No get robbed in day, only night," he said, continuing to nod, his mouth open slightly, which displayed a set of coffee stained dentures. His accent was slipping again, which Reese determined to mean the little shopkeeper felt he was again under stress.

"Just how many times have you been robbed, Mr. Tran?" Reese asked.

"Seven times," he said. Nodding once for emphasis. "Only nights. No bother Duc Tran in day."

"Did you call the police whenever you were robbed, Mr. Tran?"

The old man looked toward Reese.

"Sometimes," He frowned, "They no care; I stop calling."

What the little shopkeeper was saying was credible. Many immigrants were extremely suspicious of the police, with some justification. Reese knew that so many of these people had been abused by police in their own countries, and that fact contributed heavily to their moving to the United States.

"But you didn't hesitate to call tonight," Reese said. He had also experienced their sudden conversion to cooperation with police when they believed it would benefit them.

"Dead man on floor," Tran said. "No want dead man on floor. Police come take him away."

Reese wondered if the only service the little man felt the police would provide him would be to clean the dead people off his floor. As bad as that sounded, the detective speculated how little respect the shopkeeper would have had if the police had continually ignored his calls following a robbery. He doubted if the grocery store owner was being completely honest about his dealings with the police, but at the same time, he knew that cultural backgrounds often clouded the perception of what a police officer could accomplish to assist someone who had been robbed. While police detectives could solve a good percentage of the cases they were assigned, some cases could take many years for resolution, and a fair percentage were never solved.

Local citizens expressed frustration with the police department when it touted lowered crime rates, as many people believed strongly that the reported statistics were affected by crimes that police chose to ignore. Even more disdain fell on the department when police refused to even take a report unless the complainant originated it themselves under departmental guide lines. A large percentage of the decreased crimes stats could be attributed to the police no longer taking reports on certain types of crimes.

Reese remembered when he was in college his roommate's car battery had been stolen. His roommate had been able to supply the officer with the battery's serial number, and Reese had pointed to two men in the same parking lot installing a battery in their car. As Reese and his roommate talked with the officer, the men completed their work, closed the hood of the car and returned to their own apartment. Reese's roommate then offered to raise the hood of their car to allow the officer to check the numbers. The officer stated that if he touched the car, he would be arrested. It would be a crime to open the hood of the vehicle to remove the car battery, even if the battery was stolen from him, and he could prove it. The police officer told my roommate to contact an attorney if he wanted to go further with a complaint, but that the fastest way would be to simply buy another battery.

"The only way you are going to get your stolen battery back is, first of all, if the person or persons who stole it return it to you, or, secondly, if a truck load of stolen batteries is involved in a crash on the highway and the batteries spill out and you happen to be there and one of them has the correct serial number. Just buy another battery."

While Reese was lost in thought, Oglesby had loaded the sec ond tape into the Beta player. It was an older tape, still showing the same dreary scenes, but drawing no attention from Mr. Tran.

Fifteen minutes was approximately how long it was taking to view each film in the fast-forward mode, stopping briefly for each new face and looking at Duc Tran for his response. The squad room clock showed a few minutes after five, so they were going to have only two and a half hours to view hundreds of hours of film. Even with fast forwarding they were not going to be able to make a dent in the box of tapes.

"We need to narrow this down a bit more," Reese said. Turning to the shopkeeper, he asked, "What time did our suspect normally come into your store?"

The old man frowned, furrowing his brow, drawing his cheeks in and closed his eyes.

"Early night. Just getting dark. Always read sports page in paper. No pay. I tell go away many times."

Reese turned to the police tech.

"So, if we concentrate on just the first few of hours of each night, we might stand a slightly better chance of catching an image, before our shift ends."

Again, addressing Oglesby, the detective spoke, "Can we just concentrate on say seven to ten p.m. on each of these tapes?"

"Sure," the tech shrugged. "There are no markers to indicate time on the film so we'll have to guess. It may not be very accurate, but if you are trying to beat a deadline ..."

That last word hung like a noose over the room. There was no way of knowing how much damage they were doing by rushing through the old tapes. It would be very easy to damage or destroy the very thing they were trying to find.

That idea must have floated through Charlie's mind also because he hesitated before nodding approval.

"Let's do it. Two thousand policemen running around out there with no sense of direction scares the hell out of me."

Reese nodded in agreement.

The tapes went considerably faster after that, but with the same lack of success. Reese found himself assigned to keep the coffee flowing from the squad room coffee pot to the men assembled around the screen. Shortly before seven in the morning Mattie Reynolds came into the squad room and dropped a pile of photos, witness statements, and other evidence collected at the scene of the murder on Charlie's desk.

"Forget about getting off this morning, the chief has authorized unlimited overtime on this case, and has approved you two as the point men in this investigation," she said. Not waiting for a reply, she turned and walked back toward her office.

Limp with exhaustion, Reese eyed the mound of evidence to be sorted, placed in order and disseminated to the dozen or so detectives and special activity squads. This would take most of the day. Like Jesus before the crucifixion, he was wishing this task would pass him by. There would be no sleep today. Worse, he had promised to meet Grace Evans for breakfast before she went on a twelve-hour shift at Dallas's Southwest Regional hospital. Missing her this morning meant he would have to wait two days before seeing her again.

Several of the other detectives came in either for the morning shift or to finish up paperwork from their overnight shifts. The screen became the focal point of nearly all the eyes in the squad room, as each of the men paused on their way to or from their desks. Mattie came out long enough to pace the floor before disappearing back into her office. Reese was aware that after her second appearance she stayed behind the closed door. Through the half-drawn blinds, he could see her very animatedly talking on the telephone as the time crept closer to morning roll call.

Minutes before the roll call, Tran bolted from his chair. As a young man's image flicked on the screen, the shopkeeper shouted, "That him. That him!" He was pointing to the image of a young black teenager who appeared to be fourteen or fifteen years old.

Oglesby slowed the image until it seemed to flick forward one frame at a time. When the teenaged boy raised his head and looked toward the clerk behind the counter, his face showed clearly in the camera lens. The kid had an open newspaper in his hands.

"Get the face," Charlie said.

The film advanced until the face was clear of the newspaper. The face was slightly distorted, but still a fair image and recognizable.

"How do you do screen capture or whatever it is you do to print this out?" he asked Oglesby, pointing at the face. "And do we have any idea of how old this film is?"

The activity in the room, especially the shout by Duc Tran, drew the attention of Lt. Mattie Reynolds. She parted her way through the gathered officers to the front of the crowd.

Looking more toward Duc Tran than toward the screen, she asked authoritatively, "Are you sure that is the man that shot the policeman last night?"

Tran glanced at the image a second time and timidly pointed an index finger at the screen.

"Yes. That's him," he nodded in the affirmative.

Mattie turned to Oglesby. "Get me about a dozen copies of this immediately," she said.

One of the detectives separated from the pack, returning seconds later with the copies in hand. She scanned the photo with the practiced eye of a veteran police officer.

"Do you have any magic software down in that lab of yours that can clean the image up a bit and maybe age it a few years?"

"The quality is too bad to get a really good image, but I can get it a little clearer. I think," Oglesby replied, then, second-guessing himself, he added, "It's not going to be picture perfect. Your suspect is going to be difficult to identify from a four- or five-year-old damaged image. With this copy, I am not really sure about aging it. I'll do my best."

"Harrumph!" Maggie replied. "Work your magic then get back with me. We'll go with what we have right now. I want this picture out there in the computer screen of every squad car in the city in the next thirty minutes. Hopefully, someone will recognize this kid before anyone else is killed," she said.

The lieutenant looked at the assembled detectives in the room.

"Roll call in five minutes. Everyone except these two are going to hit the bricks today unless you bring an excuse from your mother as to why you can't go out to play," she said. "Report everything you see, hear, smell, or think you know. Work this case like the crime was committed against a member of your own family, because, and I should not have to remind you that it was. And I don't need to remind you either that with the suspect being a member of the black community, that the stakes have just doubled."

Maggie Reynolds was black, along with nearly a third of the assembled detectives.

The homicide squad was made up of thirty-four detectives, seven black, nine white, five Hispanic, a couple of Oriental descent, an American Indian, a Pakistani, some mixed, and a few who defied any classification. All, however, were aware of the implication in her statement.

The recent publicity on police shootings had shined a bad light on policemen, leading some people on the fringes of society to target officers. The department was still reeling from the deaths of five Dallas officers targeted at a *Black Lives Matter* march.

A manhunt for a black suspect was going to be like walking through a powder magazine with a lit candle waiting for the spark that would blow the city apart. It wasn't a matter of *if* the city was going to explode, but rather when.

CHAPTER 3

"I'm sorry about standing you up this morning," Reese spoke over the telephone. "I suppose you heard about the police detective shooting last night. I got stuck conducting the investigation."

"I heard," Grace replied. Her voice was low and even, but Reese caught the tremor of distress in her tone. "I've got to cut this call short. I can't take a cell phone into this ward, and I have to be on the clock in about two seconds."

"I'll try to meet up with you tomorrow," was all Reese was able to say before the phone disconnected. He dropped the cell on his desk.

"Was Grace pissed at you?" Charlie asked. "That was about the briefest conversation I have ever heard between the two of you."

Reese, who was lost in thought, took a second to process that Charlie was talking to him.

"What did you say, again?" he asked.

"I said, is Grace mad at you for standing her up for breakfast this morning?"

"No." Reese cupped his forehead in his right palm and smoothed his hair back. Another stroke scraped across the stubble of his unshaven face. He wondered if his eyes were as red and inflamed as they felt.

"She's just worried, that's all," he said. "Maybe we are both under too much stress."

Grace had just finished her nurse's probationary status at Dallas Southwest Regional Hospital and had been assigned to a floater position. Floaters were placed each shift into whatever ward or position was most critically in need of registered nurses. Grace was presently assigned to Regional's county prisoner ward. She had enough to worry about dealing with a collection of patients being held in custody for treatment while awaiting trial on charges for every crime on the books from traffic violations to capital murder. Reese was concerned because she had indicated that violence from the prisoners occurred virtually every shift. In fact, extra security personnel were assigned to the ward along with the officers who brought in the prisoners. She still sported a bruise on her cheek where a prisoner had clocked her on the side of the head despite being handcuffed to his bed with a jailor sitting only a few feet away.

She had reacted sharply with concern about Reese's safety when their discussion on the murdered detective had intensified. A segment of the Dallas populace would believe the killing of any law officer was justified. In the last few years with increased attention on looser gun laws and justifiable homicide issues, the police had been placed under a microscope by those preferring to take action on any problem or situation themselves. Those individuals would never believe they, rather than law enforcement personnel, actually were the problem.

"Why don't you just marry that girl and get it over with?" Charlie asked, looking up from the pile of evidence on his desk. His desk was shoved up against the front of Reese's desk giving them about forty square feet of space to work with on their cases.

"I'm still trying to get her to say yes," Reese said.

"You are not aggressive enough," Charlie said. "Just tell her that the two of you are going to get married and that's that, enough said."

Reese chuckled, then sighed, "That could be a real problem. Grace has an opinion about everything, which is one of the things that I like about her. She is very intelligent. Also, she thinks things out rather than making decisions quickly, except in emergency situations, of course, when her training kicks in. That is a good trait for our situation, because, of necessity, I have been trained to make snap decisions. Someone's life could depend on it. And, I also have been trained to relinquish decision-making to medical personnel in those same situations where she has been trained to take control." Reese paused.

"And how does that answer my question?"

"She will let me know when she makes up her mind."

Charlie laughed. "I bet she does."

"At least she hasn't said no," Reese said, "She just hasn't gotten around to saying yes, either."

"If she was like my Twyla, you would not have these problems," Charlie said. He continued to sift through the small mountain of information collected at the crime scene.

Three months earlier Charlie had been hospitalized for a perforated ulcer while on a murder case, and fallen head over heels in love with his nurse, Twyla, one of Graces' co-workers. Less than a month later Charlie and Twyla were married. It was Charlie's fourth marriage, and his not so blushing bride's second.

Twyla had proven to be every bit as strong-willed as Charlie. While he might think he had bulldozed his way into matrimony, she had gone into the relationship with her eyes wide open. She was in every way the perfect match for Reese's hard-headed partner. In fact, Reese had noticed the senior detective sneak in a brief telephone call to Twyla minutes earlier.

Reese picked up another witness statement and scanned through it quickly, hitting only the highlights. Later he would go back through the statement a line at a time hoping to come across anything which might help them in the investigation.

"I'm not sure these witness statements are going to help us much," Reese said, with a bit of resignation. The two had been reading the statements for a couple of hours. "Seems no one heard anything, saw anything, or knows anything."

Charlie nodded. "Sometimes it's not so much what the witnesses are saying, but what they are not saying. Maybe they are being truthful, but that doesn't explain everything. Have you noticed this?" he asked, tossing a crime scene photo toward Reese.

The junior detective picked it up and studied the photo. "What am I looking for?" he asked. The photo was of the victim from a low angle pointing upward. The stacked unit of shelves beside the body was centered on the photo.

"It's what you don't see that concerns me," Charlie said. "We assumed Detective Carver was totally unaware of what was about to transpire."

"Yeah," Reese said, "The fact that he hadn't drawn his weapon was a good indicator of that."

"Then why was he there at that time of night in the first place?" Charlie asked.

"Shopping?" Reese suggested.

"Shopping for what?" Charlie asked. "We know he was approaching the front of the store when he was killed. Look real close at it again. Where is whatever he intended to buy?"

Their preliminary investigation of the crime scene had given both detectives the opinion that the robbery detective did not have anything in his hands when the shooting had occurred. However, he had not been on duty, and there had been no report of a robbery to the police dispatchers before the shooting. Common sense would seem to indicate that he had stopped at the convenience store in order to purchase something; but, whatever it had been that he purchased, where was it? Reese and Charlie spent several minutes in silent speculation before Reese offered a suggestion.

"Maybe he was going to buy something from the front counter and hadn't picked it up yet."

"If that was the case, why was he coming from the rear of the store?"

Reese shrugged and tried again. "You think maybe he set whatever it was down on a shelf, which would have cost him time," he paused.

"Which could be why he didn't have enough time to draw his revolver?" Charlie finished.

"Yeah, but then," Reese paused once again.

Charlie did not hesitate before finishing the thought, "If he did put whatever it was back on a shelf, why is it that we can't spot anything that looks like it is on the wrong shelf, or maybe out of alignment on a shelf? If I had sensed any danger …"

Reese interrupted. "You would have pulled your weapon immediately, dropping whatever you had in your hands, to heck with putting it down on a shelf."

"And so would you, I hope, unless we were trying to sneak up on the subject quietly," Charlie continued. "Then either one of us would have carefully placed the item on the shelf closest to us, drawn our weapon, moving toward the robbery suspect with the stealth of a lion."

"And when you got shot and killed, then I would have found the item that was out of place on the shelf in the grocery store," the younger detective concluded.

"Keep dreaming, Rookie. It would be you that got shot," Charlie said.

Reese squelched a grin, but the older detective was right; he didn't make many mistakes.

Even in the clutter and disorder of the small grocery store, an object out of place would be noticed, especially in a photo, when there was sufficient time to peruse the shelves. It was much easier to determine that the two detectives were looking for something that simply was not there.

"Maybe, we had better ask Mr. Duc Tran what it was that Carver was buying, and where is it now," Reese said as he leaned back in his chair.

"Put that on our to-do list for just a bit later," Charlie said. "I am not going to wake that man until he gets a little sleep. He's barely coherent when he's operating on his normal 'awake' schedule. Can you imagine what he would be like if we hit him up on no sleep?"

"I absolutely concur with your judgement in this matter, and add that I am not sure we are going to be too coherent much longer ourselves," Reese's tone was teasing. Suddenly he wrinkled his brow in thought. "Hey, didn't that officer that arrived first on the scene say something about them having a hard time keeping Duc Tran from cleaning up the crime scene before we got there?"

Charlie paused, "Add that to our list of questions for Mr. Tran. Good catch, Partner."

Since Charlie had come back to work about six weeks earlier, Reese noticed that his old partner didn't have quite the fire in his gut that he had shown during the first three years of their partnership. Charlie had almost died from the perforated ulcer and the ensuing infection. He had emerged from his near-death experience a changed man.

The old detective had lived for years on spicy fried foods, jalapeños, and Cajun hot sauce. With Twila's help, he had made his health more of a priority. Maybe, he felt a debt to Twyla to take it a little easier. She had retired from the hospital and taken up a home nursing position to have more time for Charlie. With the more flexible schedule, she had gone on a crusade to keep him alive.

Charlie might be a charmer, but once you got to know him better, it was obvious that at times he could be a real pain in the rear.
Twyla had proven to be as tough as Charlie, and she was beginning
to make progress rebuilding the old codger.

"We need to know why Carver wasn't driving a car. No one
reported seeing a vehicle driven by either Carver or the suspect.
Maybe he had a car and the shooter took it. Right now, we have a
lot more questions than answers, and I'm getting too tired to think.
If we miss something, it might be days before we get back to it and
that, Rookie, could be too late."

Reese nodded his agreement, marveling silently about how he
had gone from Rookie to Partner and back to Rookie in a matter
of minutes. Charlie was tired. It was approaching ten o'clock, and
their shift had started at six p.m. of the previous day. Sixteen hours
was not an easy shift even without stress, but he felt a lot like a limp
dishrag himself. Maybe fresh eyes would be better. He said as much
to Charlie. The senior partner readily agreed, and both detectives
began to collect the evidence and return it to the evidence box.
They took it down to the evidence locker, where they signed the box
in. They marked the status "open access" so that anyone needing
to review the information could sign it out. Always the stickler for
details, Charlie hid a hand-written inventory of the evidence in the
box in the bottom drawer of his desk. The list probably wasn't one
hundred percent safe from prying eyes, but anyone caught looking
through his desk for any reason was going to be doing some heavy
explaining. The senior partner always kept a list of evidence items
in his desk. He checked the items against his list every time he
checked out the box.

Charlie and Reese agreed to meet back at the station at four
p.m. to continue their investigation. Reese could tell that Mattie
Reynolds was hesitant to let them go, but her hesitancy faded when
she caught Charlie's gaze. Charlie had a way with women, and

that included sixty-year-old black lieutenants carrying guns and in charge of his paycheck. Reese wouldn't have been surprised to find out Mattie Reynolds had been one of Charlie's earlier conquests, but he had enough sense to not ask.

"Get back here as quickly as you can," she told them.

Reese was concerned about his partner's health as they caught the elevator down to the main lobby. Charlie was leaning, his eyes closed, against the rear wall of the elevator, looking quite pale.

When they reached the ground floor the doors opened and they stepped out into mass confusion. The news of the policeman killed by an unknown assailant must have reached the national news wires. A CNN crew was trying to set up an interview spot in front of the elevators. Several police officers were trying to shoo them back out of the way. The lobby was crowded with representatives of local affiliates of the major networks.

Pepper Jackson, a well-known columnist for the Dallas Morning News, spotted Reese and his partner, and began pushing his way through the crowd.

"What can you tell me about the investigation into the cop being shot and killed last night?" he shouted at them, over the noisy crowd.

Rather than deflect the question, as Charlie would have done, Reese met the reporter head on.

"Jackson, you know we can't tell you anything, even if we knew about it. Anyway, we were upstairs catching up on our beauty sleep, so we don't have any idea what happened. You say a cop was shot?" Reese said, feigning innocence.

"Come on guys, I've always played square with you. I gave you plenty of press on that coma case at the hospital, you know. You two are hot stuff right now, thanks to my coverage. You have to know something."

Reese pointed a finger toward one of the hallways.

"We have a public relations department right down that hall-way. Maybe they can fill you in," he said. "I'm sure they can tell you what time the press conference will be. You know that they oversee informing the public, right? And that leaves me and my partner to the grueling tasks of the everyday grind."

"Yeah, yeah, yeah. I already tried public relations, and they don't know anything either," Jackson said. "About all we have are the victim's name, a time, and a location. They did promise us the usual press conference and told us we would be kept informed. Come on, Guys, can't you give us a little more? Even a tiny bit?"

Charlie stepped forward and waved a hand in front of Pepper's face.

"You've played this game long enough to know we can't tell you, even if we did know something, which we either don't or are not at liberty to say," he said in measured syllables. "When we find out something, we'll send you a letter by U.S. mail so you will be the first or the last to know. Maybe you should try the county morgue," the senior detective suggested.

"Very funny, Charlie," Pepper said. "The coroner informed me I wasn't dead yet and wouldn't let me in. He did offer to rectify that little detail, however, if I stuck around," The newsman smiled, "Okay, I'll just camp out and wait for someone smarter."

"You do that," Charlie replied, continuing to move toward the entrance of the building.

Pepper turned and melted back into the crowd, watching for the next available target.

Progress was slow, but the two exhausted detectives were mov-ing in the general direction of the exit. When they finally man-aged to move through the door onto the sidewalk outside, Charlie paused.

"Screw this," Charlie said. "Forget your hot shower, Reese; let's take another look at that crime scene to see if we can spot something the crime scene crew might have missed." The senior detective had put on his pensive face. "I don't have enough pieces of the puzzle to start putting it together, and I won't be able to get any rest until I do."

CHAPTER 4

The converted gas station, living its latest incarnation as a grocery store and murder scene, looked even more depressing in the daylight than it had in the darkness. Without its gas pumps, the fueling island stood naked and forlorn in front of the store as a permanent eyesore. Only the raised concrete, torn out jagged piping and the bucket to hold water for washing windshields remained.

The driveway was covered by a canopy supported by rusting pipes. The canopy effectively shielded the interior of the store from any direct sunlight. The area was now closed off to the public by a stripe of yellow police tape wrapped around the poles and anchored at the entrance to the store. A patrolman guarding the station lifted the tape for Charlie and Reese as they approached.

"Forensics made a sweep about an hour ago," the officer said. "We are keeping the scene closed until they are satisfied they have everything they need."

Standard procedure, Reese nodded. Until forensics was satisfied the tape would stay in place.

"You had any trouble so far?" Reese asked.

"Just the usual stuff," the officer said, holding the door open for them. "A film crew came by earlier, but they just took a few exterior shots and one of those talking head reporters made a few remarks in front of a camera."

Charlie, who had been one step behind the junior detective, as he passed the officer, also spoke.

"Did you happen to see a little shrimp jabbering in broken English trying to get inside?"

"Yeah, Mr. Tran came by," the patrolman said, shaking his head for emphasis. "He lives a few blocks away and he wanted to come in to re-open his store. I didn't have the heart to tell him it may be several weeks before anyone would feel comfortable enough to shop here again. I had trouble with his English, but finally convinced him he wasn't going to be able to open today nor could I allow him back inside."

"Don't let him fool you," Charlie said, "He speaks English as well as I do."

Reese resisted the urge to add that Charlie's English suffered at times.

They entered the store, and, with most of the windows covered, the dim light made it difficult to see. It was too dark to make out much detail in the pool of blood which was the most prominent feature in the room. As they were waiting for their eyes to adjust, Charlie went behind the counter and found a switch which turned on the overhead lights. The lights directly over the pool of blood and another in a rear corner of the store flickered ominously before finally settling down. They cast a feeble unsteady light on the shelves and floor below.

"Bad ballast," Charlie said. "Notice how much darker it is in those two spots?"

"That might have made it at least possible for Detective Carver to come upon the robber without being seen," Reese agreed. "But wouldn't he have been heard? These floors are not too solid."

Sometime in the past one of the tenants had added a raised wooden floor. It probably had been covered with tile, but the tile was long gone. Like most of the rest of the building, the flooring had aged ungracefully and had a slight give to the step which caused the wood slats to creak. A man of Carver's size would have had a difficult time approaching the front counter without being heard.

Charlie shrugged. "I guess that depends on how fast he was moving and how well the robber was able to hear," he said. "After all, the robber was distracted at the time, and might even have been shouting at Tran."

The senior detective searched in his jacket pockets until he found his flashlight that put out a fair amount of light. He walked over to the spot where Carver had fallen.

"Reese, come here and stand facing the front counter." The spot he had indicated was a couple of feet behind the beginning of the blood trail left by the victim.

"Tell me what you see," the senior detective said.

Reese moved into position and scanned the room with practiced eyes.

"I have a very good view of the front counter and the area where robber must have stood. It's nearly a straight angle to the cash register, so Carver would have been able to see only the back of the robber."

"No facial features?" Charlie asked.

"No. He probably wouldn't have been able to see if the man was armed or not and if he couldn't hear him, I doubt if he would have been aware that a robbery was taking place," Reese said.

"That would explain why he hadn't drawn his gun," the senior detective speculated. "So, Carver comes into the store to make a purchase and while he's here a robber comes in and when the detective walks toward the counter with the item in his hands, he unexpectedly enters into a crime scene." Charlie Dent paused and shut his eyes, sighing heavily. "If that scenario is true, Reese, where was the item he intended to buy when we came in here last night? I didn't see anything lying around near him on the floor, did you?"

Reese ran the scene from last night through his mind. The deceased detective did not have anything in his hands, nor was anything on the floor near him. Reese did not recall seeing anything on the floor anywhere last night; nothing dropped, tossed, or scattered. He guessed it could have been possible that at the last second Carver had become aware of what was happening and had put whatever he was buying back on the shelf, but it made no sense that if he was aware that a robbery was taking place, he hadn't drawn his weapon immediately. The questions were piling up, but none of them seemed to have answers.

"I think we need another look at the crime scene photos," Reese indicated.

"Let's check these shelves out first," Charlie said. "We need to look for something out of place or maybe unusual."

Reese glanced at his partner. He wasn't sure about what Charlie meant by unusual, but he didn't want to ask. He tried to remember whether he had been informed if Carver had been right handed or left. When he and Charlie had turned the body slightly to search for an identity, he remembered feeling the butt of the revolver. It was under Carver's left shoulder, which meant he had been right handed.

Reese moved toward the right-hand side of the aisle facing toward the front of the store. The unit held six individual shelves about sixteen inches apart, starting about eight or nine inches above the floor. He quickly dismissed the three lower shelves from consideration. If he had an opinion, the junior detective would have bet Carver had been standing erect when the fatal shot was fired, not crouching or bending over.

Reese estimated Carver was about his height, maybe an inch or so shorter, which would put him at slightly under six feet tall. The bottom of the fourth shelf would have been about waist level. Whatever he was looking for more than likely would have been on the fourth or fifth shelf. When people set something down they rarely reach over their heads to do so.

The store had made a few concessions to grouping items in relationship to similar items nearby. The lower shelves had been filled with charcoal briquettes, motor oil, gasoline additives, and fire starters. The collection had the appearance of being leftover inventory from when the store had been a gas station years previously.

The fourth shelf was stuffed with toilet paper in single rolls, many of which were damaged, the outer wrapping torn, dirty or both. An involuntary thought that some of the tissue looked like it might have been recycled at some point in its distant past caused the young detective to shiver. The top two shelves were covered with personal products—toothpaste, brushes, tweezers, shoe polish, fingernail polish remover, etc. At least an attempt had been made to place the items in some order.

Behind Reese on the opposite side of the aisle, his senior partner was doing the same mental inventory. The close quarters and the pool of dried blood made it difficult to move about. The straightened shelves bothered Reese. Neatness in this mess would qualify as his idea of unusual.

"Charlie, look at this," he said over his shoulder and then moved to his right so his partner could have an unobstructed view of the shelves. "Have you seen any other shelves in this store this organized?"

Charlie eyed the shelves, casting glances down the aisle at the other stacking units which were mostly in disarray.

"Something is definitely not kosher here," Charlie said finally. "I would bet that these shelves were reorganized very recently."

"Like maybe last night?"

"Yeah, like last night," the senior detective indicated.

"We need to get forensics to run a check for blood samples on those products," Reese said. "Maybe they were knocked off when Carver fell."

"Yeah, see what else you can find there. Things are not adding up."

Reese felt like a race horse hitting its stride. The two organized shelves could hold a valuable clue, not so much as what was there or missing, but that time and effort had been taken to hide evidence. So far, he couldn't see any significance to the change, but someone had felt it prudent to straighten these two shelves, and both detectives felt like it was a clue incognito.

"Charlie, let me borrow your flashlight," Reese said, reaching to grasp it as his partner offered it.

"Where's yours, Rookie?"

Reese grinned sheepishly, "I saw you grab yours and I figured it would be easier for both of us to keep up with just one. If we had both of them and one of us, you know, laid one down, we could forget it. Then Mattie would be furious."

"Heaven Forbid," the senior detective deadpanned, watching Reese for a few moments before returning to his own tasks. He could not resist a final jab, however, "Don't set that down somewhere and lose it."

Reese grinned, "Wouldn't think of it."

He played the beam over the shelves. A thin veil of dust still coated the surfaces, but by the scrape marks in the dust, it was now obvious several objects had been moved. There was no way to tell if it had been done last night or a week ago, however. It was going to take more forensics examination than just their eyeballs to get those answers. On the fifth shelf, near the front edge, the light reflected off a crude circle in the fine dust indicating something wet had been placed there recently.

The detective waved the flashlight over the water stain in several directions, hoping the angles would provide more information.

"What would leave a mark like that?" he asked Charlie.

Charlie looked at the reflected image for several seconds and then walked to the rear of the store.

Reese could hear the opening and closing of one of the freezer units before his partner returned carrying a plastic jug of milk. The senior detective set the quart jug of milk on a nearby shelf, leaving it for a second before carefully lifting it and moving it aside. A faint, barely visible image could be seen in the dust. The circle left by the milk jug was a close match to the image on the fifth shelf, but that circle was broken and didn't form a complete outline.

"Close, but not exact," Reese said.

"Look again," Charlie said. "The mark on the shelf over the victim indicates the milk jug had sweated to form the water stain. The jug would have been there longer than this one."

It took a minute longer for it to click in Reese's brain exactly what his partner was getting at. If the milk had been there long enough to leave the stain, the projected time of death was incorrect. Why had Duc Tran gone to the trouble of cleaning up the murder scene? It was beginning to look like the only reliable evidence of the shooting was the body itself. Both detectives hoped there had been no effort to tamper with the body.

Both men stood staring at the spot.

"We need to get to the coroner and establish a time of death," Reese said. "We may have it all wrong. Then we need to have another little chat with Mr. Tran about why he attempted to sanitize the crime scene before calling the police."

"Do you think…nah," Reese paused and the two partners stared into each other's eyes. Reese sighed before completing the thought that must have been on both their minds. "Tran faked the whole thing."

"Not the shooting part; we do have a dead body."

"No," Reese commented. "Not the murder, but, maybe the robbery?"

"I've been a police officer long enough to know that people do strange things when they are in shock or under duress. There is a good chance he wasn't even aware of what he was doing. Maybe he was in shock after the shooting, and he was just trying to do what he could to clean up his store."

Reese again recalled their conversation with the young officer who had been first at the scene.

"Charlie, it was Tran that was attempting to clean the store according to the officer. So, we know who moved this stuff, and, what, returned the milk to the cooler in the back?"

Charlie nodded, glancing at the recently rearranged shelves.

"What about our suspect now?" Reese asked.

"Until we find him and get some answers, he most definitely will be our number one suspect, but we need to keep an open mind about other possibilities. Someone had to shoot the detective and Tran's story is still believable. I think."

The *'I think'* which Charlie had added would weigh heavily on their minds for the next few days.

CHAPTER 5

Dr. Leonard Miller was the type of doctor who discovered late in life that he enjoyed dissecting bodies more than he did healing them; besides, the dead don't talk back. As an added incentive, his medical malpractice insurance was considerably cheaper. He liked the steady paycheck with no one looking over his shoulder.

He was very specific about the "looking over the shoulder" bit, and to most people among the living, he was about as approachable as a nest of rattlesnakes. He possibly would have become a serial killer if he hadn't stumbled into a position as the Dallas County coroner.

Reese put in a telephone call to Dr. Miller as he and Charlie were leaving the grocery store crime scene, and, true to his nature, the coroner tried to take a bite out of his hide.

"This is the fourth time you have called me asking for the preliminary report on the dead officer so far this morning," Miller growled.

"I haven't called you," Reese replied.

"Hmm, well, I actually suspected as much," Miller said over the telephone. "Especially since the last time you called you sounded very much like a girl and the time before that you sounded just like that newspaper fellow Pepper Saltine or whatever."

"Pepper Jackson?"

"Yeah, that's the one. He kept insisting he was you."

"Well, I'm me," Reese said, which met with total silence for several seconds.

"And just how am I supposed to know that. If you want the report, you are going to have to come over here and get it. And bring your photo ID," he shouted as he slammed the phone down.

Reese yanked the phone away from his ear.

"Did you hear that?" he asked his partner, who was seated in the driver's seat of the unmarked squad car.

"I think everyone on this side of town heard him," Charlie said. He started the car and headed north. "We might as well trip on over to his office."

The county coroner's office occupied a rather non-descript office building alongside Stemmons Freeway, near the area locally recognized as the hospital district. About three miles north of downtown, it was a little tricky getting to if you didn't know where you were going. Because it was the site of their Friday night poker games, Charlie and Reese knew the ins and outs, including entrances into the building which were not available to the public. Doc Miller had this thing about people slipping in and pulling open the refrigerator doors in his autopsy room.

Charlie always took the well-traveled road, which meant the partners took I-30, or Thornton Freeway, westbound through the canyon, then through the mix-master construction before picking up I-35E northbound out of downtown. Traffic was its usual fifteen miles per hour, the road was rough and unpredictable due to the construction, but Reese's senior partner still believed it was the best way to get there. With the additional stop and go traffic, due to the omnipresent construction, it took them nearly an hour to pull up to the rear of the coroner's building. Reese was convinced he could have cut ten minutes off the trip by using city streets to reach Harry Hines Boulevard, and then it would have been a straight shot to the hospital district. From there it would have been an easy connect back over the I-35 bridge, or Stemmons, and back to the office.

Reese didn't argue with Charlie about his choice of routes, however. He had learned over the years that he had more productive usages of his time than questioning his senior partner's driving. Those things included staring at the ceiling, drumming his fingers on the armrest, and silent prayers.

In the rear of the building, a rarely used sidewalk about forty feet from the main rear entrance led to a metal door half hidden by shrubbery. It was out of sight of the news media, which had discovered the investigators almost never ventured in or out the front door. The door was marked emergency exit only, but was left unlocked most of the time. The entry was still under a camera, however, so it was rare that anyone slipped in undetected.

Miller's office was on the second floor. Charlie and Reese avoided the elevators because they were visible from the front lobby, which was the limit of penetration into the building without Miller's consent. From the reaction Doc Miller had given on the telephone, Reese didn't believe there would be very many permission slips handed out today.

His office door was locked, but they could hear the doc's baritone roar and the scuffling of his feet across the room before they knocked. The door opened slightly, and Miller poked his head partially through the crack.

"You got any ID?" he asked.

"Hell, Doc. You know who we are!" Charlie said.

Doc Miller stepped aside and allowed the door to swing open for them.

"I can't take any chances," he said, "I even got a call from the mayor's mother saying he needed a copy of the autopsy, but he was too busy to come to the phone. I didn't think the mayor ever had a mother. Where do all these nuts come from?"

Reese shrugged. He wondered how many of the calls were real, or if doc was taking his normal delusions to a new level.

"You aren't wearing masks or anything?" Miller asked.

It seemed to confirm Reese's suspicions, but Texas politics had already taught him that sanity was not a requirement for holding a public position.

"We're clean, Doc," Reese said, casting a quick glance toward his partner. Charlie seemed unperturbed by Miller's reaction.

"Doc, we have a pretty good idea of how Detective Richard Carver was killed, but we are concerned about a possible discrepancy in the time of his death," Charlie stated.

Miller cocked his head to the side and raised his hands to his hips.

"I wondered how long it was going to take someone to get around to asking that question. Aren't you satisfied with the two-fifteen a.m. time of death being quoted on the news?"

Reese glanced at his partner, which confirmed his disbelief. It was unlikely that anyone in on the investigation would have released that detail, so it seemed that someone had reached the witness or had decided to make a guess as to time of death.

"We are not," Reese answered for the pair.

"Well, maybe you should have been," Miller said. "We placed the preliminary time of death at somewhere between two and two fifteen a.m. this morning, but …"

It's amazing how those three letters can chill the heart and make grown men stop in their tracks.

"My investigation seems to indicate he was shot sometime between midnight and one in the morning. The single shot fired nicked a major blood vein near his heart. I believe he was wounded and unable to get off the floor or turn over, but he was conscious and probably in quite a bit of pain before he finished bleeding out."

"Damn, Doc, do you realize what you just told me?" Charlie asked. "Could he have been saved if he had received prompt medical attention?"

Doc slumped into a half sitting position on the front of his desk.

"It took him maybe an hour and a half before he lapsed into final unconsciousness. He probably tried to move, but blood loss weakened him quickly. If medical attention had gotten to him in the first, say, forty-five minutes," he stopped and looked up as he appeared to be formulating an answer. "Yeah, I think he could have been saved."

"And he would have been conscious most of that time?" Reese asked.

Dr. Miller scratched through his hoary head of hair.

"I believe he must have been awake and aware he was mortally wounded. He would have been in great pain and possibly even able to beg for his life up to the minutes before he finally died."

"That's rough, Doc," Charlie articulated what they all were thinking.

The two detectives had one more question that needed an answer.

"Could it be possible that a witness could have seen the whole shooting and the events surrounding it and not have acted in a rational manner to save the victim's life?" Reese asked.

Doc frowned. "You'll have to ask a psychiatrist that question, Mr. Barrett. Don't we see that situation pretty much every day? I can examine a body and give you a fair picture of what occurred, but only to the physical part. The human mind behaves differently in emotional situations in every human, and each time they could react differently. Psychiatry is a tough study, and not my favorite either. No one usually needs the emotional state of a corpse. Even those brain doctors can study a person's responses and compare them with their actions in any situation, but they can't tell you how a person will react under another set of circumstances." The coroner paused. "But to answer your question, I simply don't know."

Charlie gritted his teeth, sighed deeply, and poked at Reese's arm.

"Come on partner, we need to bring Mr. Duc Tran into the stationhouse for another interview, and this time the kid-gloves come off."

The two detectives waved to the coroner, who continued to lean on his desk as they moved toward the door. Charlie was still speculating aloud as he pushed on the door and held it open for Reese.

"Shock or no shock, psycho or sane, he either lied or else his memory is completely twisted around. I think we need to consider the possibility that he lied to us about what occurred."

The detectives reached the car, and Charlie moved toward the passenger side. That was a strange move, but Reese said nothing as he sat behind the wheel and Charlie handed him the keys.

"He seemed to have had a plausible story, Charlie, but I think it's coming unraveled."

"Yep."

If the shopkeeper had been lying earlier, he was a very accomplished and convincing liar. Tran had seemed visibly shaken to the core by the sudden turn of events. His reactions were what he and Charlie had learned through experience to recognize as those of a stunned witness to a violent crime.

Could the violent confrontation have affected the old man to the point that he could lose over an hour without taking some type of action? When he called 911, why had the dispatcher routed the call to the patrolman received the call as a Priority II, meaning no imminent danger? He wanted to hear the recorded conversation between Mr. Tran and the operator. If Tran was in shock, there was a chance he wasn't aware of the passage of time, nor had he understood the cries, if any, of the fallen peace officer. The detectives wanted those answers.

Before departing from the coroner's office, Reese called Lieutenant Reynolds at the Dallas Police Headquarters. The detectives needed an update on that end of the investigation, and he also needed to inform Mattie of the possible inconsistencies in Duc Tran's witness statement.

Reese reached her without delay and he relayed the scant information they had gathered. "You've got to find some way of cooling off this rabid manhunt until we get a chance of verifying what really happened," Reese indicated.

"Slowing it down now would be about as effective as sticking your foot on the rail to slow a freight train," Mattie replied. "Is the face we identified still a valid suspect or not? Until we have him in handcuffs in the station, the hunt is not going to stop and the safest place for him is in a jail cell."

"And if not?"

"If not, I pray to God you have some way to derail that train, Reese, because suspected cop killers are usually captured dead."

CHAPTER 6

Reese insisted on driving urgently; Charlie simply shrugged and took the passenger seat. By the second block of back streets the young detective had already lost count of the number of traffic laws he had broken. It seemed all the major surface streets were packed with school buses and every block seemed to be slowed by school zones. There was no way to avoid them, so he slowed to a crawl through the zones and tried to make up the time on the few open stretches.

"We should have taken the Interstate," Charlie said, gripping tightly to the dash whenever his junior partner took a turn too fast. "It will do us no good to get there fast if we die in the process, you know."

"It's not my death I'm worried about," Reese said, between clinched teeth. His knuckles were white from the grip he had on the steering wheel. His head was beginning to ache from the pressure from his clinched teeth. The pain started in his jaws and radiated upward, where it seemed to ignite and explode from his mind outward through his unblinking eyes. He was aware he was holding a death grip on the wheel. In the back of his mind he sensed the lack of time, which at this moment was their mortal enemy.

"What do you think, Charlie, have we released the hounds on the right fox or is an innocent man in danger?"

"I don't think it's going to matter to us one whit if we don't get there alive," Charlie replied.

Strangely, although his partner had often criticized Reese's choices in driving routes, he had never complained before about the way Reese drove them. In difference to his partner, the junior detective slowed a bit and attempted to keep all four tires on the pavement. Reese felt that Charlie was also feeling the tension building from recent developments.

Charlie was on the radio communicating with the patrolman standing guard outside the grocery store.

"We need a location on the store owner, Duc Tran."

"He hasn't been by the store since I talked to him earlier this morning," the metallic response poured from the radio speaker. "I guess I managed to cool him off earlier."

Charlie signed off before speaking again.

"Or scared him into hiding?" he said in a barely audible whisper. He slammed his hand down on his leg and turned to Reese. "Can't you make this thing go any faster?"

Reese responded by switching on the cruiser's flashing lights and accelerating a good twenty miles an hour over the speed limit. Still several Dallas drivers tempted fate and roared around the unmarked car at even greater speed. After one obnoxious driver in a Lexus sped passed them at least fifteen miles an hour faster, Charlie glanced nervously at the speedometer.

"Don't baby my car. Go faster," he said, reaching over to give an extra tug to his seatbelt.

Breakneck speed does little to save time, especially when it is approaching four in the afternoon. Dayshift had ended at Love Field and the onslaught of airport traffic quickly filled any open slots left by workers from nearby industries, bringing traffic to a near a standstill. Flashing lights and touches on the siren gained very little cooperation from the afternoon commuter crowd and the detectives could only inch forward.

"I warned you, didn't I? You should have stayed with Stemmons to I-30," Charlie reprimanded.

"If we had, we would still be trying to get into the canyon," Reese said. The canyon referred to a dry creek bed which the highway department had converted into a clogged interstate. "We wouldn't have gotten through any faster."

Charlie appeared to be pouting, but he backed off.

"Just get us there as quickly as possible."

Charlie had gotten Duc Tran's home address last night in the brief interrogation he had conducted while Reese was locating Walter Oglesby and setting up the security tapes for viewing in the squad room. Reese could sense the agitation from his senior partner, but he knew it wasn't directed at him personally. Charlie was questioning himself. He was concerned that he might have missed something in the interview which should have triggered further investigation. Instead, he had accepted the story the storekeeper had presented. The two of them were under tremendous pressure to solve this case before the city erupted in violence. The fact that the main suspect in the death of the officer was a black man was likely to cause increased friction within the community. The "Black Lives Matter" reaction which had swept the country following the deaths of black men killed by police under questionable circumstances had everyone on edge. A similar over-reaction was likely if the investigation determined someone in the immigrant society was the shooter.

Before they arrived at the store, Charlie was on his cell phone speaking to the lieutenant.

"I don't care what the evidence we have on this case shows," Charlie said. "We need to take this case a little more deliberately. We can't just rush to judgment."

Charlie paused, listening.

"Mattie, we need a search warrant on Duc Tran's home and we are going to need backup," the detective said. Charlie must have noticed Reese's interest in the call because he switched the phone to intercom.

"We've nearly got to have a smoking gun to get a judge to sign off on a search without probable cause," Mattie Reynolds was saying. "What are we looking for?"

Charlie exhaled an old-man, asthmatic sigh. "If we are right, we are looking for the smoking gun."

There was hesitation on the other end of the line, before Reynolds came back. "You suspect our storekeeper may have fabricated the whole robbery story?" she asked.

"We have no concrete evidence which would indicate that, but there are too many inconsistencies in his version of the events," Charlie said.

Reese knew how hard it was for the long-time homicide detective to make that statement. Charlie had questioned hundreds of witnesses and suspects and prided himself in being able to read through the bull they spouted. Not to say he hadn't made mistakes in the past, but they both had given a compassionate read on the old Vietnamese storekeeper, and now they suspected they had not questioned him thoroughly enough. Charlie had always said that Lady Justice never offered commiseration to anyone, but the detectives realized they had bought into the story hook, line, and sinker.

"I'll meet you there," the lieutenant replied. "I'll have your warrant. I'm also issuing an APB on Tran. I have a few questions I'd like to ask him myself."

Knowing it would take at least an hour for Reynolds to obtain the proper warrants, Reese headed directly to the store. The forensics team was back on location and the team leader, Bjorn Halsteen, met them at the door. Halsteen, a transplanted Chicago native of

Danish stock, stood about five ten, with wheat blonde hair, golden beard, penetrating green eyes, big smile and white teeth. The smile and teeth were not visible as he held the door open for them.

"We had taken a photo of the watermark on the shelf when we were here earlier," Halsteen said in an apologetic voice. "At the time, we didn't see the significance of the mark and probably wouldn't have since it was dry, but I can guarantee you that nothing is going to get past us again." His voice was harsh and firm. "Do you have any other ideas of what we might be looking for?"

Charlie nodded. "Look for a gun, small caliber, maybe a .38, and signs of activity which would indicate why the man who was supposed to be a witness waited over an hour while our detective bled out on his shop floor before calling 911."

"So, the old man is the primary suspect now?" Halsteen asked.

Exhaling loudly, Charlie bowed his head forward and glanced to the spot on the floor where Carver had fallen. "That's what I need for you to find out for me."

Halsteen, who had the reputation of being one of the smartest men in the police force, glanced at the specialists under his command.

"If we must take this whole building apart one brick at a time and run it under a microscope, I will guarantee we won't miss anything again," he vowed. "Are you going after the old man?"

"Search warrant is on its way, we'll let you know if we find the smoking gun in his home. We've got to account for the missing hour somehow. Maybe he stashed a weapon back at his house before making the 911 call."

"Then we will check every inch of the ground between this store and his house," Halsteen said.

The pair of detectives left the crime scene team at the store and went outside to wait for Lt. Reynolds to arrive with the search warrant. Despite the rush hour traffic, Mattie had made the I-30 corridor trip in under an hour with warrant in hand.

She pulled up beside them and lowered her window. "Sorry for the delay. Judges are scarcer than hen's teeth to find after quitting time, but I finally found one that would sign-off on the warrant. Maybe Mr. Tran will cooperate and explain the discrepancies in his story, but we are prepared," she said, waving the legal document in the air. "I called in two other detectives as backups."

Reese followed the lieutenant's car with Charlie taking a sullen shotgun position. The nearby house reference must have been calculated as a straight line because Tran's house was a block behind the store and in the middle of the second block back to the south. The other detectives had taken up position in an unmarked car in front of a neighbor's house. Nearly all the available parking was along the street. Most of the driveways along the block were a pair of concrete ribbons disappearing between the houses. Shrubs and trees had overgrown several to the point that if you looked up the drive you could make out the outline of the family car carved in the foliage.

The east Dallas neighborhood was old, probably built up in the late 40s or early 50s and it had fallen into a state of disrepair. Tran's house was a small two-bedroom frame house, maybe 800 square feet, with crumpling asbestos shingle siding, bright blue painted wooden framed doors and windows. A screen door on the front of the house looked like a Dallas Cowboy linebacker had plowed into it at full force. The door was still closed, but the gaps around the frame made it useless as a weather barrier. The whole property looked like it was one step ahead of a city condemnation order. The roof was bowed across the crest and it looked like the asphalt shingles had not been replaced in twenty years.

Not that they considered Duc Tran much of a flight risk, but the Lt. sent their backup up the driveway toward a separate single car garage. The walkway to the back door was visible from the edge of the structure. Charlie and Mattie flanked the front door, while

Reese proceeded to the door and knocked loudly. There was no answer. The knock seemed to alert several neighborhood dogs, whose angry barks ruptured the calm.

"Kick the door," Mattie Reynolds commanded. "We have plenty of probable cause to conduct a search."

It took almost no force for Reese to level his shoulder into the door and spring the lock. The deadbolt lock had not been engaged. The door swung open with a creak and the bottom of the door dragged across a thread-bare carpet which stopped it before it was fully open.

The interior of the house was dark, causing Reese to squint in the dim light. Entering the door, he held his pistol out in front of him, while Charlie was completing the same maneuver only barely above the floor level.

"Clear," Reese called out as soon as he cleared the doorway and was sure no one was in the room.

Charlie peeled off to the right, heading for the point position toward the hallway leading to the bedrooms.

Mattie charged straight ahead, moving toward the kitchen and back door.

"I'm clear," she called out after sticking her head into the Pullman-type kitchen. The dining room she had to pass through was little more than a tiny space with a corner table and two wicker chairs pushed back against the outside wall. She proceeded to the back door and unlocked it to admit the other two detectives.

Reese waited until he saw the first officer approach the doorway before turning his attention toward Charlie. Fewer than ten seconds had lapsed before his senior partner moved into the hallway with Reese, covering him from behind. The door of the first bedroom was cracked open and it took less than three seconds to scan the interior for occupants before moving on the rear bedroom.

The second door in the hallway was closed and again they

assumed a high-low position before pushing into the room. The bedroom and attached bathroom were empty.

"All clear," Charlie shouted. Both men shouldered their weapons before returning to the small living room.

"I've seen vacant houses that looked more lived-in than this place," the lieutenant said. "Did Tran have a car?"

"If he did, he's got it with him. The garage is empty—at least, no vehicle," one of the backups said. "I'll check with DMV to see if he has one registered, but from the evidence and pooled oil in the driveway, I'd say he does and it's a clunker."

"I have an uneasy feeling about this," Mattie said, slipping her own weapon, a Police Special .38, into a belt holster which fit in the small of her back. "Take this place apart; I'm beginning to buy into you and your partner's new conspiracy theory, Charlie. I got an APB out on our so-called witness. I want to know where he is and what he is doing."

"Are you going to cancel the APB on the original suspect?" Reese asked.

"We really can't do that either," she answered. "Right now, we don't have any evidence that counters anything Duc Tran has told us. I want them both picked up, and then we will sort this out."

The detectives were very intent on what they were looking for—a small caliber pistol or any evidence Mr. Tran kept a weapon. He was not licensed to carry one, but with the erosion of gun control in Texas, a gun was easier to purchase, either legally or illegally, than to buy a pack of cigarettes.

However, after an hour, no weapon had been found and Tran had not returned. Charlie had given up and was fighting to stay awake. Reese wasn't faring much better. Mattie cornered them in the back bedroom where they were searching.

"Go home and get some rest," she said. "I'll see you at roll call in the morning."

Charlie started to protest, "I'll rest when I die."

"You've already tried that on me, Charlie," the lieutenant countered. "You and Reese have been working for over twenty-four hours."

Both detectives paused, evidently too tired to process the request mentally.

"Well, git, the both of you," She made a shooing motion with her hand. "I am not going to pay you overtime to sleep on my watch."

Reluctantly, Reese said, "Let's go, Charlie."

"I'm working on it, but my legs ain't listening," Charlie placed his pen in his notepad and shut the tablet.

"I'll call you if we come up with something important," Mattie said. "We can handle it for a few hours without you." Left unsaid was that the lieutenant was quickly approaching the twenty-four hour mark herself.

Reese wasn't sure about the lieutenant's optimism, but he was sure he wanted to sleep.

CHAPTER 7

Reese was completely exhausted by the time he dropped Charlie off at his small house in Oak Cliff. He fought sleep by blaring the country music channel on the radio for the thirty minutes it took to get to his apartment complex off Webb Chapel and Park Lane. Entering the apartment, he tossed his key chain onto the edge of the couch and sat facing the blank screen of his television set. Despite the hour, he flicked on the news. The rash of talking heads was discussing the manhunt underway for the as yet unnamed suspect in the murder of Dallas Police Officer Richard Carver. The story had reached the national news.

The TV was showing a scene outside a modest brick home in far north Dallas and a female reporter kept referring to the family of Detective Carver. The news media had not picked up on Carver living alone in a small apartment only a short distance from where he died. On the TV image of the home he could see the movement of drawn drapes on the front windows. The robbery detective had two sons, one a patrol officer in the northwest division and the other, a long-haul truck driver. The trucker was on a run out of Boston, and was now rushing home to be with the family. Reese wondered how he had been informed. Probably, some reporter stuffed a microphone in his face and asked him how he felt about the murder of his father, who had been shot down and left to die on a dirty floor in a small convenience store.

Disgusted, Reese changed the channel, only to hear a nationally known crime show host ranting that the murderer of Officer Richard Carver didn't deserve a trial; rather when the creep was caught, he deserved to be strung up in the city square.

"If you leave it to the courts, it may be fifteen or twenty years before justice is served, if ever. He needs to die now ..."

Reese turned the television off abruptly, interrupting the commentator's tirade. No justice at all would be better than the suggested violence being spouted by the vigilante masquerading as a news commentator. This was more of an entertainment segment than serious reporting. The only thing the media was doing right now was enflaming the angry passions of those hurting the most, and that could lead to a more serious problem than the department was already facing.

He had no stomach for food, but risked a quick peek in the fridge. He decided to skip supper, and instead, sprawled out across the bed without bothering to undress. Moments later, he sat up and removed his gun and badge, and then he lay down and removed his pants. That was as far as he got. The ten-thirty p.m. bed-time was early for him, but he hadn't slept in over thirty hours, and his eyes were closing before his head touched the pillow.

Reese needed Grace right now. He could feel the anger building up inside him. Grace had the ability with just a few words to keep him grounded and sane in a very insane situation. Unfortunately, she was in the middle of a twelve-hour shift at Dallas' Southwest Regional Hospital. Reese knew he was not listed among the hospital administration's favorite people. He ruffled feathers during a previous case that involved a coma patient who mysteriously disappeared from the hospital. The fear that they might retaliate against Grace for something he did or said seemed a real possibility to him. If he had not been sleep deprived, he would have recognized the paranoia in that scenario, but the events of the last twenty-four hours had rendered him beyond logical thought. Eyes already closed, he reached for the phone; but sleep took over before his fingers punched in her number.

Hours later, Reese was jarred awake by loud pounding on his apartment door. In a haze, he stumbled into the living room, and before he turned on the light, peeked through the peep hole. Charlie Dent was standing on the narrow ribbon of concrete slab which doubled as a front patio. Daylight was filtering through the heavy drapes over his window, and laying streaks across the aged gray shag carpet covering the living room-dining room combination. Newer light blue carpet had been laid in the bedroom, but the kitchen and bathroom were tiled with plain grayish white linoleum that was starting to curl at the edges.

Reese flicked on the light and thumbed the door locks. Swinging the door inward, he stepped back for his partner to enter.

"What time is it?" Reese asked, turning toward the small Pullman kitchen. He turned on the water in the sink and located a pan on the counter that looked clean. Filling it with water, he placed it on a burner and turned on the heat.

"Late enough that everyone is worried about you," Charlie said.

He closed the front door and picked up a pile of newspapers from the couch, tossing them into the corner of the room. He sat down on the couch and put his feet on the coffee table.

"When you didn't call Grace at six-thirty this morning, she called you a couple of hundred times. You never answered, so she called the cavalry, meaning me and Twyla, to find out whether you were dead or alive." Charlie paused and gestured as if waiting for applause for his wit.

Reese was fumbling in the cabinets to locate cups, so Charlie shrugged, and continued.

"I think she was about to file a claim on your life insurance policy. Twyla said I'd better get over here before she sent the meat wagon."

When the water was boiling, Reese poured it into a couple of the cleanest cups and added some freeze-dried coffee. He carried the cups into the living room, placing one on the table in front of his partner.

"Have you ever thought that maybe Twyla is waiting on your insurance policy to pay off as well?" he asked.

"Yeah," Charlie said. "When she dragged me out of bed this morning, I had the sudden premonition that she was going to help fate along a bit."

The senior detective sipped carefully, then made a face and placed the cup none too gently back on the coffee table. "Ah! Too hot!" he complained. "You in cahoots with her?"

Reese grinned, excused himself and headed toward the bathroom.

"Have you talked to the Lieutenant yet this morning?" Reese asked, minutes later as he rejoined Charlie.

"She still hadn't made it in when I called about half an hour ago," he said. "I talked to Waters in the squad room and he said she was out nearly all night with the search warrant. He said she had nothing to report."

"Then where do we stand?" Reese asked, reaching for his cup, also on the coffee table. He swallowed nearly a third of the cup. "Nothing wrong with this coffee."

"Well, shoot, Rookie," Charlie countered. "Hell, if I know where we are. I got from Waters that they are still pursuing the guy fingered by the shop keeper. I guess they still consider him the prime suspect. We are sitting on a powder keg right now and the match has already been lit."

Charlie gingerly sipped the brew, then, satisfied it was cool enough, drank several swallows. "Ain't nothing wrong with it now that it's cooled down."

"What about the discrepancies we uncovered in Tran's story and where is our chief witness, anyway?" Reese moved to the bedroom with his coffee.

"When I was a kid, we lived in the country on a farm," the senior detective said, starting another of his long-winded stories, "and we had this knot head of a dog. That dog fixated on one thing at a time. I remember once he spotted a rabbit in some high weeds back behind our chicken house and he took up chase. The dog, Bruiser, was one of those Mexican dogs, you know, a Chihuahua, who in addition to not having any brains, had no legs to brag of either. During the chase, that dog ran through a patch of weeds and ran head on into a rabbit in a hutch and both animals were knocked silly. Old Bruiser stumbled to his feet, took a long look at the stunned rabbit a couple of feet away, and must have decided that wasn't the rabbit he was after. He left it there and took up the chase for the first rabbit again."

Reese was fascinated by the revelation. "So, what's the moral of this story?"

"Right now, most the police department is acting like that brainless dog. Nothing is going to distract them from their quarry, even some basic little truths. You and I don't trust the statement made by that terrified little man, but like the dog, the police now have a target and nothing like a few missing pieces of the puzzle are going to stop them from chasing their suspect to ground. For the first time in a long time, I hope to hell we are wrong. I hope the guy everybody's looking for is guilty. It would be a lot easier."

Reese, quickening his pace, left Charlie in the living room while he took a quick shower and scraped off a couple days' worth of beard with a dull razor. Because of Grace, he had made several improvements to his wardrobe and could dress in a clean, comfortable suit. Less than fifteen minutes later, he walked back into the living room.

"Let's go," he said.

"What have you got in mind, partner?" Charlie asked, as he stood and carried the empty cup back into the kitchen.

"I don't think there is anything we can do to speed up the search for the suspect, but I think we ought to get more background on Tran. He lied to us and I want to know why. Maybe it was just a case of nerves, but what if it was something else? I would like very much to know where he was last night when we served that search warrant on his house. I want to know where he is right now," Reese said.

"Well, that's not asking a whole lot," Charlie said.

He followed Reese out the door, waiting patiently as the younger detective locked it. Both men walked to Reese's car, then Charlie hesitated.

"What am I going to do with my car?" He asked.

"You parked legally?"

"Yep, visitor slot over there."

"Leave it. It would be better for you if someone did steal it. Then you could get newer wheels with the insurance."

"On whose money, Rookie?"

Both detectives snickered as they climbed into Reese's car and buckled up.

"Besides," Reese reminded him, "You won't let me drive your car, and I'm not getting into a car with you behind the wheel again."

The drive in to the police headquarters building was uneventful. The clock over Lt. Reynolds' office door showed a few minutes after ten o'clock when they checked into the squad room. Since most of their duties were done outside any set schedule, no one noticed the time of their arrival. Reese had been mentally calculating his overtime, and he figured he had nearly twenty hours of comp time coming from this week alone and it was only Thursday. Theoretically, they did have time off, but as crime goes, the reality is they were always on duty. Lt. Mattie Reynolds's duty was to give the detectives a swift kick in the seat of the pants if they weren't accomplishing something worthwhile.

Reese hated sitting in the office, especially doing paperwork, so he would not have complained if the lieutenant walked in and kicked him back to the streets. The first phone call Reese made was to the patrol division guarding the crime scene, only to be made aware that Mattie had released the guard after the forensics team had completed their second sweep, which was sometime shortly after midnight. A call to the crime scene team brought the disappointing results that no weapon had been found.

Forensic team leader Bjorn Halsteen came on the line sounding like he had gotten no sleep last night.

"We were able to trace the watermark you found back to a quart of milk in one of the coolers in the rear of the store. It had our victim's prints on the jug and on the cooler door handle so we are pretty sure he made the watermark."

"Why would someone put the milk back in the cooler?" Reese asked.

"We assume they wanted to keep the milk from spoiling," Halsteen speculated. "We also got a good palm print of the victim on the plastic cover of a toothbrush. It was back in its proper place except for the color. The handle of the brush was a muted green color and it was stuck in a slot of red ones."

"What does that mean?" Reese asked.

"It probably means nothing. The storekeeper could have been in a hurry or maybe he or the victim was colorblind."

After hanging up, Reese proceeded to call the grocery store. The phone rang nine times before it was answered by call notes. By then, Reese was too frustrated and angry so he decided not to bother leaving a message.

"Tran didn't return to the store," he told his partner, cupping the receiver in the palm of his hand.

"Did you really expect he would?" the senior detective asked.

"No," Reese admitted, "I was just hoping."

Charlie had spoken to one of his numerous contacts who had given him the name of a leader in the Vietnamese community. He was a senior partner in one of the major downtown law firms. He agreed to meet with them, but couldn't arrange a time before tomorrow.

While waiting for Charlie to finish his arrangements, Reese placed a call to the Department of Motor Vehicles for registration and license plate number on Duc Tran's vehicle.

His call was put on hold for several minutes so he sat listening to a recording listing office hours and special instructions before a supervisor came on the line.

After explaining the purpose of the call, Reese detected a bit of reluctance from the supervisor.

"Can you give us anything else to go on, like a partial number or model of vehicle?" the supervisor asked. "Just the name of a suspected owner isn't much to go on."

"Sorry," Reese answered. "That's all we have, and we were just hoping for a miracle on your end."

Reese knew it was a long shot in tracing Tran's car. From the oil stain on the driveway and the grass that had been growing up in the pavement cracks, more than likely the vehicle was rarely if ever used. DMV could come up with a plate number in short order, provided it was registered under Tran's name and a score of other factors. In Reese's mind, the old Vietnamese store owner was building a profile as someone who didn't follow through on anything which could more than likely included insurance, registration, inspections, and general upkeep on a motor vehicle. The detective held out little hope on this line of questioning, so he was mildly surprised in DMV returning his call an hour later.

"We found a record of a Duc Do Tran registering a Datsun

210, 1975 model, ten years ago," the DMV supervisor said over the phone. "We can't tell you if that is the car you are looking for, but it was registered from the same address."

"Has there been any activity under the current title?"

"It would have been nearly old enough to be a classic when he bought it. I doubt if it was running very good then, and since he hasn't kept up the registration, I would have to assume it's not running now. Not only has the car not been registered since, but there is no record in our department of a transfer title, so I would have to assume if it is working, he's a lot better at dodging traffic cops than I ever was." The supervisor was unable to provide Reese with any other details, suggesting he check local arrest reports on unpaid tickets.

Reese decided this line of inquiry was going nowhere. If he had been stopped by the police, if the records still existed, if the car was damaged in a fender-bender, if an insurance claim had been made, if a policy had ever existed. Too many ifs and not enough solid information were revealing too little results. The supervisor gave him the last license plate number issued on a Datsun 210 and wished him good luck.

Maybe that would be enough to post on the computer system. Even that was a supposition because Reese didn't think anyone could count on getting by with ten-year-old tags.

He suggested going with what they had and concentrating on identifying the suspect Tran had pointed out for them. Charlie reluctantly agreed, setting aside the investigation into Tran's background.

"Even if Mr. Tran was correct in his identification, I'm not sure how effective a witness he will be for us," Reese said. "The chief and District Attorney are going to want a lot more evidence than we've uncovered so far."

"Maybe not, Partner. The murder of a police officer is a capital murder case. It won't take much evidence to get a conviction on this case," Charlie said.

He set a writing pen aside and stared at Reese with hard-set eyes. "They are going to come at this guy hard and furiously. Emotions are going to be a more important factor than evidence. I'm surprised the police patrol cars are not out on the streets with hangman's nooses dangling from their rearview mirrors."

Reese was shocked. "The police want this guy, sure, but that doesn't make them vigilantes."

"I'm not saying that, partner," Charlie raised his hands and patted them downward as if consoling an upset child. "I'm just indicating the rules of evidence are likely to be a little more flexible and justice may be meted swifter."

"You are making it sound scary," Reese said.

"Maybe it is," Charlie theorized. "Let's just say if justice were a two-bladed sword, you are likely to find one side is a little sharper and swifter than the other."

"Can we get a better image of that original surveillance tape photo than the one we had the other night?" Reese asked Charlie.

"We'll know in a second," he said, calling downstairs to Walter Oglesby's office. Charlie spoke into the phone, then leaned back and sat clicking his ballpoint pen.

"They are getting someone to '*look into*' it for me," Charlie said sarcastically to Reese. "It seems Walter doesn't work both day and night shifts at the same time like we do so information has to be passed along."

Charlie diverted the conversation back to the phone.

"Yeah, bring up what you have, please. And hurry, you are de-laying my afternoon nap." Charlie dropped the phone back into the cradle. "Can you imagine, they wanted me to come down there to get it? You'd think those inflated brains of theirs interfere with their ability to walk."

Reese glanced over his slightly pudgy partner with the flat feet and decided the best course of action was to reserve judgment and keep his mouth shut.

"Uh-huh, I can see that being a problem," he said instead.

One of the crime lab rats, a kid barely old enough to shave, came into the squad room, spotted Charlie and Reese, which wasn't a difficult task considering at that exact moment, they were the only ones in the room. He weaved a path to them and plopped several photos on their desks.

"I've been able to clean it up quite a bit, and if you will look at these, he fumbled through the stack and withdrew a pair of photos, I used a special program, which I wrote, to age the suspect about five years. Halsteen indicated that was the age you suspect most likely for the perp."

Reese noticed that his partner barely looked at the rendered photo before turning his attention to the enhanced security video shot of a black teenager, maybe fourteen or at most fifteen. He was a good-looking kid, already developing the shoulders and size which would make him a good football player, or, he thought, an excellent bouncer at a strip club in a few years. Even though the suspect had just been rousted by the small Vietnamese grocery clerk, there was no look of guile Reece could detect on his face. He might have been slightly contrite about being called out, but he saw no signs of anger, neither in facial expression nor body language.

Charlie must have noticed Reese studying the face because he moved it closer so all three men were looking squarely down at it.

"What's your take on this?" the senior detective asked. "If you met this kid in a dark alley would you be afraid?"

"I would be a fool if I wasn't a little bit apprehensive, but honestly even with all his size and the setting, for some reason I don't think I would be overly alarmed," Reese said.

"Exactly," Charlie said. "My first reaction would have been, what no books? We already know he's a reader, Tran told us so. At that age, kids are either thinking about college, maybe developed an interest in a job or craft, running with a gang, or are already full-blown crack-heads with a budding rap sheet guaranteed to make any probation office or case worker cringe."

While Reese felt Charlie's assessment of today's youth was a little harsh, the senior detective had brought out several valid points. The suspect didn't appear to either of them to be fitting in the pigeon hole of a person they thought he would have to be to shoot a cop. Years on the streets had taught both detectives to read any situation very quickly, and, while they weren't perfect every time, the partners were well ahead of the curve when it came to profiling.

"You think we might be able to pick out a face from a high school yearbook for our suspect?" Reese asked. "You know, the reading would seem to indicate school was still in his future."

"That's exactly what I'm thinking," Charlie grinned. "I'll bet the Dallas library system has every yearbook printed during the last few years. Once we get a name, it shouldn't be too difficult to find him if he's still in the area."

"There must be forty or so high schools in the Dallas area," Reese said. "That's a lot of yearbooks."

Charlie nodded, "But I'm betting we are not going to need any other than within, say, two miles of Tran's store. I can't see a four-teen or fifteen-year-old kid walking more than a couple miles in this neighborhood after dark, just for a quick glance at a newspaper. With the time of day being consistent, I would conjecture the kid was walking home from an afterschool job, which means he probably lived nearby; therefore, he probably went to school nearby, also."

Charlie had a valid point, Reese determined. He opened his computer to a city map and quickly narrowed the field of likely high schools. There was still the possibility that the kid never finished high school or wasn't photographed, but this was the best they had to go on. About the only school which fit the needed description was Woodrow Wilson High School on Glasgow and even that was a stretch because of distance. Reese was surprised by the dearth of high schools in the southeast quarter of the city.

They decided to check the yearbooks at the school rather than stumble through hundreds of books at the library. It narrowed their scope, but if this failed they could always spread their nets a little wider. Percentage wise this was the best opportunity to locate the identity of the suspect. Maybe, Reece suspected, they should have concentrated on establishing an ID of the suspect as their priority, but other people were already on the search and neither of them felt like they were on the right track. The possibility someone else had seized on the idea that the suspect could be identified through high school yearbooks was a high probability. They had used it numerous times before, and likely the detectives were plowing the proverbial ground again, however, both Reese and his partner felt like they had the best chance of locating him.

Since school was not scheduled for several more weeks and summer school was concluded for the year, Reese called ahead and got an amiable custodian, who agreed to keep the building open until five-thirty. "We had to add a couple of classrooms for this fall and we are unloading and setting up desks, but if you'll stay out of our way, I see no harm in letting you search through the yearbooks in the library," the janitor said. "We got to close the doors at five-thirty, however. Regardless of how far we are behind, the district doesn't want us working overtime."

Woodrow Wilson High School was a three-story Elizabethan structure built in 1927-28 and now held nearly 1,800 students in three grades. The student population had shifted sharply in the last two decades and was now over sixty-six percent Hispanic students. The black student body, which hopefully included our suspect, made up about nine percent of the total students, so we had narrowed it down some, but it still left us with approximately a hundred students to eyeball, with only slightly improved odds that the two detectives were even searching the right school.

Arriving at the school thirty minutes later, the janitor, a black man, about forty-five, dressed in dusty overalls which were splotched with paint, was waiting for them at the main entry off South Glasgow.

"I can direct you toward the library, but you are going to be pretty much on your own," he said. "I've got a crew working on the far end of the second floor and I'm afraid they are a lazy lot. If I don't keep on them, they take a break until I get back. I can't trust them to work on their own."

He pulled a handkerchief from a rear pocket and mopped across his face.

"As you've probably already noticed, they won't allow us to turn on the air conditioning until the weekend before school starts, and then pray it works. It was down the first three days of class last year. What a mess."

Reese and Charlie followed along behind the janitor, listening to a continuous monologue for several minutes before the janitor stopped and pointed out a direction for them. "The name will be on the door and it's unlocked for you. I'll send someone to let you know when it is time to close up." He bowed and shook their hands, "Good luck to you. Let us know if there is anything else we can do to help."

Reese watched the maintenance man retreating down the dark hall for a second before catching up with Charlie. Their footsteps echoed on the tile floor, resounding through the nearly vacant building.

"I dreamed about sneaking into the high school building after hours when I was a kid," Reese told his partner.

"And was this what you expected?"

Reese laughed. "No, my high school was a lot smaller than this one. We only had a hundred and nineteen students in our graduation class and we only had three grades in the building so the whole student body was less than one of Woodrow's classes."

Once Carlie and Reese located the library, it took a while to locate the yearbooks, which were stashed in a corner of the reference section. Like most libraries, the school library was more concentrated on computers and high tech learning than in the giant tomes we had carted around in school while working on our projects a generation earlier. Well, maybe a generation for Reese, but secretly he harbored suspicions that some of Charlie's books were carved in stone.

He would have guessed that most of the yearbooks from 1928 to present were in the stacks, but low priority had been given in keeping them straight. After a bit of fumbling, they managed to find most of the volumes between 2008 to present. The book for 2011 was missing and several others had been damaged, either by rough handling or vandalism.

Piling the volumes, they found on a table, Charlie started with the older books while Reese grabbed the 2014 Wildcat yearbook and started with the senior section. Matching a face in the yearbook proved to be a little more difficult than Reese had expected. After looking through over four hundred members of the 2014 senior class, he had found at least three boys which could have been a match for the face on the security tape. Most of the boys in the class wore similar type hairstyles, clothing, even the same bored expression as if getting photographed was a real ordeal.

Finally, he selected one of the students, a boy named Bryan Alderson and held the open book over to Charlie, who peered down at the small one inch by one and a quarter inch shot for several seconds.

"Don't think so," he said finally, "This guy is a little too narrow between the eyes and he looks like he's practicing for a poster on the post office wall. I bet we will see him again, but not today."

Reese had less confidence in the other two candidates, a feeling which the senior detective echoed minutes later.

"I think you are looking at the right age group so keep at it. I'm going to skip forward to the 2010 volume. My gut reaction tells me he's in here somewhere."

The freshmen pictures would have been students in the fourteen or fifteen age range and Reese's partner zeroed in on the class. The directory stated there were five hundred seventy-three members of that class. Because of the number of pictures in the lower classes the pictures were even smaller, appearing only slightly larger than a thumbnail, which accounted for the thumbnail print moniker.

If his picture was in the 2010 tome, there was an excellent chance it was also in the 2011 volume. Only after a brief search did Reese realize that it was a missing book. Picking up the 2012 volume, he mentally calculated that his best bet was with the junior class, so he flipped through until he found where they started and slipped the flier into the book so he could make a better comparison. If the flier was a true representation of what he looked like then, it was almost frightening how much a teenager could change appearance in just a few years. These kids, while probably only a couple years older than the photo appeared to be morphing into adults as he watched. It was also noticeable that the junior class was smaller in numbers than the sophomore or the freshman classes which was a glaring example of the dropout rate. A large percentage of those dropouts were probably now clogging up the juvenile courts and detention centers. Along with the good kids, each year brought in a new crop of delinquents, a high percentage of those being dropouts, not only from school, but also from society.

Reese was scouring the faces in the yearbook for nearly twenty minutes when Charlie called out from the other side of their shared table.

"I got him," he said. "He is in the freshman class in the 2010 book, which would make him a junior in your 2012 volume. Check out Kindred James."

CHAPTER 8

Reese Barrett was already searching in the 'P' names of the junior class which meant he had overlooked the face or Kindred James had dropped out or transferred during the last couple of years. He flipped back a couple of pages and scanned downward. The name jumped out at him, but the face that went with it had changed significantly. He studied the face for maybe thirty second as the features seemed to rearrange themselves and the image of the face in the surveillance tape filtered through.

"Yeah, that's him," Reese admitted.

James had put on maybe sixty pounds and seven or eight inches in height during the missing year, Reese estimated, from the limited view the thumbnail photo presented. The face was fuller; having lost some of the innocent baby look as he had developed, but the eyes had stayed the same. His skin had darkened with the added years and he had chosen a mini retro Afro hairstyle which had all the curls, but was worn close to the scalp. His shoulders had widened into formidable platforms. If Reese met him in an alley, he decided he would use extreme caution.

Reese showed Charlie the later photo, which Charlie took in with a well-practiced eye. "He's a big one, isn't he?"

They both grabbed for the 2013 yearbook, a contest won by Charlie, but only because he was closer. Reese waited patiently until he flipped to the seniors' section, which provided larger photos and a brief biography of each of the graduating students. Kindred James was not hard to locate. Included in his bio was his class standing, 22 out of a class of 446, selection as a Top 100 Texas high school football recruit and listing as the number three high school football defensive tight end in the state. He had been offered several scholarships, both athletic and academic.

Reese looked over at his partner. "Well, I certainly didn't expect this," he said.

Charlie nodded. "It most definitely doesn't match any profile for a cop killer that I ever heard. I'm not ready to anoint him for sainthood, but I am willing to give him the benefit of the doubt. We need to get him in for questioning as quickly as possible before ..." the senior detective allowed his words to trail off into silence.

Before the cops get to him, Reese understood.

"How should we handle it?" the younger detective asked.

"We need to contact the lieutenant and start developing as much background information on this guy as possible," Charlie sighed. It was one of those deep cleansing breaths which were supposed to make you feel better, but he didn't look very happy about it. For the first time in a long time, Reese could detect an undertone of doubt; maybe even fear emitting from the almost unflappable senior detective. The hardness of his jaw and the stiffness in his face told another story.

"I hope you haven't made any plans with Grace because this is going to be another long night."

Assenting silently, Reese rose to close the books and reshelf them, but Charlie stopped him.

"Grab the three volumes we know his picture is in and leave the rest," he said, reaching out a hand to grab one of the open books. "Let the librarian put them back. These three are now evidence."

The detectives left the library about 5:15 and met the janitor coming to get them a few doors down from the library.

"Did you find what you were looking for?" the janitor asked, pointing at the three books Reese was carrying. "No one is supposed to remove books from the library without permission, you know?"

"Police evidence," Charlie said.

The janitor mused, "Then I guess you found it. Looking for anyone I might know?"

In a school of seventeen hundred students and hundreds of teachers and support personnel, Reese guess the odds were rather thin that the janitor could remember a student who graduated two years earlier, but he decided to ask. "Do you remember a student who graduated in 2013 named Kindred James?"

The man in overalls stopped, turned and scratched his head. "Now that's a name I haven't heard in a while. Why would the police be looking for a kid like him?"

An unspoken signal shifted between the two detectives before Charlie spoke. "We need to question him in a murder investigation."

"Are you talking about that policeman that was killed the other day?" The janitor stepped back and whistled. "I would never have expected Kindred to be mixed up in something like that. He was always such a good kid. You know he almost single-handedly led Woodrow to the state championship game in football his senior year. He was a terror on the football field, but one of the nicest kids you would ever meet."

"Sounds like you know him," Reese said.

The janitor had resumed the walk down the hallway, stopping to use a key on his belt to open a fuse box on the wall and flicked several switches. The hall lights behind them went out, casting the long hallway in darkness.

"It was more like I knew of him," he said. "Most of the kids that come through this school are quickly forgotten, you know. There are just so many of them and most would never stoop so low as to speak to one of us old fuddy-duddies. Kindred was different. Of course, I remember him from the football field, but sometimes one of these kids just kind of sticks in your mind. I had to run him out of the library more than once to close the school at the end of day. He was definitely a good kid and I hope he's not involved in your murder case, Detective."

By then, they had reached the main entry and the janitor un-locked the door to let them out.

"Don't forget to return the books when you are through with them," he said, relocking the doors behind them.

Walking back to the car, Charlie appeared to be very angry, an attitude which carried over as we crawled into the car. Temperature outside the car was in the upper 90s and inside the closed car it had to be well over a hundred and thirty. Charlie stabbed at the window control savagely as soon as Reese had turned the key in the ignition. Before the car could move, he had cranked the air conditioner fan to blow at it coldest setting and implored for Reese to get the car moving. "Don't roll the windows up until we get moving and have a chance to blow some of this hot air out of here," he snarled.

"Don't bite me," Reese said, easing into the street, "I'm on your side."

Mollified, Charlie seemed to calm down a bit, but the under lying anger was still there.

"I have handled dozens of cases over the last thirty-five years and nearly every time people are willing to testify the suspect could walk on water. The victim is always the closest thing on earth to an angel. And accomplices are always just along for the ride. You know what I mean? You've seen it dozens of times yourself. Even murderers are simply misunderstood individuals, victims of a cruel upbringing and an evil society. Nothing they ever do is their own fault, at least per the testimony."

Charlie cupped his face in his hands and Reese was unable to determine he was in grief or simply taking advantage of the cool air pouring out of the vent only inches from his face.

"You okay?" Reese asked, slightly concerned about his partner. When Charlie had returned to the squad after the medical layoff, he was a changed man.

"Yeah, yeah, I'm okay," Charlie waved a dismissal with his hand before raising his head and leaning back in the seat. "I'm just very tired and this thing is hitting me all wrong," he said hesitantly. "We normally get the testimonies after someone is killed or charges are filed. Getting an unsolicited response concerning the flawless character of someone I'm tracking for murder just got to me for a minute."

Reese echoed the thought. "We already have serious doubts about this case. I'm with you on this. We have got to get this guy in for questioning as soon as possible."

"Get us back to the station," Charlie said, "I'm going to call Mattie Reynolds to get her opinion on this turn of events."

"She just going to tell you to do your job and get the answers," Reese said.

"Yeah, but maybe she can do something to cool this manhunt off and give us time to build or refute this case," Charlie said. "If that name leaks out, we might not get a chance to question him."

Shoot on sight might not be the official policy of the Dallas police department, but among the two thousand or so officers there seemed to be a segment who believed it was best to equal the score. Perhaps to save the county the expense of a long drawn out trial, or, more possibly, to avoid a plea bargain, which could eventually put a murderer back on the streets. The *bargain* portion of that equation would weigh heavily on their minds, if they caught the suspect in their crosshairs. On a couple of cases, Reese had the murderer in his own sights and had felt the almost irresistible urge to pull the trigger.

Reese shivered with dread as he was slowly slipped away from the "comrades in arms" mindset of the police force. Although there was a lot of room for doubt in this case, he was beginning to develop some of his partner's paranoia about what would happen if trigger happy police officers spotted the suspect before the detectives could determine completely the facts in this case.

"Do we need to contact the lieutenant?" Reese asked.

"I think we need to meet her at the station," Charlie said. "She knows better who to trust in that building and it's way too much for us to handle alone. I'm going to ask her to meet us there to look at what we have and what we suspect. I wish to hell I knew where our witness is staying and why he's unavailable to us."

"Think he may be dodging us?"

Charlie's face had grown cold and was the color of chiseled granite. "Yeah, I do."

It was after six p.m. when the homicide detectives pulled into the police parking lot behind the police station. Despite the day ending and shadows growing longer the temperatures outside had failed to moderate, the air conditioner in the car was beginning to win its battle against the unseasonal heat. The difference was enough to cause both detectives to pause a long second before plunging back out into the heated air. Charlie had called ahead, asking Mattie Reynolds to wait for their return without specifying a reason. Reese hoped she would be puzzling over some of the questions he and Charlie were asking.

The squad room was nearly deserted with only four of the case detectives in the office. Two were in the office with the lieutenant. Charlie and Reese caught her signal to wait a minute before approaching her. Their desks were about midway into the room, so they plopped down and waited. A couple of minutes later the two detectives in with Reynolds came out and headed for the streets. The lieutenant signaled for Charlie and Reese to come to her office and began closing the blinds. As they entered, she locked the door.

"I'll have to admit that I feel like a co-conspirator right now, but I got your rather cryptic message, and I can tell already I am most likely not going to like what you two have to say," she said, walking back behind her desk and sitting in her chair. Much like the woman herself, the office had taken on an unusual character. The desk, a heavy oak monster, heavily scarred, was reportedly inherited from her father, who had been a detective in robbery division. The chair was a heavy wooden contraption which had been modified by heavy duty swivel castors added to the four legs, which made it awkward and prone to tipping, which fit her personality to a tee. Leaning back in the unsteady chair, she glared at Charlie, "Okay, spit it out."

Charlie flipped open the yearbook with our suspect's senior picture and pointed at the tiny photo before sliding into a chair in front of Reynolds' desk. Reese's senior partner was not a large man, but his movements were those of a bigger man and he was sweating profusely despite the cool of the room.

"Our 'suspect' is a twenty or twenty-one-year-old man named Kindred James," he said. He did little quote marks in the air when he said the word: suspect.

The lieutenant had located the picture and was studying it intently. She looked up at Charlie, "But?"

The senior detective seemed to burrow down into the soft leather of the seat. Mattie Reynolds locked on him with a practiced eye.

"Charlie Dent, I have known you a long time and never once have you come to me in this manner without a 'but' attached. Speak up."

"We don't believe he's the right man," he said.

"And you are afraid if you release the name that you are signing his death warrant," she said. She pushed away from the desk and stared across the room, her eyes elevated as if scanning the room for bugs—the electronic type.

"I can understand your fears. If you have seen the news, you have heard that the media, political figures and the community are one hundred percent behind condemnation of the murder of Officer Carver. Even the 'kill the pigs' hate groups have decided to sit this one out."

"We are concerned about those not willing to allow the slow wheels of justice to turn, but rather prefer to impose their own version of justice, which is quicker," Reese ventured.

Charlie nodded in agreement.

"That is a stiff indictment, Detective, insinuating that harm would come to him while in police custody. We have a very honorable department here, Gentlemen. I can't believe there are vigilantes in this department," Mattie said, her voice, although not one decibel louder, was tensed, sending out words with sharp, barbed edges. She sounded dangerous, like a feline predator crouched, hissing its warning.

"There are always those who feel it is their right to exact judgment," Charlie said, solemnly. "And, perhaps we are speaking of the whole of the department rather than the smaller segment under your command."

The lieutenant placed her hands on her hips and strolled about five feet away from her desk before returning, placing her knuckles on the desk, and leaning toward Charlie. "What did you hope to accomplish by presenting this scenario to me?"

"We want Kindred James to be downgraded to a person of interest, rather than a confirmed suspect," Charlie said evenly. He seemed unaffected by her show of power. "We would like to be present if an arrest is necessary, but we would rather the option be presented to him to come in of his own will. I'm assuming law enforcement has not been able to account for the whereabouts of our flighty witness to collaborate his statement identifying this suspect."

"No, he's still playing hide and seek."

The lieutenant moved her head from side to side, "He has had ample time to leave the city. We are reaching out to the Vietnamese-American community for their assistance, but so far he has not been seen," she paused, perching once again on her chair.

"Are you hinting that he may have pointed out an innocent man to cover for himself?" she raised an eyebrow. "That's a lot to read into a reaction which you don't understand."

"Nevertheless, we believe it's a strong possibility," Charlie said, not backing down.

CHAPTER 9

"I can tell you right now that the chief will not allow us to withhold any information we have as to the identity of this suspect," Mattie Reynolds said. "We are going to be crucified by the department, the policemen's unions, the media, and the citizens of this city if we don't make an arrest soon. The police force has already burned through over 10,000 hours of overtime and the chief is catching a lot of heat because we haven't made an arrest."

"It's only been two days. What are they expecting from us?" Reese asked. "The picture we have of him now doesn't resemble the pictures on the surveillance tapes and I would venture an opinion that in the past two and a half years he has changed even more," Reese said. His voice was a lot calmer than he felt inside. "He might be unrecognizable on the streets."

"If you think that is going to slow this freight train down, you are gravely mistaken," Mattie replied.

"If we put his name out there," Charlie inserted, "A half dozen officers are going to slap themselves on the forehead and say, *'I recognize that guy now. Let's go take him down.'* That scares me, Mattie."

The lieutenant stopped and looked around the small glass-lined office. Sighing deeply, she fixed Charlie in her sight. Reese was sure his partner was going to melt under the glare, before she broke her gaze.

"Some of them may not buy into the release that he is just a person of interest, especially since we have been circulating that surveillance photo for the last twenty-four hours under the assumption that he is the perp. And I really don't want to state what I know is true, but I'd rather not even know, that some are wanting the opportunity to get the high-profile publicity and award by being the one to bring down a cop killer."

The detectives waited as the lieutenant picked up the phone, sighed heavily, and asked to speak to an assistant chief. She relayed the information, as well as her misgivings, about releasing the name of the man they suspected of being the actual murderer. The room had grown increasingly tense for Reese. He felt like now he was the one drowning in sweat as Lieutenant Reynolds appeared to be in mortal combat over the telephone.

"I understand the need to move quickly on this investigation, but sir, I feel, and my top investigators agree, that it would be a mistake to release the name of the suspect before we have cleared up some details on the shooting. We have no hard evidence on this case, just an eyewitness report which we find rather suspicious. The account doesn't match the evidence, and I need more time."

Mattie's face had become flushed and rigid. Reese had seen this expression before. He could sense the emotional outburst growing inside her small frame. The junior detective was always amazed at the amount of venom she could generate.

She appeared to be on the edge of exploding. She tightened her grip on the receiver until the knuckles on her hand stood out in white relief from her dark fingers. "Until we have an opportunity to question the witness further, I feel it would be a grievous mistake to execute an arrest now," she said.

Tears appeared in the lieutenant's eyes and Reese looked away. "I don't give a damn whether it is expedient, Chief," she clenched her teeth.

Charlie and Reese had seen her step up in support of members of her squad before, but this time, she would not give ground.

"This is wrong and you know it. You are going to have two thousand officers out there ready to shoot to kill at the slightest provocation. They are not going to be interested in evidence or probable cause. Emotions are high, and, unfortunately, are likely to overrule calm judgment in a confrontation. The officers are angry, heck, we all are, and we want the person who killed our detective to be punished. I am concerned that any one of them might not be thinking clearly enough to exercise the normal considerations an officer needs to before taking deadly action." The lieutenant paused, breathing a heavy sigh as she listened.

"Yes, sir, I am afraid someone will search him out to kill him and you should be too. I do fear that it may be a situation where someone feels the necessity to shoot on sight. Can you live with that possibility if you are wrong? At least, my plan will allow us to err on the side of caution."

Mattie was on the phone for nearly a minute longer, saying nothing more, just listening to the disembodied voice on the other end of the line. Lowering the receiver slowly into its cradle, she gripped the desk in front of her with both hands and shook her head.

"He's releasing the name and the latest photo you have found," she sighed. "He was not willing to cooperate with any other request."

The turn of events was hitting Reese hard. He was angry, and he was not ready to calm down, even though he could do nothing further until he had a cool head. He had felt like a spectator in the earlier conversation and nothing that was being said was changing the frustration of feeling like he was helplessly watching events unfold from the sidelines.

"What about our missing witness?" Charlie asked. The senior

detective seemed to take the rejection calmly enough, but Reese and Mattie both knew he was boiling with anger.

"I which I were a magician and could pull him out of my hat, but I can't," the lieutenant said. "Nor do I believe we are going to be able to locate him in time to defuse this situation."

"So, there's nothing more to do?" Reese did not mask his frustration.

"I'm going to request that any information developed on either man be given to me as quickly as it is developing. I want all information coming to me. Not everyone out there is going to be a vigilante and there is a chance our fears are unfounded. We will hope a cooler head spots Mr. James first."

Reese could read the words between the lines; Lieutenant Reynolds didn't believe what she was saying either. Since the patrolmen were not going to have access to the information the pair of detectives had accumulated, there was no way an officer would believe any defense the suspect might offer.

"Other than a three-year-old picture and a name, I have no intention of passing along any further information to the brass just now," she said. "If they wouldn't trust my word earlier, they are certainly not going to believe anything else I would say to them. I hope you are right about his changing appearance, because that, and the three of us in this room, are about the only things he has going for him."

An hour later, Reese and Charlie had developed very little more information about Kindred James. Per the DMV, he had never owned a car nor had ever applied for a driver's license. He had no priors with the state, although the juvenile records would have been sealed if there were any. He had no priors, no arrests, nor any stops. Certainly not the profile of a robbery or murder suspect. Even if he had a juvenile record, the man had been clean for over two years.

Before graduation, he had accepted a scholarship for football at the University of Oklahoma, a football power team in the Big Twelve conference. The yearbook they had brought had an article about his football success and future. Per the yearbook, he had caught the attention of several major football powers, but a lot of that attention had subsided when he blew out a knee during his senior year in high school, and had missed three games. Oklahoma University had been only one of two schools that had pursued him up to signing date his senior year.

Equally unlucky for the detectives was the fact that they had been unable to establish an address for Kindred James. An 'after hours' call to the district office had resulted in being rebuffed by the Dallas Independent School District, which was unwilling to furnish the last known address of any student, or even acknowledge that such information might exist. The post office provided an address, but it hadn't been used in two years. They also struck out on determining next-of-kin, and therefore, it appeared Mr. James wasn't even popular with bill collectors, because no mail for him had been delivered during that same two years.

A call to the Oklahoma University campus in Norman, Oklahoma, however, indicated he was a student in good standing, and was a member of the football team. Speaking to the coach, they found that he was expected back on campus next Monday to start three-a-day football drills preparing for the fall season. They listed his address as the sports dorm, but it would not be open until the weekend, nor did they have current information on how to reach him. At least they would know where to find him next week, if no one found him before then.

By nine o'clock Reese was nearing exhaustion. Leaning back in his chair, he waited for the kinks to work themselves out of his back. He had been hunched over the telephone and computer for hours. Yawning, he stretched and looked across the expansion of his and Charlie's desks. The senior detective was slumped over his desk, snoring loudly. The junior detective waited a moment before slapping a hand down on his desk, which brought an instant reaction from the old detective.

"I just had to rest my eyes for a second," he said, looking about bewilderedly as if trying to establish where he was and what he was doing. "Have you got something?"

"Only a desire to pass out," Reese indicated. "I feel like a bull charging into a brick wall over and over. I might be moving the wall, but it's going to kill me before I break through. Ninety percent of my phone calls are going unanswered or else not accomplishing anything. I suggest we go home, come back in the morning and hit it again with fresh eyes and brains."

Reese was sure he knew the thoughts that were going through Charlie's head. The same thoughts were circulating in his mind. The picture and name were out there, and sooner or later someone was going to connect them with an individual, and things would happen rather swiftly beyond that point.

The urge to keep at the investigation was a strong driving force, but Charlie and he were both mentally drained. Any further efforts by them tonight would continue to be counter-productive. Mental fatigue and exhaustion leads to too many mistakes, lost time, skipped information, and simply being blind to the evidence in front of them.

Reese rose from his chair, closed a yearbook which had been open in front of him, and looked at his partner. The senior partner was on the verge of passing out again.

"My turn to play chief nag," he said. "Can you get up by yourself or do I have to call Twyla down here to drag you home by your ears?"

That brought a smile to Charlie's face and he nodded and slipped the pen and note paper into a drawer, then locked it.

Satisfied, Charlie stumbled to his feet. "You know, of course, that she would have done it, too," he said. "That woman is fiercely protective of me for some reason, which I fail to understand."

When Twyla first met Charlie in the hospital, she had instantly bonded with the gruff old man. While not a big believer in love at first sight, Reese had seen all the signs in her. Charlie took a while longer, but he had been very ill. There was an instant attraction between them from the first moment they met, though, which was almost awkward to watch. Charlie, who had been constantly in the pursuit of a fourth Mrs. Charlie Dent had missed the first cue, maybe the second and third for all Reese knew. Twyla, however, remained persistent in her pursuit. When Charlie finally honed in on the signals, he didn't put up much resistance.

"I'm surprised she hasn't called you tonight to find out when you were coming home," Reese said as the pair left the squad room.

"She has," Charlie mumbled, "Twice."

The heat of the day had carried over into the night and even though it was after ten o'clock the temperatures felt like they were in the upper eighties. The air had enough humidity to make it extremely uncomfortable outside.

Reese was thinking about Grace when he reached his car. He had been thinking about the nurse most of the last few days while schedules and events had conspired to keep them apart. Unlocking the door of his unmarked patrol car, he slumped behind the wheel, rolled down the windows to let the hot air out and cranked the air conditioner to its highest level, before beginning the drive home.

Before he turned off the ignition, Reese reached for his phone. Grace's number was on speed dial.

She answered on the third ring. "Hello, Reese, I was beginning to wonder if you remembered my number," she said. She sounded breathless, but she indicated she had already gone to bed.

"Sorry," Reese apologized. "This investigation has got me tied in knots. I lost track of time."

"That's not much of an excuse," she replied.

Reacting a lot more contrite than he felt, Reese apologized a second time. "It's only a few minutes after ten, how about I pick you up for a late-night dinner on the town."

Grace broke out in laughter. "Do I need to dress or is this a come as you are date. This time of night you have a choice of Denny's, IHOP, McDonalds', or Taco Bell. Which is your pleasure?"

There were other options, but he was relieved she didn't pick some place that would require him to change clothing or start spending next month's paycheck.

"IHOP it is," he said. "I'll be at your apartment in twenty minutes."

CHAPTER 10

It took Reese twenty-five minutes to reach Grace's apartment complex, but only because he chose to leave his complex by the back way. After ten o'clock at night the residents of his complex had taken to avoiding the area near the laundry mat. Cocaine addicts laid out their lines of drugs on the closed lids of the washers and snorted them up through rolled up dollar bills. He knew they could see him coming from half a block away and could easily dispose of the evidence by flipping the lid. He took a certain perverse pleasure in driving by knowing they had just been forced to ditch a load into a washer.

Several of the more defiant druggies stood in the alley as he drove passed. Reese had proved his point, so he drove slowly by the gathering without stopping. As soon as he turned at the end of the block he knew they would go back to their drugs unhindered, but they would not be able to completely retrieve the powder, and every grain lost was money from their pockets and less release from their habit.

Leaving the complex, Reese stopped and charted the car's mileage on his travel log. Grace, who lived in a safer neighborhood near Brookhaven Community College, had heeded his advice and had waited inside the locked apartment until he knocked on her door. No place was safe for a single woman, especially one as pretty as Grace.

She came out dressed in tennis shoes, blue jeans, and a t-shirt printed with *'If you want to feel safe, sleep with a nurse'*. She did a pirouette after locking her door.

"I hope you don't mind casual," she said. "I had a whole day off with nothing to do but sleep, so I took full advantage of it. After all, there was no one to bother me." That last remark was strictly for Reese's benefit, a sharp reminder that he had failed to call her all day.

"I get the point," Reese responded, apologetically. "I let the time get away from me."

"That means I get waffles with extra strawberries for dessert," she said, smiling.

Reese wanted to play the game, but he was having a difficult time tracking the conversation. It occurred to him that he could not remember eating anything at all during the day, and the endless cups of coffee were beginning to wear on his stomach.

"I asked you out because I thought it was your time to buy," he teased.

"Not on your life," she replied, "and because of that remark, I am going to get a large orange juice to go with my large milk."

"Ouch, hit a man while he's down, why don't you?"

Grace smiled and Reese caught it in the streetlight as he turned north onto Marsh Lane, heading to the restaurant on Beltline in Addison. Grace had lived a hard life, widowed at 25, losing not only her husband, but also her young son to a drunk driver. The drunk had wiggled free of justice due to a technical error in the investigation, and a bleeding-heart judge more strongly attuned to criminal's rights than victim's rights. Reese was also keenly aware that he had been the policeman who had botched the investigation, and that if anyone had the right to hate him, it was Grace.

Three months earlier, approximately three years after the car crash, the two had been thrown together during another investigation. He had discovered it was more than shame he felt, he also held a deep respect for the young woman. Above all, he wanted her to be happy. In a sense, she was saving him from the cynical life of self-loathing that he had created for himself after the incident.

The traffic light at Marsh Lane and Beltline turned red just as they got to the turn. Reese was the third car back from the light, but for a Thursday night, and despite the late hour, there were a lot of cars on the road. They were forced to wait for an opening in the flow before turning right. Reese's cell phone rang as they waited. He fished it out of his pocket, glanced at the caller ID and handed the phone to Grace.

"It's Charlie, can you answer it?" he asked handing it to her. He kept his eyes on the traffic.

Grace answered, "Reese Barrett's phone, this is Grace, his personal secretary. Why are you calling this time of night, Charlie?"

She listened for a moment before turning to Reese, and then speaking. "Charlie says to turn your police radio back on. They think they have located the cop murder suspect and are going to make an arrest."

Startled, Reese flicked the radio to life, quickly pinpointing the isolated frequency band. He listened long enough to get a general location, before flicking on his lights and siren, which bought him an immediate entry into the busy traffic lane.

"Sorry, Grace, supper is going to be a little late."

He estimated they were about ten miles from the intersection of Skillman and Audelia, where police were closing in on a string of apartment complexes. Evidently, the officers had not yet pinpointed the exact location of the suspect.

"What do I tell Charlie?" she asked, still holding the cell phone.

"Tell Charlie to relay to the patrolmen to back off. The man they believe is a suspect is only a person of interest," he said.

Grace relayed the information, listening a moment longer before hanging up.

"He said, he already has, but they were not interested," she said. "He's on his way to the location, as well, but he doesn't know if either of you will get there in time."

Reese glanced at Grace sitting calmly beside him.

She caught his eyes with hers for only a second before he had to turn his attention back to traffic. Her gaze never faltered.

"In time for what, Reese?"

Reese was grim as he thought what might be happening. He could not hide his fears from Grace.

She looked at him expectantly. Reese knew she had to be scared, even not being totally aware of what was going down. His terse behavior had to have triggered some anxiety for her, but she reacted with trained calm. He was sure his driving wasn't helping her to remain calm, as he tried to blast a path through the busy thoroughfare. She was turning out to be quite a special lady.

"I'm afraid I don't have time to drop you off at your apartment. It looks like you are in for a little ride."

"Is there going to be trouble?" she asked.

He hoped not, but deep down in his gut, he expected there would be. If the man the police were closing in on was the cop killer, the suspect would have nothing to lose by shooting it out. If Kindred James was an innocent victim in this investigation, there was still no way to predict how he would react when they closed in around him, or as Reese feared, how the officers would react. One of their own had been killed, apparently ambushed, and they would be taking no chances. The detective suspected that, with even the slightest provocation, the police would blow him away.

"Probably," Reese swung the unmarked car southward at the tollway, and then picked up LBJ freeway eastbound. "Charlie and I need to get there before there is trouble, if we can."

A steady chatter was coming over the police radio. Police had closed off the triangle represented by the major streets of Forest

Lane, Audelia Road, and Skillman Street. That area was nearly solid apartments and for years had been one of the highest crime areas of the city. Not too long ago, the police had sealed off one of the many complexes within the area, and had executed nearly a hundred search warrants at one time, which resulted in nearly as many arrests for drug dealing and possession. For the last couple of years, the police had increased their patrols in that neighborhood, and the constant 911 calls had settled down a bit. To Reese, though, it made him wonder why anyone would want to live there.

It occurred to Reese that police were casting a broad net to find the suspect, which could indicate they had credible evidence that he was in the area, but had not been able to narrow their search down to a specific complex or apartment. There still might be time to defuse the situation if he or Charlie Dent could reach the area before the suspect was traced to a specific location.

Reese was fearful he might not get the chance, hitting the first roadblock on Forest Lane, still a half mile from Audelia. A patrolman approached his unmarked car, keeping a shotgun trained on him. "Street is closed," the officer stated sternly.

Aware that emotions were running high, Reese, who certainly didn't look the part of a detective in the flashing red lights of several squad cars, kept his hands in sight and spoke loud enough to be heard. "I'm going to reach into my pocket and pull out my badge and ID," he said, "I am Reese Barrett, the homicide detective assigned to this case."

The officer glared at the ID, studying it for a full second before lowering the shotgun.

"Can you give me an update?" Reese asked as he replaced his badge and ID.

"We believe the suspect is hold up in an apartment on Audelia near Skillman. We are beginning to draw the roadblocks in closer to that location, now."

"Who's in charge and where can I locate them?" Reese asked, silently praying that Charlie had gotten through and hopefully was talking some sense into whoever had assumed command of the manhunt. Apparently, a corporal was the highest ranked officer on this end of the roadblocks.

"They are set up in Kinko's parking lot near where Skillman crosses Audelia just off LBJ. It might be easier to come in from the other side," the policeman instructed him. "There must be twenty cars in that area."

"I'll take my chances," Reese said. He eased the squad car around the roadblock and drove toward Audelia, turning right for the three or four block drive to the intersection the officer had indicated. Audelia crossed Skillman at a partial traffic circle about a block east of LBJ. The officers had it well surrounded and the three major streets offered the only paths in or out of the area. Reese slowed his speed and engaged his flashers to avoid further hindrance.

Grace had plastered herself to the passenger's seat of the car, taking everything in, but not uttering a word. Her eyes were large and her lips had faded to the color of parchment. The absurdity of chasing a man down to put him in prison or execute him must seem very surreal to her, Reese thought.

Right now, it seemed rather ridiculous to him, also. Much like a game of "Red Rover, Red Rover, Let Johnny Come Over" the police had formed a line waiting for 'Johnny' to come running out in a vain attempt to break through their line. The trick of the game was to attack between two of the littlest kids in line, so it would be easier to break through. But this time, it was no game, and the runner stood no chance.

"I wish there had been a way to avoid dragging you into this," Reese said, reaching out to her. His fingers felt only cold, unyield-ing skin. "When we get there, I want you to stay in the car. Other policemen will be around so you should feel safe. If there is any shooting, get down." His own words had to sound surreal to her because they felt that way to him. Reese was worried about her safety and she tensed, understanding his concern.

Police cars were still coming in, as if everyone wanted in on the apprehension of a cop killer. With all the flashing lights, dying sirens, and officers taking up position behind squad cars, drawing weapons and donning flak jackets, the scene appeared macabre even to the homicide detective. With this many people involved, the scene seemed to be quickly changing from a manhunt into a mob scene.

"Is it always like this?" Grace asked in a whisper.

"No, this is not normal."

Reese and Charlie had apprehended several murder suspects over the years, but he had never seen anything like this display. Most homicides are domestic arguments that have gone a little too far. It seems almost a relief to a murderer when he or she is arrested, because usually a suspect is given the chance to confess, which releases quite a bit of anxiety. On occasion, he or Charlie had to shut the suspect up to keep them from telling everything before they were given their Miranda Rights.

Failure to read them their rights quickly would become a major issue when the defendant came to trial. Sharp tongued lawyers are all over protecting the poor murderous defendants against the cruel law, which wants to remove them from society just because, in a brief lapse of judgment, they ended another person's life. The victim is dead, but the courts, most notably the defense team, puts the victim, who is the silent witness, on trial, denying them the opportunity to be defended against the very person who killed them.

"No," Reese continued, "SWAT is not here at all, and they are supposed to be contacted first. This has gone way over the line of reason."

He found the parking lot at the intersection was crowded with police cars and he was unable to drive through the crowd into the lot to get closer to the police department's mobile command unit. Finally, he was directed by the officers who were handling traffic to park along the side of the street. He would have to walk the rest of the short distance to the command center.

"Stay in the car, please" he instructed Grace again. "You don't need to be a part of this."

Crossing the street, Reese dodged between two patrol cars and across the lot. Approaching the command vehicle, he asked an officer to point out the one in command. The officer pointed to a small group of officers. Reese approached and flashed his badge again to gain entrance into the inner circle. The captain in command was one he recognized, Andrew Baldwin, who was in the command structure, but he was limited in street situations. Actually, he was the head officer in the neighborhood watch program. a seasoned bureaucrat, but not in a position that faced this type of situation. Reese had always considered him more of a public relations man than a leader. He had risen to the top of the police department by staying out of challenging situations. The detective believed that Baldwin had risen to the highest level of his incompetence. How he came to oversee this situation was a mystery.

"Captain, I'm detective Reese Barrett of violent crime. I'm assigned to this investigation," he said, above the voices of the crowd. "Have you been in contact with Sergeant Charlie Dent or Lieutenant Mattie Reynolds?"

"No, this just came up and we haven't had a chance to make any notifications, yet," the Captain said.

Reese felt like pointing out that he had picked up the information from the police band nearly thirty minutes ago, plenty of time to contact those involved in the investigation. None of the swat team was present, even though they should have been a first responder for an expected violent arrest. Evidentially the captain had neglected to inform them either.

"Maybe you should," Reese said, "the investigating team now believes your suspected cop killer is a person of interest, not a prime suspect."

"That is not the information we were given, Detective," the captain said. "Now let us do our jobs."

Unless more seasoned and cooler heads arrived in the next few minutes, Reese feared a mob scene.

"How did you learn of Kindred James being in the area?" he asked, deliberately calling the suspect by name, hoping to humanize the target of the manhunt.

That didn't appear to faze the captain. "One of my neighborhood officers spotted him, recognized him and contacted me at home. We were in the area within minutes."

"Why was no notification given to homicide, which is conducting the investigation?" Reese asked. It was obvious, however, that Captain Baldwin wanted command of the manhunt. The apprehension of a murder suspect, especially a cop killer, didn't occur often and Captain Baldwin was basking in the spotlight.

"It wasn't necessary. I have this well in hand," the Captain said, "As the senior officer present on location, I'm in charge." His rebuke was both heated and final as he turned his back to the young homicide detective.

Reese wondered just how far the capture of James would go toward covering up the captain's failure to use proper police protocol.

Reese dialed his partner to fill him in on the situation. Charlie was caught in traffic near the Skillman intersection. The police were turning the eastbound traffic on Skillman south onto the interstate access road.

"They have one hell of a mess out here, but I should be there in a few minutes."

"I'm not sure there isn't a bigger mess here," Reese informed him. "Homicide, SWAT, and command have not been informed of the current situation. Andrew Baldwin was contacted at home by a patrol officer, and he has taken control without notifying proper channels. Most of the police element present are patrol units, which are coming in from all areas of the city."

"Crap!" Charlie responded, "I'll call the lieutenant; you contact police headquarters, request SWAT and if they ask questions, tell them what's going on there. If no one has already stepped up and followed correct police protocol, it's up to us to do so."

A quick call to headquarters brought the information that they had just been informed of the manhunt in progress and that SWAT and a negotiating unit were in route. Their estimated time of arrival was seven minutes. Reese personally hoped that the police chief was aware that a certain captain had greatly overstepped his authority. The chief doesn't like to be bypassed, and so he would, the young detective envisioned, personally step on the captain's neck after doing several 'untoward' things to other parts of his anatomy. Reese decided to allow higher authorities to inform Captain Baldwin what was in store for him, which didn't include an 'at-a-boy' award, or a promotion, and certainly not an invitation to attend the chief's weekly luncheon.

A couple of things became instantly aware to Reese. If Captain Baldwin was aware that negotiators and SWAT were coming, it would take the situation out of his control, and he was apparently not going to allow that to happen. The captain began spreading those under his command throughout the neighborhood rather than closing off any means of escape for the suspect.

Against his better judgment, the homicide detective sought out Captain Baldwin again.

"Captain, I just got word that a SWAT team is in route to handle the arrest. You need to pull these men back and secure a perimeter."

Baldwin was annoyed. "I don't think we should wait that long, I'm going to flood the neighborhood with officers immediately," he said. "We'll have that killer out of there by the time they arrive."

"Your men are not trained to facilitate this type of arrest," Reese protested.

"Back off, Barrett," Baldwin shot back. "These men are police officers and they handle situations like this every day." He looked around the assembled officers as if seeking approval. He appeared to still be campaigning for support for his actions. "Stay out of the way and let them do their jobs."

The last remark from the captain sounded much like a political campaign statement to Reese, almost as if the officer was trying to sway an opinion to his favor against the individual officers' better judgment.

The detective made one more play, stalling for time. If he could hold their attention until SWAT arrived, clearer heads could resolve the issue.

"I'd like to go on record opposing what you intend to do," Reese said.

Baldwin growled, "Do you know what insubordination is, Detective Barrett? It's opposing the commands of higher authority. And right now, I am the highest authority on the scene, so it's my call. Got that?" He punctuated his words by jabbing an index finger at Barrett's chest. Mollified, he turned back to a dozen or so officers, who were not manning the roadblocks, "Move into position," he commanded.

Reese noted some reluctance from several of the officers as they swept passed him to leave the parking lot. The officers appeared to be avoiding exposure from the street lights, keeping to the shadows as much as possible. Most moved out on foot, but a few took their patrol cars, fanning out without lights or sirens, almost as if in stealth mode. Reese decided he had not heard all the instructions the captain had handed out, but they were unlikely to apprehend anyone by approaching in this manner.

As the crowd in the parking lot dispersed, Reese spotted Charlie Dent coming toward him through the cars. It was evident the older detective had run part of the way; he approached breathlessly.

"SWAT is still a couple minutes out and Mattie is about to have a cow," he said, between gasps for air. "She said to get that bastard Baldwin off her case."

"I tried, but the captain has gone Hollywood on us. He's not listening to anyone except that little gerbil in his head which he has mistaken for his brains," Barrett said. "He threatened me with insubordination charges if I interfered in his takedown."

"Then when I spit in his eye, it ain't going to make him wonder what's going on?" Charlie asked, now breathing easier. "I always thought that guy was a real SOB."

The older detective's eyes were just slits, telegraphing his anger.

"The more I think about it, the more I am convinced we have the wrong man as a suspect. Right now, I'm hoping Kindred James is anywhere but home."

"We still need to bring him in tonight for his own safety," Reese said.

CHAPTER 11

"I have spotted the suspect," an excited voice shouted over the radio. "He's coming out of the Doral East Apartment complex."

"Is he coming through the main gate? Where? I'm right on it, but I don't see him," a response came back.

"No, about a hundred yards north of the main gate. Someone has torn a hole in the fence behind the bus stop. He's coming through the hole."

"Stay on him. I'm on my way," responded another voice, one Reese recognized instantly as Captain Andrew Baldwin. Not content to be just in command of the apprehension team, the captain evidentially intended to be the arresting officer. He appeared out of the crowd, running toward a squad car.

"Where are you parked?" Reese asked Charlie.

"Too far away," the senior detective replied.

"I'm just around the corner. Let's take mine," Reese said. "Grace is with me so you'll have to ride in back."

Hustling to catch up with Reese, Charlie snapped, "Not on your life rookie. You get in back and I'll drive."

Among the horde of phobias, the old detective had developed over the years was the fear of being trapped inside a burning car. The rear doors of our squad car only could be opened from the outside. The phobia was sharp enough that most of the time Reese's partner refused to fasten his seatbelt and was in utter disdain of the state law which mandated it. Luckily, cops do not arrest cops so his paranoia had not become a major issue. Fortunately, the fear of being trapped was only about moving vehicles, and did not extend to matrimony, because Twyla had the old man tied up tighter than a drum.

"I can get us there quicker," Reese countered.

"Yeah, but I want to get there alive," Charlie said between puffs as his air began to fail him.

Grace appeared remarkably calm as the two detectives rushed out of the darkness and piled into the car. Charlie grabbed the keys and was kicking up gravel by the time the rear door slammed shut beside Reese, sealing him inside.

"Better get down, Kiddo," Charlie said, pushing the gas pedal to the floor.

Grace slid down into the floorboard and placed her head on her arms on the seat.

"Pedal to the medal," Charlie added quietly.

Whatever phobias Charlie had, they didn't extend to fear of running over people; several officers had to bail out of the middle of the street as he swung out onto Skillman and headed north.

At a distance, we could make out several officers converging on a covered bus stop about two hundred yards away. Captain Baldwin had beaten most of them there. He was the closest officer, and was angling his car into the curb just south of the bus stop. His headlights lit up the area of the damaged fence in stark relief from its dark surroundings. The officer had stepped out of his car and was crouched behind the vehicle.

Charlie was closing the distance rapidly, but the little drama in front of the detectives was moving too fast. The bus stop shelter was one of those with a Plexiglas front and steel benches against a rear wall. Someone must have shouted, or maybe the suspect simply turned to look when the headlights lit up the area and the tires screeched. He must have suddenly realized he was the target of the police, because no one else was in the enclosure. He could have just been curious as to why the officers were lining up in front of this bus shelter. Whatever his reason was, as Charlie and Reese watched, Kindred James rose and stepped forward, sticking his head out of the enclosure.

"God, please don't let him move," Charlie groaned.

His prayers went unanswered as the suspect turned his head toward the closest officer and opened his mouth to speak. As he did, all hell broke loose.

Charlie and Reese were still too far away to prevent the horrible chain of events that was unfolding before them. Disaster struck as several of the officers fired almost simultaneously. The suspect did an awkward dance before falling backwards to the floor of the shelter. By the time the first sound of gunfire reached them, the suspect was down and officers were strafing the shelter, reloading and firing again. The Plexiglas front of the shelter disintegrated into a fountain of plastic shards and smoke from dozens of bullets.

Charlie Dent set his own boundaries for the shooting scene, sirens blaring, scattering officers as he drove the squad car between the shooters and the shelter, hitting the curb and rebounding back into the street blocking the shelter and fallen man from the onslaught. His sudden maneuver must have driven a bit of sanity or fear into the gathered officers because the firing stopped. Charlie stepped out into the street facing the officers, giving them one of his patented glares before opening Reese's door. For a split-second Reese feared the old detective was going to draw his weapon and do some shooting on his own into the crowd of officers.

Reese ran to the shattered shelter. Climbing over the splintered plastic and steel he had dropped to a knee beside the fallen suspect and felt for a pulse on his neck. A shock ran all the way up his arm and into his heart as he felt a weak throb.

"He's still alive," he shouted. "Get an ambulance here!"

He had totally forgotten about Grace until she forced her way into the shelter beside him and moved him aside.

"Get me some more light down here," she stated calmly, taking charge of the situation. She ripped the victim's shirt, exposing his chest, which was undulating like a freight train over a stretch of bad track. Blood fountained out of a lower chest wound like a mini geyser, and she quickly wadded the shirt, pressing it over the bullet hole. "Hold this as tight as you possibly can," she ordered Reese in a voice that sounded like a mother bear protecting her cubs. "If you let go, he will die in less than a minute, do you understand?"

Reese could only nod and obey.

At a distance, the sound of more sirens could be heard echoing across the neighborhood. Grace glanced in the direction of the sirens, and then continued her triage on the wounded man. From his vantage point, Reese could count six bullet wounds, which, by itself was a minor miracle. He estimated that well over a hundred rounds had been fired, all from less than fifty feet from the shelter.

Besides the gushing wound in his lower chest, there was a crease across his head at the temple. Reese had no doubt that if Kindred James had not been turning his head when the shot was fired, the bullet would have caught the suspect directly between the eyes. It would have been a great kill shot, one only a true marksman could have made. Angrily, Reese reminded himself to check into who the shooter was. He wanted to shove his face into the bloody wound. The crease in the skull started at James' brow and plowed a groove toward the back of his head, like a channel parting the flesh to the bone. If it had been the only wound, it would have left him with a headache like nothing he could have ever experienced before.

Kindred James was never going to get the chance to tell his side of the story. Even if he lived, and Reese could not believe in that possibility, but if he lived, how would he be able to defend himself in court.

Reese knew enough about head injuries to know that head wounds bleed profusely, but that shot was not the one that would kill him in the estimation of the young detective. The hole in his lower chest was the worst Reese could see, and the blood had continued to soak through the wadded shirt, which was saturated beyond its limit, and over the detective's hands.

"I can't stop the bleeding," he said. "I don't think I am even slowing it down."

It was hard to hold the shirt in position because the blood was making his hands slippery.

"Apply more pressure," Grace commanded. "You've got to slow the bleeding down or he will die."

"I'm crushing his chest, already," Reese lamented.

"He can live with busted ribs, but if you don't slow that bleeding, he will be dead in a matter of minutes."

Reese pushed down with all his might. Beneath his hands, he could feel one of the ribs collapse under the pressure and snap with an audible pop. The detective suddenly felt very sick at his stomach.

"You just bought him a couple extra minutes. Don't let up on that pressure whatever you do," Grace said.

Captain Baldwin stuck his head inside the shelter. "If that bastard is still alive, get some handcuffs on him and give me his gun. I need to turn it over to the shooting investigation team," he said.

"What gun?" Reese responded. "The suspect that you just ordered shot to hell was not armed, Captain. He came out of this shelter empty handed."

"That can't be right," Baldwin said. "He was carrying something in his hand when he went into the shelter. I have officers swear that he had a gun."

Charlie had entered the bus stop from the other double door pointed at a wrench lying in a corner against the far wall from the suspect. He pulled an ink pen from a shirt pocket and threaded it through a hole in the handle and held it up without touching it. I'm not sure what type of bullets you expected him to shoot at you with this thing, Captain."

"What is it?" Baldwin asked.

"Looks like a twelve-inch pipe wrench to me," Charlie replied. He held it up higher so that there was no doubt to what he was referring to. "You felt your life was endanger because of this?" Charlie made no attempt to hide the distain in his voice. "These things are so off balanced that I doubt if he could have hit you even if he had thrown it less than ten feet."

"It can still be classified as a weapon," the Captain said.

"Maybe, if it could have been if he had come at you with it in his hand, but he was smart enough to leave it in the shelter ten feet from where he could reach it, Sir." The word 'sir' spilling from the senior detective's mouth sounded like a verbal slap.

Charlie was on the other side of Grace and Reese from the captain. Otherwise, Reese suspected, the senior detective might have attacked the captain.

Captain Baldwin must have realized he was on shaky ground, because he backed out of the shelter with a stunned look of realization.

"I need the names of all the officers involved in this shooting, along with weapons, and body cameras," he ordered to the officers, whose number had swollen to more than thirty policemen. "I also needed to know the names of any officers who believed the suspect was armed."

Charlie stepped from the shelter, "And you will be turning them over to me until someone from internal affairs or the shooting review board takes over. I would advise you to stand back, because this is now an active crime scene."

"I am quite capable of handling this, Detective," Baldwin said acidly. "I am the senior officer present and I am still in charge."

"Your weapon has been fired," Charlie said. "You are in no position to handle any type of investigation with any degree of impartiality."

The captain looked down at his gun, which he still held in his hand. Reese caught the cloak of self-doubt cross over the man's face, as if, for the first time, he realized what he had done. The man had gotten so tied up in the situation that he was not thinking rationally. The only other alternative Reese could think of was that the captain had known exactly what he was doing when he led the assault. Whatever the situation may be, the veteran police detective was glad he and his partner were not on the weapons fired review board.

Before he could speculate further, SWAT had arrived and began clearing a path through the mingling officers away from the scene. Overhead a helicopter lit up the street and police units began backing up to clear a landing space. The Medivac Copter settled in a dust storm about a hundred feet from the shelter. It did not kill its engine, only feathered down to slow the rising dust kicked up by the props.

Medical City Hospital was closer, but Southwest held the contract for treating county prisoners. Whoever had ordered the evacuation plan and the bypass of the closer hospital in deference to Regional must have been assured that the extra minute or so to cross the city was justified. While headed for the secured jail ward, Kindred James was certainly not a flight risk any more.

"Move aside," said a uniformed EMT and Reese looked up to see if the man was referring to him.

He was speaking to Captain Baldwin.

The EMT motioned for Reese to stay. The medic quickly scanned over the injuries.

"I need a neck-brace and backboard in here, stat. There is a good chance he took a bullet to the spine and he is bleeding out quickly," he shouted instructions over the crowd noise.

The medic pulled a strap tightly around the torso of the wounded man, and then tore into a package of gauze and started separating them. He furrowed his brow, apparently rethinking the process needed. He then wadded the gauze pads into a large mass about the size of a softball.

"I'm going to work this bandage over the wound you are holding. When I say now, yank the shirt out, grab the ends of this strap," he pointed them out with a flick of a finger as he instructed Reese, "And cinch the hell out of it. Don't worry about hurting him; I'll adjust the pressure if necessary. Then back out of the shelter and give me a little more room."

Reese glanced at Grace, near the bench seat, at the head of the fallen man. Like him, she was coated with blood. She had rammed a finger into one wound and from the strain on her face he could only assume that in that uncomfortable position she had used the finger to clamp off another severe bleeder. Despite our efforts, the victim looked like he had experienced a close encounter with a vampire, and had lost.

Another EMT had circled through the second door of the shelter and was attempting to start an IV, but had a lot of difficulty before finally hitting a vein.

"His veins are almost totally collapsed; we got to go with him right now or we are going to lose him," the second EMT said. "Get him on a board and let's move it, now."

"Now," the EMT that Reese was working with shouted.

Reese yanked the shirt, the wound pooled blood as the EMT

moved the ball sized mass over the open bullet hole, and Reese yanked on the straps.

"Good, I got it from here," he said. The EMT motioned for Reese to give him a little room as the board slid across the floor toward them. "Help us flip him on the board and we are out of here," he shouted.

Grace gave no indication she was letting go with her finger, the medic glanced at the wound. "Don't move that finger, you are going to need to go with us to the hospital," he said. "This victim has no more blood to lose."

Outside, Charlie had grabbed a couple of policemen and volunteered them to help with the gurney and clearing a path for the medics who made a run toward the helicopter as soon as they had the patient strapped to the gurney. Grace was dragged along in the mad rush.

The captain attempted to cut them off at the helicopter.

"As the arresting officer, I need to travel with him to the hospital," he said.

The Medic that Reese had worked with shoved the captain aside. "We only have room for medical personnel," he said.

He was the last one to climb aboard. He rotated his hand over his head before closing the outer door. The engine revved up, and the churning blades tilted the helicopter forward and lifted off the ground, leaving a cloud of dust and an angry police captain ducking and running for cover.

"Well, I guess the captain lost again," Charlie said, "Now the fun begins. The judging team has arrived."

An internal affairs officer that both Reese and Charlie recognized as Luther Nichols, a former homicide detective, approached the two detectives.

"Hi, Charlie, I understand you are the go to guy on this shooting."

"Probably," Charlie said. "Although, I'm sure Captain Baldwin would prefer to have that honor."

"A couple of patrolmen informed me that the captain was an active shooter in the takedown, so that rules him out," Nichols said. "Were either of you involved?"

"Close enough to see it happen, but not close enough to do anything about it," Charlie said. "That's my car between the shooters and the man who was shot."

"Then, you can't be involved in the investigation, either," he said. "I must warn you that until the shooting investigation is completed you are barred from making any public statement concerning what happened here tonight."

"It was our case until it got hijacked," Charlie indicated. "I should have shot the bastard myself."

"The suspect?"

"No, I am referring to that pompous ass masquerading as the man in charge. We tried to get him to back off until cooler heads arrived." Charlie was getting warmed up. "But, he was so intent on overseeing the operation that he wouldn't listen to us about how to handle the takedown. Maybe he was seeing his name in print."

"That's quite a charge to be insinuating against a fellow officer," Nichols said.

"Maybe, but he didn't have to shoot the kid," he said.

Nichols continued to stare at Charlie. Reese moved up beside his partner as a show of unity.

"You don't think it was a justifiable shoot?"

"No, I do not. The suspect was unarmed, and came out of the bus shelter at the officer's command, looking like he didn't have a clue about what was going on. There were no sudden moves on his part, lighting from my headlights and the captain's car provided a clear view, plus he would have been a fool to attack a half dozen officers with drawn weapons." Charlie paused for a breath.

He was gasping and Reese again worried about the health of the senior detective, fearing he had rushed back to work too quickly following his recent surgery. His face was flushed and he was sweating heavily, but he was bringing it under control.

"You asked, so I will tell you that nothing about this incident was justified," Charlie said.

CHAPTER 12

Someone had talked. That much was obvious when Reese opened the front page of the Morning News when he reported for duty the morning after the shooting. He sat in the squad room at his desk concentrating; it was shortly after seven o'clock. The front page of the News contained a picture of the chaotic scene from last night adorning the top center of the page followed by a lengthy story with Pepper Jackson's byline quoting unnamed sources in the Dallas Police Department. The story filled in a wide right column. The headline read, 'Accused Cop Killer Captured in Deadly Shootout.'

Reese looked up as Charlie dropped into the chair behind the desk facing him. A couple of other detectives, filing into the squad room before roll call, walked by and offered congratulations on closing the cop killer case. Reese looked at his partner, who had the same gloomy expression that the junior detective figured was on his own face.

Charlie slapped his own paper on the desk, sighing, and looking at Reese.

"Has Kindred James died yet?" he asked.

Reese's mind wandered back to the horrible events of last night. After they had been released from the scene, shortly after three in the morning, Charlie had driven them down to a nearby gas station and allowed Reese to wash off James' blood from his hands and arms. His coat, he decided, was ruined, but he rolled it in paper towels to carry back to the car. Charlie brought him a plastic bag from inside the store, and he placed the coat in it, tying it so the blood would not touch the inside of the car. The rest of his clothing would have to be discarded later. Reese drove Charlie back to get his car. Investigators were still at the shooting scene, but the two homicide detectives had seen enough for one night. They quickly discovered that their presence at the shooting meant they had been relieved of any part in the apprehension investigation. One of the investigators informed the homicide team that they would be contacted in a few days for anything they could add to the incident. Neither Charlie Dent or Reese Barrett were sure what to do next. They had sat numbly in the car for some time.

It was nearly four in the morning before Charlie climbed from the squad car and headed across the street where his car was parked in the median of the closed street.

Reese turned his car and headed across town to Dallas Southwest Regional to check on Grace. She was again going to have the right to be angry with him. Tonight, she had seen things which no one should ever have to encounter, and she had left the scene without saying a word to him, and she was soaked in blood. She had been a real trooper through all this, but Reese wondered if she would ever speak to him again. He didn't think she would agree that tonight had lived up to the promise of showing a girl a good time. He had heard nothing from her since they lifted off in the helicopter from the middle of the street near where the suspect had fallen.

After arriving at the hospital, he asked for her in the emergency room and a compassionate nurse directed him toward the surgery waiting area. Reese found her curled into a tight cocoon in the corner on a chair with a cushioned seat, but no arm rests. She had changed clothes into a spare uniform and she was still damp from where she had attempted to wash off the blood. Her shoes were on the floor beneath her chair, and her knees were drawn up to her chest. Her head was drooped down over her knees. A white hospital blanket was folded in the seat beside her, with a pillow in a white case sitting on top of it. The nurses in the surgery ward were taking care of their fellow nurse the best they could by trying to make her as comfortable as possible.

As the young detective approached, Grace raised her head, revealing she had been crying.

Reese asked the same question Charlie had asked in the squad room, "Is he still alive?"

She nodded, sniffling.

"He's in surgery now," she said. "Police are bringing his mother, but they haven't gotten here yet and I didn't want to leave him alone. They wouldn't let me stay with him in surgery. They didn't seem very confident in his chances for survival."

If Kindred James turned out to be a cop killer, Reese knew he should have felt nothing but relief that he was off the street, but he had held the man's life in his hands and he realized that he didn't want to let go, either.

Charlie cleared his throat, "How about a refill on the coffee, Partner?"

Remembering the scene at the hospital had distracted him from the reality of the morning after. It took him several seconds to realize his partner was waiting for an answer.

Reese responded, "He went into surgery about three, and he's in very critical condition. They pumped him full of blood and slowed the bleeding, but surgery is going to take most of the morning, and odds are heavy he'll not make it."

He tossed his cup half full of cold coffee into the trash can beside his desk as he stood.

"I'll spring for the coffee, Charlie," he said as he turned toward the break room.

One of the detectives was standing directly in front of him when he turned, one of the rookies. He handed Reese a cup, then set Charlie's on the desk in front of the senior detective.

"Thanks," Reese said, totally confused by the gesture.

The kid nodded and made a hasty exit. There was only a moment of silence between the two partners as they both sipped from their cups, then Charlie spoke in an agitated tone.

Shoving his copy of the newspaper toward Reese, he growled, "Have you read the B.S. our unnamed source dished out? He claims the suspect charged out of the bus shelter waving what appeared to be a gun and that officers had no choice but to open fire."

Reese, who had already found himself close to tears, was also angry.

"We found only the pipe wrench, and it wasn't anywhere near close enough to him so that he could have brandished it," Reese said, his voice rising.

Charlie held up a hand, waving it in defense, "Don't bark at me, Reese. You are preaching to the choir on this one. I found the wrench, remember?"

"What happened to the police policy that no one involved in a police shooting can be questioned concerning their role in the case for 72 hours, huh?"

"I guess it doesn't apply if an officer volunteers information," Charlie said. "They have always told us to keep our mouths shut if we ever got in this situation. I think it is designed to give the officer enough time to see the evidence against him and come up with some story to match it."

Charlie raised a hand to silence his partner. He spoke quietly, "Partner, we need to lower our discussion, there are too many ears here. Grab your cup and let's find an observation room in interrogation."

Reese complied, following the older detective to a private area where they could talk without being heard.

Reese said. "If they hadn't shot James all to hell, they would have had him in interrogation, and kept him there until they found something to charge him with."

"I agree," Charlie said, "But don't be too quick to condemn the departmental policy. It may be useful to you some day. Policemen are only human, and sometimes we make mistakes in judgment, too. When emotions are raw, people tend to say things they regret later. Daily, we are put in situations where the slightest mistakes can result in deaths. It's only fair that we have a get-out-of-jail-free card."

"How fair is it to people like Kindred James, who has already had his trial, his sentencing, and probably his execution. I'm betting he didn't even have a clue as to why."

"I agree with you, but if you go out there with that attitude, they will eat you alive," Charlie indicated. "All we can do is let it play out and try to lay low."

"No," Reese said. "We can still go out there and prove either he killed Detective Carver or not."

"I'm with you, but I'm betting the police department and the unions are going to oppose us with everything they have if we don't come up with what they want to hear. Former cops don't fare too well in prison."

"We would still have to convince a Grand Jury to indict the officers in the shooting, and you know as well as I do that it will never happen. They have a track record of almost always coming down on the side of the police."

Perceived threat was a one-way street as far as juries had shown in the past. District Attorneys had a reputation of never prosecuting police in a shooting case. Every officer was well grounded in the concept that justice for them was different than for everyday offenders.

"You are forgetting that we still work for the police department," Charlie reminded Reese, much like he would have admonished a child. "They are supposed to be on our side and our side is claiming they had no choice but shoot the suspect. A lot of misinformation is already out there, as reflected in this story. There's a chance they are never going to look at the other side. Tensions are going to be running high for the next few days anyway."

Charlie folded the newspaper and pressed it flat with the palm of his hand. He looked old and very tired.

"Detective Richard Carver's funeral is scheduled for Monday and the department wants to believe the case has been solved and the killer captured. If we start countering their preconceived version of what happened, they are likely to come at us hard."

"They have no reason to doubt us," Reese countered. "I, for one, saw what I saw."

"Agreed," the senior detective said, "But Pepper Jackson's newspaper story is already hinting that we may have tried to interfere in the capture of the suspect. Right now, people want to believe what they read."

Charlie shook his head from side to side, much like a big bull stunned and in enraged by the injustice of the news coverage.

"Why in hell did that kid have to have a pipe wrench in that bus shelter with him in the first place? They are going to make a lot of mileage out of the fact that it could have been a potential deadly weapon."

"But he wasn't carrying it when the shooting occurred," Reese protested.

"Jackson just told a couple of hundred thousand people that he was, and just how many of the policemen that were there are going to admit shooting to death an unarmed man who was offering no resistance. We might not have liked the way he was taken down, but you and I are about the only people in the world right now questioning his guilt. Hell, let's face it, Reese, we could be wrong."

"Right or wrong, he didn't deserve what happened to him," Reese said.

The two men were sitting on either side of a table just large enough for a desk phone with a lot of buttons, and their two coffee cups, which were now empty. The room was small, with an observation window peering into an interrogation room on the other side. In the interrogation rooms, instead of an observation window, there was a mirror. The glass was one way. Reese stared silently at the empty room through the square.

Charlie looked defeated, laying his hands out flat on the small table and staring across at Reese.

"I agree, but it's a matter of perspective. If you asked Carver's family, they are probably ready to believe whatever happened to the suspect is totally justified. I doubt if any one of them is mean or vindictive, Partner, they just want justice, and James' death, whether right or wrong, would fill that need for them."

CHAPTER 13

Lt. Mattie Reynolds arrived in the squad room minutes before the seven-thirty a.m. roll call looking like she was on the edge of exhaustion. If she had arrived at the shooting scene last night, Reese and his partner did not see her. With all the confusion, and nearly a hundred police officers and department officials searching for answers, it was understandable if they missed her. From her appearance, however, Reese judged that she had gotten little or no sleep, and was running on frayed nerves and adrenaline.

The roll call was merely a way of passing on departmental instructions, information on ongoing investigations, and types of communication which could be handled as a group rather than one-on-one. Last night's shooting played a major part in the discussion, but Reese could tell the lieutenant was cool and reserved about the celebration.

After the meeting, she called Charlie and Reese into her office and shut the door. She sat back in her desk chair and sighed, deeply.

"Before we get started, will someone get me a cup of coffee? Black, no cream or sugar," she said.

She waited as Reese got three cups of coffee from the squad's communal coffee pot and returned.

"I've been in discussion since five a.m. with the police chief about your supposed interference with the police in making an arrest on Kindred James."

Charlie, who was in the process of sampling the hot coffee, jerked up out of his seat, spilling coffee everywhere.

"I hope you straightened his ass out," Charlie Dent said. "Neither of us did anything to interfere other than telling that pompous captain that Kindred James was a person of interest in this case, not a suspect."

"Well," Reynolds said, removing her glasses and wiping her eyes, "The chief has elevated James back to the position as the only suspect. He wanted to set you two down, but I convinced him to leave you on the case. I'm not sure I did you any favor. I think he's hoping you two will hang yourselves."

Replacing the glasses, she looked from Charlie to Reese. "He's probably going to come after you—if—if you fail to build an air-tight case against Kindred James, whether he lives or dies. Already the chief is getting calls from Black community leaders concerning the amount of force used in his apprehension. If the information gets out that we had reason to suspect our original ID was tainted, and I believe it will, this town is going to split wide open in racial violence. The scenario of white cops shooting black men is not play-ing well with the American public right now. Just ask the people in Ferguson, Missouri, about that one.

"To refresh your memory, Ferguson is probably about eighty-five percent black, with a police force that is at least eighty-five per-cent white. There was an incident when a black man resisted arrest, and he was shot and killed by the white cops trying to arrest him. The black population rose up in protest. That is when the 'Black Lives Matter' slogan was born."

"What were we supposed to do?" Reese asked, earnestly. "I, for one, couldn't just stand by and let it get out of hand."

The lieutenant snorted, "That was done long before you got

there. Just by being there you made yourselves targets. Captain Baldwin is trying to raise red flags about your actions, for instance, questioning his authority, thereby convincing some of the officers to doubt their own duties. Did you know that of the dozen or so officers in the immediate vicinity of that bus stop, only five officers discharged their weapons? The captain is hollering that your interference kept many of the officers from realizing the danger, thereby endangering the lives of their fellow officers by not firing on the suspect. He's half convinced the chief of that, and the only thing saving your asses was that you were not in the immediate vicinity when the takedown occurred."

Charlie appeared to be thoughtfully absorbing this revelation as routine, while Reese was becoming increasingly agitated.

The senior detective said quietly, "Then he's discounting everything we said or did by claiming we were either not in the know or were too far away to see what was going on?"

"Yeah," Mattie Reynolds said. "His attempt to kick you to the curb and down play your role in the shooting saved your bacon, whether intentionally or accidentally. But it leaves you in the dubious position of meddlers, so that anything you say against the chief's fair haired boy, unless you can prove it beyond a doubt, is going to come back on you with the full weight of the department. If you go after the captain for his actions, there is a good chance he will take you down with him. Did you know that Captain Baldwin is being looked at as a potential assistant police chief when the next slot becomes available? Getting credit for taking down a cop killer is likely to move him to the top of the promotion list."

"It couldn't happen to a worse guy," Charlie growled.

While the lieutenant came just short of nodding in agreement, she did pause and appeared to be refocusing her direction.

"I need you to find out everything you can about Kindred James. Dig into his life back to when he was in diapers. We need to know what his home life was like, who his friends were, if he's ever been in trouble before, and what a six-foot-four-inch black man, who probably weighed two hundred forty pounds, with greased lightning reflexes was doing carrying a twelve inch pipe wrench around in the middle of the night."

"Has forensics been able to develop any other evidence on Carver's death?" Reese asked. The only ties he and Charlie had developed had been the ID of the suspect from a six-year old photograph by a witness who had apparently skipped town. They had nothing currently to indicate Kindred James had ever been within five miles of Duc Tran's grocery during the last six years.

Reynolds gave a discouraging nod.

"All they have is a theory about what may have gone down. Without a witness, we can't even believe that is a strong possibility. This investigation was literally bulldozed through before we could develop any type of a supported case."

"And if James dies?" Reese asked.

The frowns on Lt. Mattie Reynolds' and detective Charlie Dent's faces told the story. The lieutenant was the first to speak.

"If he dies, they will slam the doors closed on this case and it will disappear from the media faster than used toilet tissue." She hesitated long enough for the junior detective to allow the knowledge to sink into his thick skull. "Gentlemen," she continued, "From the last status report I received on James' condition, I believe your time is very short to get at the truth of this matter."

Mattie's dismissal felt like marching orders to Reese and his partner was taking it nearly as badly as he was. They wandered back to their desks in a bit of a fog. Powerful forces were allied against them, and the only safe way was to go along with the direction the case had turned. Reese was aware that the accusations made against him and Charlie would vaporize like a morning mist if they simply played along.

Reese slumped in his chair and stared across the abutting desks at his partner. Charlie had shown some weakness as far as he was concerned in the office with the lieutenant and for the first time in a long time, he was unsure what to expect from the aging detective. Charlie had been a mentor and friend, but the older detective was only a couple years away from full retirement. The loss of his pension and reputation were a powerful incentive to ease up on this case.

Somehow, the image of the kid, ambushed from every direction by overzealous police, yet still fighting for each breath as he lay on the concrete floor of that bus stop shelter, would not fade in Reese's memory. What did Kindred James have to gain by robbing a failing grocery store which probably had less than a hundred dollars in the till? Robberies and even murders had been committed for less. But they were being expected to believe a killer, despite having a distinct advantage in the store, had murdered a cop, and then had fled without taking anything, leaving a witness to the murder and attempted robbery unscathed. The entire scenario made no sense.

The question of why their suspect had not attempted to evade police as they closed in on him was begging for an answer also. While not all of the cars closing off the neighborhood were running sirens, almost all were flashing lights which could be seen for blocks. For Reese, the only thing that made sense in that instance was that the young man had no knowledge of the robbery or cop killing. He did not know he was the focus of a major manhunt.

Kindred James had walked into that shelter like someone who had nothing to fear.

He had emerged like someone who did not know what was happening. His behavior was that of an innocent man, not of a man guilty of killing a man in a foiled robbery attempt just hours earlier.

"Where do we go from here?" Reese asked.

"We are going to need to talk to Kindred James' mother as soon as possible, but things are going to be very emotional down at the hospital. Under the present conditions, I don't think any conversation is going to be very rational or productive," Charlie said.

Reese had also arrived at the same opinion, and he nodded his agreement.

"I've got that Vietnamese attorney checking into Duc Tran's background," Charlie continued, "I need to get back with him today. Hopefully, he can give us some idea where our missing witness might be found."

"It bugs the hell out of me that Duc Tran was so anxious to get back into his store, but when he was told it might be several days before forensics was complete, he chose to disappear without a trace."

"You're thinking he had some reason to be concerned about the delay?"

Reese drummed his fingertips on the desktop.

"I just don't like the sudden one hundred eighty-degree change in attitude," he said, unable to explain his thoughts without entertaining the idea that everything the little, old shopkeeper had told them was a lie. "I've still got a lot more questions than answers."

Charlie responded with a grunt, which sounded to Reese as if it was coming from a mother bear. Charlie was probably as angered and frustrated by the sudden twist of events as Reese felt.

His senior partner was a slow burning volcano ready to boil over the top, who had been known to blow up violently on occasion. Reese wasn't fearful of the coming explosion, but when the time did come he planned to avoid the wrath by being behind his partner rather than facing him.

"If Captain Baldwin inserts himself into this investigation, he's likely to stomp all over James' mother at the hospital," Reese said. "If he contaminates her story about his background, it's going to be twice as hard to find the truth."

"You think he's going to do that?" Charlie asked.

"I think he is capable of doing whatever it takes to keep a favorable image of Kindred James from emerging out of this investigation."

Charlie having assumed his philosophical mood, nodded in agreement as if he were a new doctor listening to a patient, but when he spoke his words bore a note of urgency.

"We contributed to some of this confusion with the quick ID of a suspect, based on shaky evidence, but we have been given a second chance. This time we had better do everything right, Reese. With the initial suspect in custody or worse," he emphasized, "We need to re-examine this whole case and come up with the truth. We are likely to step on a few toes and put our careers in jeopardy. Are you ready to make that level of commitment?"

Reese felt completely unsteady with a trembling in his lips as he tried to speak. He forced himself away from his desk to stand.

"When I was kneeling on the concrete floor of that bus stop shelter, I could feel the blood soaking into my pants leg. I broke his rib mashing the shirt we stripped off his body into a gaping chest wound trying in vain to slow a fountain of blood. At that point I had no doubt in my mind that the kid was innocent of the murder, and I'm not willing to step away until I know whether my feelings were correct. Whatever it takes, I have to know for certain whether the right man was gunned down last night."

CHAPTER 14

Marquis Pham Do turned out to be a second-generation Vietnamese-American, who had flourished in the American society. The civil suit corporate attorney agreed to meet with us in a health club in the underground tunnels of the office building where his partnership occupied nearly an entire floor of one of the high-rise buildings. Reese and Charlie arrived shortly before twelve and found a table in a small corner of the gym where natural health foods and drinks were being sold.

Charlie looked over the limited menu, making awkward faces at the offering, but finally settled on a small apple and walnut salad with a cup of unsweetened hot green tea for lunch. Reese took a tuna salad on toasted rye and bottled water. Only about a dozen people were in the gym and it wasn't hard to recognize Do when he entered. A generation in the American culture had not eradicated the physical appearance of the man, but the process of change was evident. He was still slightly short at maybe five foot seven or eight, with a slight build and Vietnamese coloring, but everything else was totally westernized.

The two detectives must have stood out from the regular gym crowd because Do waved to them, before stepping to the bar; returning in a minute with a glass of vegetable juice, with a few additives. Reese was not interested in the identity of those additives.

"I apologize for having to meet you like this, but I have to be in court at two p.m. and this is the only chance I have of getting a little exercise," he said, with an accent which could easily be placed in North Texas. "After you called, I did a little investigating on Duc Tran," he nodded toward Charlie, being very astute about which of the pair had called earlier. "Tran was listed on the national register for several years trying to re-unite with his wife and six children. They fled South Viet Nam when the northern invaders moved on the southern capital. They had not been lucky enough to get on one of the evacuation flights, so they tried to escape along with over a million other boat people from the country. Somehow, they got separated and the boat with his family on it never reached a safe port. No one knows what happened to the boat or the people, which wasn't an uncommon occurrence at the time. China and North Viet Nam were both very active in capturing the boats, as well as pirates. Some of the boats leaked; there was no water to drink, nor food to eat. Many people starved. There were a dozen other factors making any successful escape a minor miracle."

"Sounds like you know quite a bit about it," Charlie said.

"Thanks, but not really," said Do. "My family was among the lucky ones. My father was on the ambassador's staff, stationed at the embassy in Washington when South Viet Nam fell. He did what he could to help settle the thousands that made it to the United States. I was born at the big refugee camp in Louisiana and later we moved to Dallas. My knowledge of Viet Nam was limited and my parents wanted it that way. My knowledge came through education, mostly from history books and the internet."

"What can you tell us about Duc Tran?" Reese asked.

Do raised his glass of juice, sipped, and set it aside. "This stuff tastes terrible by the way. My wife says I need to lose some weight. If I keep drinking this stuff, I should have no problem."

"As to Tran," he continued, "I wasn't able to find out much. He was a fisherman turned soldier in Viet Nam, and he went back to fishing when he reached America. He settled along the Louisiana coast, but lost everything when Hurricane Katrina hit. He evacuated to Dallas, and never returned to Louisiana. There is some indication that he was a little bitter about the government reneging on their promise to help him out after the disaster. They probably tried to help, but he clung to the old ways, which included distrust of any government, so he probably never followed through on getting assistance."

"Would that make him bitter?" Charlie asked.

Marquis Do closed his eyes and leaned back for a moment. "Bitter enough to kill. Is that what you are asking?"

"Hypothetically," Charlie responded.

"Well, hypothetically, I guess anyone could be angry and bitter enough to kill, but Mr. Tran hasn't been a blip on anyone's radar screen in over forty years. I can't see him stepping out of character that much without extreme provocation," Do offered.

"If he was just confused and distressed, looking for a place to maybe hide for a while, where do you think he might have gone?"

"You are suggesting that I hazard a guess about something I know nothing about," Do said. "I've never met the man, and I know very little about him or his country. I'm an attorney, not a psychiatrist, Gentlemen. I have no clue."

Reese spoke up. "Let's put it another way, again hypothetically, if you were in his shoes, knowing a little bit about his culture, where would you go to not be found?"

"That's not much easier, but I'll try," Do replied. "Appearance wise, he's going to stand out like Steve Urkel at a fashion show. Probably he will seek out a group of Vietnamese, because he would feel safer and more able to blend into the crowd. My contacts say he's pretty much a loner with little interaction among the local ethnic community, but recognizable. If I were him, I think I would probably seek out other former refugees, but probably out of state. I don't think he would go back to the coast, although that is only a personal feeling. Try looking for him in one of the major cities, maybe Oklahoma City or Kansas City. They both have large communities of Vietnamese."

Charlie finished his notes, pushing his salad aside. "We will try your advice," he said. If you do get information on his location, please contact us."

The lawyer pushed his chair back and stood, as Reese handed him a business card.

"I will, Gentlemen. Now, if you will excuse me, those extra pounds are still hanging around, and my wife is not getting any happier," he said the last phrase punctuated with a smile as he turned and headed across the room. "Oh, feel free to finish my juice, it's nasty."

After they left the gym, Reese contacted Dallas Southwest Regional Hospital to check on the progress of Kindred James' surgery. He identified himself as the homicide detective conducting the investigation into the death of a police officer and that James was the primary suspect. The doctor he was finally connected to was not very sympathetic toward the police, but was willing to confirm James was out of surgery, and had been moved to ICU in critical condition.

"Every hour he stays alive improves his chances of survival, but, honestly, it's much too early to know how it will go," the doctor informed Reese.

"When will we be able to ask him a few questions?" Reese asked.

The physician hesitated before responding. "I'll have to tell you the same thing I told the other officers. Odds are against him waking up. If he does, it could be days, a week, or never."

Reese thanked him and severed the connection.

"Well, partner, it looks like you're right. Someone else is trying to open up their own investigation."

"Did they identify themselves as police officers?" he asked.

"The doctor implied so. He didn't offer me names, just 'other officers.'"

Charlie chose to take the driver's seat when they reached the squad car. Kicking the seat back a couple of notches, he slid in and plugged the key into the ignition, but did not start the car.

"Someone is worried about what our suspect has to say, so they've gone outside channels to start their own investigation."

"Baldwin?"

"Not likely," Charlie replied, "even he's not a big enough fool to get within five miles of that place after the lieutenant talked with the police chief. The hospital is to Baldwin like kryptonite is to superman right now. He might be behind the scenes of a clandestine inquiry, but if it is traced back to him, the chief is going to land on him like a rabid dog."

"Should we go to the hospital?" Reese asked.

"Not yet," Charlie said. "We can't talk with the kid right now, so they can't either. I'll check in with the lieutenant." He grabbed his cell phone and dialed her office in the police station.

"Houston, we have a problem," he said, quoting a line from a popular movie. "Without naming names, Lieutenant, I need to report that someone is conducting an outside investigation and could muddy the waters."

He listened for a second.

"No, I don't think so. Baldwin might be a pompous ass but surely he's not that stupid." Charlie cupped the phone closely for a minute longer before signing off. Turning to Reese, he said, "She disagrees about the intelligence level of Captain Baldwin, says he's ever bit that stupid."

Next, they checked for results on the APB they had issued days earlier, when Duc Tran was first discovered to have skipped. On a hunch, Reese had inserted the attorney's thoughts that Mr. Tran might seek out the Vietnamese community in Oklahoma City or Kansas City.

"Couldn't hurt, and Marquis Do might have pegged it," he concluded.

Charlie looked doubtful, but let it pass. "I want to check with the forensics people again, but first I want to reassure myself that Tran hasn't slipped back into his old stomping grounds. Wouldn't look good for either of us if we chase the witness all over the country only to find him behind the counter of his store, now would it?"

It was after two in the afternoon when they turned onto the street leading passed Duc Tran's modest two-bedroom home in East Dallas. The house was dark, the driveway was empty and no tell-tale trail of engine oil indicated Tran's ancient car had returned since that night of the search. Reese got out at the house; gathering up a couple of newspaper fliers left on the lawn and tossed them behind a bush to the side of the front door.

Several days' accumulation of mail was crammed into the small black metal mailbox on the back wall of the small porch. Obviously, the mail had not been picked up for several days. He flipped through the handful of envelopes, and determined that most of it was junk mail, addressed to 'recipient' or 'box holder'. The door was locked, so he walked around to the back, checking the kitchen door and peeking in a crack into the separated garage. The garage was empty. Everything had the feeling of abandonment, and Reese was willing to bet that mold was already climbing up the stained walls to reclaim the homestead for nature.

It reminded him of his own return to Dallas after taking Grace to Amarillo, to take her nursing licensing test. Instead of returning home to a warm, cozy retreat, he had found the experience of stepping into his apartment strangely disturbing. It almost seemed as if the surroundings had already accepted his departure as permanent, and had to readjust to his return. Of course, he had hoped for a much different homecoming, but Grace begged out of committing to their engagement, leaving him a bit confused and unsettled. For now, she seemed satisfied for their relationship to just be one of friends dating, which threw everything a bit out of kilter for him.

Returning to the car, Reese shook his head. Still feeling the almost supernatural chill which pervaded the atmosphere, he took a last glance at the poor, sad house. Reese slipped back into his seat in the car, and turned to Charlie.

"Nothing," he said. "Let's go check the store."

The distance was less than three blocks, but the route required several turns to travel the short distance. Reese wondered if it was quicker to drive to the store, or whether it could be walked quicker. By cutting through the alleys and crossing a vacant field, the distance between the two locations would be much shorter. Traveling on foot, Tran would have been able to reach his house from the store in two or three minutes.

Coming around the last ninety degree turn, Reese spotted a kid throw a rock toward the closed store.

"Let's stop that kid," he said.

Charlie accelerated, swerved into the parking lot, crossing the boy's path. The young man was maybe twelve or thirteen. He jerked his head up suddenly. Reese and Charlie could see the panic in his face, and both had the feeling that the boy was about to bolt. Reese bailed out of the car before it came to a complete stop, and moved to intercept the youth. The boy must have been aware that the two men approaching him from both sides were policemen and he looked like he was torn between fleeing the scene or wetting his pants.

Reese reached him first, and clamped a hand on the youth's shoulder. The detective spun him around.

"We are police officers. I would advise you not to attempt any-thing stupid just now."

Despite his youth, the kid had already developed a defiant attitude.

"Like what, huh? Breathing? Standing here? What are you go-ing to do, shoot me?"

Charlie stepped up beside Reese. "You think you got it all fig-ured out don't you?"

"Yeah," the kid said, "Everyone knows what white cops do to black men."

"Then you'd better thank your lucky stars that you aren't a man," Reese said, releasing his grip on the shoulder of the young boy's jersey.

The boy was black, about five foot two, a hundred pounds, dressed in Nike basketball sneakers, baggy pants and a bright red football jersey, with the interlocking OU, Oklahoma Sooners logo. The number eighty-eight was printed on the back. The boy stepped back, but made no attempt to flee. Perhaps he recognized the fu-tility of running, or he decided that he could possibly talk his way out of the situation.

"Is that Kindred James' number?" Reese asked, pointing to the number on the jersey.

"No, the black brother is not a big star, yet, so they don't have a jersey with his number, but they will. He's going to make it big someday," he said, as if realizing what he was saying. "Well, maybe he was, anyway, before the cops shot him up," he added timidly.

Reese watched the boy's shoulders and demeanor sag.

"What's your name son?" Reese asked.

The pre-teenager instantly bristled.

"I ain't your son," he said. He stiffened and his tone was bellig-erent. "No honky has the right to call me son."

"Give me your name or I will make one up for you and it will not be flattering," Charlie added. "Neither one of us wants to fight you, but I can guarantee if we do, you are going to lose."

"Yeah, just like Kindred," he replied, his eyes flashing in anger.

"I'm still waiting on a name, and I don't like to be kept waiting," Reese said. He felt no anger, at least not toward the kid, only a sense of deep seated resentment. He suspected he would have reacted in much the same way if he were in the same circumstances.

"LeVartis Thompson," the boy replied.

Reese nodded. "LeVartis, did you know Kindred very well?"

"Not really," he said. "He was like a hero in our neighborhood a couple years ago, but he moved away after graduating from high school. He didn't come around much anymore, but he was hot stuff around here."

"Hot stuff?"

"You know, everyone looked up to him. He was a big football star in high school and I even went to one of his games."

The age difference was catching up with Reese again, and he calculated that LeVartis Thompson would have had to have been about ten years old when he saw Kindred James play at the high school game. The ten years' difference in their ages nearly precluded any chance LeVartis and Kindred knew each other well. Reese was having a difficult time realizing the photo of the fourteen-year-old boy in the corner grocery store surveillance tape was the same person as the twenty-year-old man he had struggled to keep from bleeding out on the concrete floor of a bus stop shelter.

"Did you know where Kindred lived?" Charlie asked.

LeVartis eyed the senior detective suspiciously, but answered anyway.

"He lived one block down and two blocks over from my house. I never saw the inside, but the whole thing looked like it would fall down in the next storm."

"How about Mr. Tran? How close did he live to Kindred?"

"I don't know where the old Cong man lived," LeVartis replied.

"Cong man," Charlie said. "I take it you don't like him very much."

LeVartis shifted his eyes toward the ground. "No one liked him, especially the kids. Old man Tran hated kids and he was always running us out of his store. He kept accusing us of stealing stuff."

"Were you?" Charlie asked.

"Well, I didn't but some of the others bragged about stealing candy and chips."

It wasn't hard for Reese to see through the little façade LeVartis was putting up to separate himself from the thefts, but that didn't concern him or his senior partner.

"What happened when he accused you kids?" Reese asked, knowing very well that the sharp tongued little vandal was among them. "Did Mr. Tran get violent about the thefts?"

"He would run out from behind that counter, screaming at us in some weird language and throwing stuff," LeVartis said.

Reese quickly noted that the young delinquent was so intent on recalling the excitement that he failed to distance himself from the theft.

"What did he throw at you?" the detective asked, deliberately stating his question to include the youthful offender in the group. He watched LeVartis closely as the kid realized he had said more than he should.

"I didn't actually see it," he said, backing away from his earlier statement. He waved his hands in a denial. "I heard about it from some of the kids that he threw whatever he got his hands on when he took out after them. Sometime it was candy which they snuck back and picked up off the parking lot after he went back inside the store."

"And you are saying you didn't have anything to do with stealing from the old man?" Reese asked, keeping his eyes locked on the young boy's face.

LeVartis shook his head.

"Why were you throwing rocks at the store windows when we came around the corner?" Charlie asked.

The senior detective reminded Reese somewhat of an angry bear as he stared down the juvenile delinquent. LeVartis said nothing as Charlie reached out and turned down a front pocket of the kid's pants and dumped a couple of rocks onto the cracked asphalt. "I suppose you always walk around with rocks in your pockets."

LeVartis remained silent, staring toward the ground.

Charlie put a hand on the kid's shoulder. "Go on; get out of here and no more rocks. We have your name, kid."

LeVartis looked like a deer trapped in headlights, uncertain whether to stand still or run for it. Playing out an unveiled threat, Charlie gave no indication of which action the kid should take for a second before moving his hand and turning his back toward the kid. Charlie was a crafty old codger, knowing full well that Reese still had eyes on the kid and would quickly respond if a threat arose.

The young vandal hesitantly moved away from the pair keeping eyes on them until he realized that they were through with him. He turned and ran from the parking lot.

"It wasn't worth the effort to call a patrol to take him in," Charlie said. "I'll bet he thinks twice about throwing stones for a few days, though."

They walked to the front of the store to survey the damage. Reese decided LeVartis was never going to make a baseball pitcher. At least two rocks had been thrown, one striking a window frame and the other hitting the wall below the large glass window near the front door. Neither rock had done any damage. The crime tape had been removed, but the store was still shuttered and secure. No one had evidentially entered the store since the team executing the search warrant had been there. After checking the locks, the detectives returned to the squad car.

"I didn't think Mr. Tran would come back, just wanted to make sure," Charlie said.

"At least we got a good read on the character of the storekeeper and our chief suspect," Reese said.

Again, upon reaching the car, Charlie chose to drive, and for a fleeting moment Reese wondered if the old detective was afraid of his driving.

"Yeah," Charlie indicated, "Sounds like a lot of anger has been building up in the old man for a long time. I got the picture of someone who is a bit of a loose cannon, too small to stop those around him from tormenting him."

Not sure where this conversation was going, Reese speculated, "Maybe he went out and got himself an equalizer?"

CHAPTER 15

Charlie and Reese drove back to the forensics' office in silence. While both had harbored a suspicion that Duc Tran might have been the shooter, they had tiptoed around coming out with a statement. Reese's words had a chilling effect on their conversation. Reese had not wanted to believe the little Vietnamese emigrant was capable of being a killer, even though the signs were certainly present.

With the hero worship LeVartis Thompson had expressed toward their suspect, Reese had few doubts that if Kindred James had returned to the old neighborhood, Tran would have been aware. Any bad blood between Kindred and Tran was nearly ancient history, having occurred at least two years in the past. If that was true, then why had Tran pointed out James as the armed robber in the store?

"What did the background check on Mr. Tran show about prior incidents?" Reese asked Charlie.

The senior detective was attempting to merge into heavy traffic on I-30 headed toward downtown and waited to answer until he had shoehorned the squad car in to a nearly standstill right lane headed west

"Everything we have so far shows him to be squeaky clean," he said. "He has no priors; some complaints, but nothing serious. No indications he has ever owned a weapon or attempted to intimidate anyone with one. He's been robbed four times in the last few years at that location, twice with firearms."

Reese recalled Tran indicating he had been robbed seven times, but that he hadn't reported some of them, since none of the earlier robberies had been solved. He had said he quit reporting because the police didn't care. The old man seemed to have developed a deep seeded distrust in policemen.

"What are the odds that the old man bought himself a gun and tried to even the score?" he speculated.

Charlie snorted. "He probably had enough provocation, and with most of your gun dealers willing to look the other way, getting a gun would have been no problem," he said. "Whether he thought it was enough reason to buy a gun and shoot a cop is another matter."

The stop at the forensics lab came a few minutes after five in the afternoon. Instead of walking into a nearly deserted office, Charlie and Reese heard phones ringing, and there were at least ten people visible, doing various tests and computer searches.

The detectives spotted Bjorn Halsteen, the forensics' team leader, talking on the phone in the center of the crowded office space. He looked up as the two detectives approached, holding up an index finger for them to wait as he dropped his eyes to a note pad in front of him. He scribbled a couple of lines, then ended the call.

"Sorry, for the delay, but this place is suddenly a madhouse. Seems like the whole city is about to go up in flames. We are working around the clock trying to get ahead of the suspect shot by the cops in that shootout," he said.

"I assume you mean one-sided shootout," Charlie said, bluntly.

"Yeah, we found no indications that the suspect was armed with anything other than a twelve-inch pipe wrench. And I understand that it was found beside the suspect after the takedown," Halsteen said. "I can't imagine what he thought he could do with a wrench against nearly a dozen police officers."

"Nothing," Charlie said. "He didn't have possession of the wrench during the shooting incident, and it wasn't anywhere near him. Reese was the first officer in the bus stop shelter and I went in the other door at the same time. I discovered the pipe wrench on the bench a good ten feet from the suspect. Do you have the wrench?"

"No, internal affairs is investigating the police involved shooting and they took possession after we ran fingerprint tests."

"Any chance we can get a look at it?" Reese asked.

Halsteen looked from Charlie Dent to Reese. "You have less chance than a snowball in hell, Gentlemen. Once it gets in the hands of internal affairs the only way you can see it is if it's used as evidence in a trial."

Reese had half expected that answer, and a quick glance at Charlie indicated his senior partner was thinking along the same lines.

"You said you checked the wrench for fingerprints," Reese said. "Did you turn up anything interesting?"

"Nothing, special," Halsteen indicated. "It's hard to raise fingerprints from a wrench of this style because of the beaded, rough textured surface. We lifted a couple of partials around the ratchet. Evidence would indicate he carried the wrench by gripping it across the balance of the wrench, which would make it easier to carry, but certainly not the best way to use it as a weapon." Halsteen must have noticed the blank faces staring at him and he quickly flipped a page on his pad and drew a representation of the wrench.

"To carry it, it's best to grip it right about here, which is approximately the balance point," he pointed to a spot right below a large screw on the wrench, used to adjust the width of its jaws. Moving his hand down the length of the wrench, he added, "Because a wrench is heavier on one end, to use it as a weapon, it would have been better to grip it at the tip of the handle and use the heavy head of the wrench for striking. We didn't find any prints on the handle so it was probably wiped down prior to the bus stop."

"What does wiping it down show?" Charlie asked.

"Probably nothing, but it does indicate that after it was wiped down, the wrench was not used as a weapon."

"How much of this does internal affairs know?" Reese asked.

Halsteen sighed. "Less than you do, apparently. They know about the fingerprints which indicate he was carrying it, but if what you are saying about where it was found," he shrugged his shoulders and hesitated, as if seeking assurance.

Neither of the detectives spoke.

The veteran forensics expert frowned. "Oh, my, this is going to put a whole new wrinkle in this case. It sounds almost like you are indicating that some of the evidence was manipulated by someone in the department."

"We were there and we did not see the wrench in Kindred James' possession when he stepped out of that shelter," Charlie said. "I had my partner locked in the back seat, which is another story altogether, but we had a bird's eye view of the shootout. We were just too far away to stop it. Also, we have a civilian witness to back up what we saw."

Reese could only hope Grace could corroborate their statements. In the heat of the moment they had not questioned her closely about what she saw. The Baldwin faction seemed unaware of her role in the shooting. They had ignored her so far and Reese hoped to keep it that way.

"They have already released the information that Kindred James threatened police with the wrench. At least one patrolman is willing to testify that he thought the suspect was holding a pistol," Halsteen said. "He claimed it was impossible to distinguish exactly what it was because of the darkness."

"Captain Baldwin and I both had headlights on the suspect

when he came out of the shelter, plus there was a street light outside the shelter," Charlie said, with a heavy sigh. "He was lit up like a Christmas tree when he came to the entrance."

"Why weren't all these pieces of evidence in place when we arrived at the scene?" Halsteen asked.

Charlie looked at the medical examiner, "I would think that would be rather self-evident."

Halsteen's demeanor changed rather quickly as the implication filtered through his brain. "You know of course that this information is not likely to make it to a grand jury, don't you?"

Solemnly, Charlie admitted it was unlikely. "We are also aware of what it will do to this city if the fact that several white police officers opened fire on an unarmed black suspect, firing off, uh,"

"...thirty-six shots," Halsteen interrupted, completing the sentence. "Most courtesy of Captain James Baldwin."

"Kindred James looks like some new type of Swiss cheese," Reese said in the ensuing silence. "He's still alive, but he may not be for long."

"Sounds like he needs to be in some sort of custody situation to protect him from the police," the forensics officer said. "You know, of course, in addition to internal affairs, others in the department are seeking information in this case outside your investigation?"

"We are aware," Charlie replied using his benign growl.

Reese chose this second to shift the conversation back to the death of detective Richard Carver.

"We have been instructed through our department to prove that Kindred James was in fact the one responsible for Carver's death," he said. "Where are you on completing that forensics investigation?"

The forensics expert did a double-clutch hesitation, almost as if he had shifted gears and hit reverse by accident. For the moment, it appeared as if he was relieved to get away from the conversation on the police shooting. It seemed he was reluctant about being dumped into another hot-bed investigation, this one also very troubling.

"I feel like I'm on a merry-go-round that is broken, with no end to the ride," Halsteen said. He shuffled through several file folders on his desk before turning in his chair and opening a file cabinet behind him. He pulled out a bulky file. Homicide procedures dictate that only one case could be out on a desk at a time, so, Reese speculated, forensics operated under different rules. Spinning back around, Halsteen opened the file and dropped it on his desk. "We have only the preliminary report complete. We will know a lot more when the weapon is found."

"I take it that you didn't discover anything when you did a search of James' apartment?" Reese asked.

Shaking his head, Halsteen responded, "We are still going through the evidence collected and running our tests, but did we find a gun? No. So far we have found nothing which ties him to the grocery robbery-murder."

"For the moment, let's concentrate on Carver's death," Charlie said. "What can you tell us from what you have found so far?"

"Well, we know he was shot one time with a weapon firing a .38 caliber bullet which struck him in the upper chest. The bullet missed the major organs, but severed a blood vein near the heart. He was incapacitated, but because of his position, and other factors, it probably took him quite some time to bleed out. Cause of death was blood loss due to the severity of the wound. I would estimate it would have taken him over an hour to die, but he may have been, and, in my opinion, was unconscious most of that time. The coroner says he was unable to help himself."

"Then could you say that, if found in time, that he could have been saved?"

"Possibly, but that statement is not entirely correct. A .38 bullet makes a large wound, and sometimes they are hard to plug, especially if the one who was shot was on blood thinners, and Carver was. He could have been taken to the best trauma hospital in the world and they still might not have been able to save him."

"There was an awfully lot of blood for only one hole, as you put it," Reese said.

"The flat position that he fell onto on the floor probably slowed the blood flow, otherwise it would have allowed the heart to pump blood straight out of the body. It was almost like someone had inserted a wick into the cavity. Gravity moved the blood fast enough that there was no clotting factor."

"How close to the victim was the shooter?"

Halsteen flipped through the file and pulled a photo diagram of the front of the store. He laid it in front of the two detectives.

"We estimated Carver was right here," he said, pointing to a few feet in the rear of a large blood pool, which was quite evident on the wooden floor of the store.

"When he was hit, we believe he fell here," he pointed toward the center of the largest pool, "he was probably unconscious after he fell, or perhaps just unable to move. Later, he moved slightly forward toward the front counter, but he didn't make it very far. From the amount of spent powder found on his clothing, the shooter would have been at least eight feet away from the victim at this angle." He pointed at a spot against the front counter, which indicated the shooter would have to have been pressed up against the counter.

"Could the shooter have been closer to the victim when the fatal shot was fired?"

"No, any closer and the concentration of powder residue would have been higher. We have tests which can pinpoint the distance between pointblank up to about six feet in the case of a small caliber weapon like this. The powder disburses rather quickly beyond that point and would be inconclusive."

"Then it couldn't be any closer. But, the shooter could have been farther away?"

"That's possible. If we apprehended someone immediately after a weapon is fired we can place them in the room, but the concentration of spent powder would be too low beyond a certain distance to provide us evidence on the victim."

"So, everyone in the room would have had some type of residue on their clothing?"

Halsteen looked at Charlie. "You're pulling my leg, right? You know the answer, the highest concentration would be near the fired weapon, but everyone would be contaminated to some measure."

Charlie smiled. "I just wanted to hear you say it. When you tested the clothing Duc Tran was wearing, did you find any powder traces?"

"I was getting to that," Halsteen replied. "None of the clothing in Mr. Tran's home had any powder traces, which means either he disposed of his clothing or took it with him. The only other explanations possible would be, one, that he wasn't there, or two, he was directly shielded from the scene when the shot was fired."

"The shooter would have been facing away from the man at the cash register to get off the shot that killed Detective Carver. You would have to ask yourself what type of robber would turn his back on the clerk, and then leave him alive after firing the fatal shot. That scenario makes the shooter sound not very smart, but if we have established anything so far, it is that Kindred James was a very intelligent young man."

CHAPTER 16

Talking with the mother of a suspect who has just been shot down by the police is like pulling teeth from a crocodile or crossing a minefield blindfolded. Even if you survive the attempt, the attack on your psyche is going to leave lingering side effects.

The two uniformed deputies from the Dallas County Sheriff's Office in the hallway had distanced themselves as far as possible from where the mother was waiting, surrounded by friends and activists, who appeared like flies buzzing around the room. One of the officers pretended to wipe his brow to indicate they were feeling the heat emerging from down the hallway.

"Go easy," he admonished them. "The last officers really stirred up a hornet's nest in there."

"No one should have interviewed them," Charlie said. "Did you ID them?"

"Only well enough to recognize they were from the Dallas Police. Why? Is there a problem?"

"We don't know yet," the senior detective said. "Don't let anyone have contact with the prisoner without contacting Lieutenant Mattie Reynolds in the homicide department from now on, will you? Pass that instruction on to your reliefs and supervisors."

Reese spoke as they walked by the two deputies.

"I wasn't looking forward to meeting with the family before, but I'm downright terrified now," he said.

"Yeah," Charlie growled. "Keep your gun down and maybe we will get out of the room alive."

Reese and his partner found Kindred James' mother in a private waiting room outside ICU surrounded by nearly a dozen Black Community leaders, NAACP representatives, and Civil Liberties Union attorneys; all seemingly intent on ambushing the next policeman who walked through the door. For once Reese was glad he was behind Charlie, who had taken a deep breath and charged into the fray.

Every eye in the room turned toward the two detectives, and the room grew deadly quiet. There was not even the sound of breathing; it was as if everyone in the room was holding their collective breath. Seconds later the air rattled as the group let out a massive exhalation.

"Haven't you done enough harm for one day?" asked one of the community leaders.

Reese had seen him rattling his saber at city hall once or twice before at hot issues emitting from South Dallas, but the junior detective did not know his name.

The gathering moved to form a protective barrier between the victim's mother and the detectives. The movement was fluid, but it temporarily left a small black woman alone at the back of the room, making identification easier.

"If you are referring to another investigating team, no other team was authorized to conduct an investigation of Kindred James and his role, if any, in the murder of a policeman in East Dallas three days ago."

That statement alone was enough to bring the temperature up ten degrees in the crowded room. Enough of those near the pair caught the '*if any*' phrase that any movement to intercept the

detectives slowed. They stood like wary boxers, unsure about delivering the next blow, even though they knew another attack was
coming toward them. Whatever had been said earlier must have
been a straightforward condemnation of Kindred without any attempt to recognize that there might be another side to the story.
Regardless of what they said those in the crowded room were not
likely to reach out to the detectives as long lost friends, it was evident they had decided to reserve a judgment of condemnation
for a minute longer. Reese was also aware that anything taken the
wrong way by the crowd could turn them against the detectives
faster than a flash fire.

"We need a few words with Mrs. James, but it's not necessary
that we do it in absolute privacy," he said, gauging the response to
his statement. Private would have been preferred, but it was much
preferable that the hospital was still standing when they finished.
"Maybe two or three of you can assist Mrs. James. We will make
our questions brief and …" He was temporarily at a loss for a word
to describe the emotional impact, but he settled on the word, " …
discreet."

By putting them in the so-called driver's seat, it was quickly
obvious who the leaders were and who were the followers. The
firebrand, who had flared when they first entered, took one of the
slots, a man, who Reese took for a NAACP attorney another, and
one of the louder Civil Liberties crowd set themselves apart from
the others, probably convinced the whole setup was their idea.
Reese would like to have lost the civil liberties guy, which he saw
as a negative influence on the others. If any trouble erupted from
this situation, he believed there was no question the civil liberties
guy would be the catalyst.

Reese was accustomed to the scent of fear, but the reaction he
felt as he and his partner eased their way through the group was
something different. They yielded their ground grudgingly and

laced the atmosphere with an unnatural heat which bred a primal sense of hate. If the men and women in the overfilled room were a jury and he was the one on trial, the detective felt like his fate was pre-ordained. They walked lightly, aware that an inadvertent brush against any of the angry individuals could lead to more than a little inconvenience.

Mrs. James was sitting with a group of three women in the far corner of the room. She was a short woman, being maybe five foot four inches, but middle age had not been kind to her because she had put on a lot of weight and the swelling in her legs underscored some serious health problems. She was easy to pick out of the group because her broad pleasant face had been twisted into an angry rage, and her cheeks glistened from tears still flowing nearly a day after finding out what happened to her son.

The other women reached out to her, even as they moved aside for the entourage of police detectives, politicians, and naysayers. The civil liberties representative slipped ahead and grabbed the chair next to the grieving woman, reaching for her hand in an over patronizing show of support. By the almost startled look on her face, Reese surmised she was partially offended with his familiarity toward her. That told the detectives a lot about her character. Reese sensed that she would have preferred to be alone with her circle of friends, rather than being fondled over by the group of firebrands crowded into the waiting room.

Charlie stepped to the forefront, because, as he had explained before to his junior partner, in her culture, the senior would assume the leadership role automatically.

"Mrs. James, we are sorry to impose on you now, but it is important that we have certain information about your son. My name is Charlie Dent and I am a senior sergeant in the Dallas Police Department Homicide Investigative Squad." Pointing toward me, he said, "This is my partner, Reese Barrett."

She stared at them with jaundiced eyes, following every move they made as they made their way closer to her.

"My Kindred, he was a good boy. How could you do this to him?" she said. Her voice was hoarse and Reese sensed she was all screamed out. "He never hurt a soul in his whole life. My boy would never attack those police officers like they said he did. He wouldn't have."

"Like who said, Mrs. James?" Charlie asked.

"Those detectives that came to the hospital this morning said he attacked the officers with a wrench. Later it was all over the news. Why are they lying to me? Why are you here? To add more lies?"

Delicately, the senior detective approached the grieving mother. "We are here Mrs. James because even though it is difficult on you; there are things you can tell us to help clear up the mystery in this situation," Charlie said, quietly. "Our job is to determine who murdered a policeman and bring him to justice."

Charlie was on very fragile ground with every word coming out of his mouth. Both he and Reese were aware that none of the men surrounding them were fools. The level of tension in the room backed up the detectives' certainty that members of the group were ready to pounce on any statement even slightly out of line. The detectives were not there to enforce the deniability of the earlier detectives, but at the same time, they didn't dare to come down as too condescending.

Any position other than neutrality could, and probably would, have dire consequences. Too much encouragement for the mother, too much sympathy, would bring them down as opposing their fellow officers; too little would only intensify the wall of hate being cast up around the group in the waiting room.

The lead detective slumped into a chair facing the grieving mother across a narrow walk space. "I know it's not easy for you to hear what we have to say."

"You have nothing to say that I want to hear," she said, her voice trembling as if the words being spoken were not words she would naturally have chosen. Her words held the fire the two detectives had expected to hear, but the mother was beyond rage and was simmering on violent response. Reese expected her to lash out at the lead detective, but he was aware that Charlie would not flinch if she did.

"Mrs. James, I can't imagine the pain you are going through right now, nor are we here to judge your son," Charlie said, in calm, quiet voice which belied his normal bellicose nature. "We understand Kindred James is lying a few feet from here fighting for his life and we have no intention of adding more pain to this situation than is already present."

She looked up abruptly and stared at Charlie. "You can call it a situation? My son is in there dying for a crime he did not commit and you dismiss it as a *'situation.'* Kindred never hurt anyone in his whole life, and it's not right that it comes to this: him being shot down like a dog by the police."

A murmur of sympathy rose from those surrounding the small group in the corner.

"Maybe situation is not the best word to use," the senior detective said. "We are not here to debate whether it was right or wrong. My partner and I are concerned about why this confrontation happened in the first place, Mrs. James." Charlie hesitated, and Reese could tell that he was gauging his next response.

"If we know more about Kindred, we can better understand exactly what happened and maybe we can get some of the answers you seek," Reese said. He hoped his words put some of the emphasis back on Mrs. James.

Outrage cannot exist with understanding and he was aware that what she needed more than anything right now was to understand why it happened. Only knowledge would help her channel her outrage in the proper direction, and right now she was ready to strike out at everyone and everything.

Talking about Kindred, what type of a person he was in the past, what he liked to do, who his friends were; all of this might open her up to some of the tougher questions. At least this was what Reese reasoned.

Charlie picked up on what Reese was suggesting, and asked, "We know some of Kindred's background, his love of football, academics, and I'm assuming there are only the two of you in the family?"

She sniffled and buried her face into a tissue, which one of the men shoved in her direction.

"Can I ask you what your first name is Mrs. James?" Charlie asked. "I don't think I even asked you before we sat down for the interview?"

"Eleanor."

"Like President Roosevelt's wife," Charlie suggested.

Eleanor James nodded, "My father always thought it was a beautiful name and he wanted me to have it."

"It is a beautiful name, Eleanor. Did Kindred's father suggest your son's name?"

Wrong cue. Her nostrils flared heatedly as she looked at the two detectives with jaundice eyes.

"Kindred ain't never had no father," she said angrily. "He ran out on me when I first got pregnant. I raised my boy all by myself."

It took a bit more coaxing, but she finally calmed down enough to answer. She had been in her sophomore year of high school when she got pregnant. The father had been one of the football players, who decided she was good enough to bed, but not good enough to wed. He graduated from high school and skipped town days after getting his diploma. That was the end of their relationship. She had neither seen nor heard from him again.

Her family had treated her much the same. Her loving father forced her from their home while she was five months pregnant, refusing to acknowledge her or her son after he was born. Contact with them remained problematic.

The name Kindred came from the fact the baby was the only kin she had left after all others had rejected her. It was an often-repeated story she was telling them, one that had played out many times in the past. Cast out and left alone by those she loved, she had struggled to raise her son, living in cheap motels, dropping school to work as a day maid, taking the infant with her to work, not always getting the good jobs, because they did not want her to bring the child, and she had no place to leave him. The early years had been ones of base survival.

"That little man worked as hard as I did, just to survive, Officers." She reached out to the detectives as if seeking approval. "There is no way that my son, Kindred, would ever be involved in a crime. I taught him too well that there is always a better way."

"Was Kindred in a financial bind which may have caused him to try to make an easy score?" Reese asked, bringing an immediate rebuke from his senior partner in the form of a steely glare.

The question went unchallenged by Mrs. James although the ACLU attorney reached out and gripped her arm.

"You don't have to answer that question, Mrs. James. The detective is wrong to insinuate that Kindred robbed that store and shot that officer."

Reese bowed his head. "I'm sorry Mrs. James. I was merely trying to establish if there was any reason he could have changed."

Eleanor looked Reese's eyes and he felt like she was peering at his soul.

"God tests his people with hardships, but he has promised that we will not be tested with more than we can bear. Kindred has been tested from birth with poverty, rejection, discrimination, and misunderstanding. He came into this world being treated as a second-class citizen, and only because of his character has he risen above that pit, Officer. There is nothing on this earth which could have led to him to steal from those who have little more than he has, and certainly not to kill anyone. There is no excuse for killing. A mistake has been made, one which may cost my son his life, but I am telling you that he is not the one who made it." Her words carried more venom than a rattlesnake.

"One more question and we will leave you alone, Mrs. James," Charlie said. "What was your son doing last night with a pipe wrench at the bus stop?"

Eleanor James sighed heavily and placed her hand over her heart.

"He borrowed it from one of his friends at work to fix a leaking pipe under our kitchen sink. We have been trying to get maintenance to fix it for several months, but evidently, we are low priority. Kindred said he could fix it, but he kept putting it off until this week because he didn't have the right tool. Tonight, was going to be his last night at work until next summer so he finally got around to borrowing the wrench. He fixed the leak, and was taking the wrench back."

"Did he wash the wrench before he took it last night?"

"The wrench, yes, but you know how kids are, the kitchen sink was a real mess, but he said he didn't have time to clean it because he was going to be late for the bus."

"So, he ran out with just the wrench to catch a bus?"

"He even forgot the lunch I made for him," she said. "They were going to have a going away party for him at work, but I thought he needed some real food. I made him chicken salad with sweet pickles and Doritos. That was his favorite."

Eleanor James provided us with the name and location where Kindred was employed until last night—a machine shop in Garland in the industrial area near LBJ freeway.

"He started working in the shop part time during the summer between his sophomore and junior year in high school," she said. "My son was a good worker and they took him back every summer."

"Did he always work nights?" Reese asked.

"Kindred preferred the nights. He said machine shops get awfully hot in the summer and it's a little cooler at nights."

Despite leaving Mrs. James no worse off emotionally than she was when they arrived, the two detectives had noticed slight erosion in the fragile restraints which kept the two sides apart. Some of the people in the room were beginning to grumble vocally about the homicide detectives asking too many personal questions. Reese was relieved to escape the repressive atmosphere developing in the small waiting room.

"There is going to be a riot before this investigation is over," Charlie indicated as we slithered out of earshot of the gathering. The senior detective had never been the one with the optimistic attitude, but now his face read like a forecast of stormy skies with lightening, thunder, and pain.

"There are some agitators in that room who are willing to drive this into a full-scale riot. I'm not sure that I blame them," he said. "However this investigation goes, we are not going to make everyone happy. Right now, those people are being force-fed a one-sided story. Even if Kindred James was as guilty as hell, he should never have been taken down by a mob."

Reese shivered. "I think I was developing a good case of pneumonia in that room," he said.

"Yeah, me too," Charlie nodded. The expression on the face of the old detective had gone stone cold. "I suspect the cold vibes being given off by certain people are making many others very uncomfortable right this minute."

They continued down the hallway with Reese slightly in the

lead, heading toward the hospital's prison lockup ward, for county prisoners undergoing treatment.

"We need to check on the condition of our suspect," he said to Charlie.

"And I suppose the fact that a certain Ms. Grace Evans is on shift at the jail lockup ward, and the fact that you haven't seen or talked to her in several hours, never figured into this decision?"

Reese held his hand up and pinched the air about a quarter an inch across between his thumb and index finger.

"Maybe a little bit," he said.

Charlie spaced the palms of his hands about two feet apart.

"I think more than a little," he said. "I'll check on the suspect while you check out his nurse." Charlie flashed a small smile, but tonight it felt strained to Reese.

"When I saw her last night, she was really shaken up," Reese murmured. "I never would have wanted her to see that side of police work. She denies it, but I know she still has an occasional nightmare about when her husband and son were killed. Once the initial shock wears off, I'm not sure how she is going to react to this incident."

Charlie sighed. "I hope you are worrying too much about her reactions last night. I believe she is made of sterner stuff than you are giving her credit for," he said. "There is nothing glamorous to nursing: bedpans, vomit, blood, torn limbs, and death. Like my Twyla, I don't think she would have made the cut to be one of the bedpan rustlers if she couldn't handle it. She handled it like a pro last night; she saved that kid's life."

CHAPTER 17

Grace did not appear to be handling things very well when Reese finally caught up with her. She looked like she hadn't slept in two days, which he couldn't be sure wasn't true. She had been almost ready to drop from exhaustion when he left he at her apartment shortly after dawn this morning. Now, fourteen hours later, she looked even worse.

Her reaction toward Reese and his partner was even more startling.

"Reese, you are going to die on your feet if you don't get some rest."

"I was concerned about you," Reese said, realizing suddenly he was very tired. Somehow, it felt good to him that each of them were thinking of the wellbeing of the other over their own needs. "I guess I don't have to ask how well you are holding up."

"Oh, everything is just peachy," she said, wiping her hands unconsciously on the front of her scrubs. "Start out the day with your hands buried inside a shooting victim, who resembles a piece of Swiss cheese, fight with all you got to keep him alive, fend off the family, who will do anything to be with him, and it may all be for nothing, Reese."

Despite the separation nurses had been trained to emotionally maintain from the patient, she started to cry. She was failing to do the one thing she had been told never to do, to become emotionally involved with her patient.

"He got out of surgery about two this afternoon, and they just took him back in because of internal bleeding, again. I don't think he is going to make it."

"I just left his mother a couple of minutes ago. Are they going to inform her that her son is back in surgery?"

"They should already have. Reese, this whole day has been a rush from one crisis point to another and you can almost see him slipping away. I'm not sure that it wouldn't be easier on her to delay telling her, again, maybe give her a little time to adjust before throwing her into panic again."

"Surely the doctors will tell her in the easiest way possible," Reese said.

"The hospital called me back in to work shortly before he came out of surgery, so I'm working a seventeen hour shift tonight. I'm not even sure what work schedule I have. They make mistakes and have personal judgements which are not always with proper procedure," Grace said.

Reese read a second meaning into what she was implying. "Are you insinuating that some of the staff are refusing to care for Kindred James?"

"Well, maybe not a refusal, more like reluctance," Grace said.

"Even working short staffed, I don't see that as an excuse not to follow procedures," Reese said, "He's a human being, her son, and withholding information from her just to make things a little easier on themselves would be one of the cruelest things I could imagine." He watched as Grace nodded, and then bowed her head. "Keep your chin up, the hospital has to know you are one of the best."

"I'm just glad I'm not the one who has to tell her," she said.

"Did you get any sleep after I dropped you off at your apartment this morning?"

"I couldn't sleep," she sighed, "I kept thinking about all that blood and I could feel every pulse his heart made. If everyone was forced to watch someone die in this way, there would never be another murder."

Grace had spoken those words with conviction, but Reese knew that even that experience wouldn't deter some people from brutal killings, that there are people beyond redemption. It might decrease the number of murders for a time, but there would still be those who do not value human life as Grace did.

Reese agreed, sympathetically, but he knew it was more a dream than reality. During his nearly twelve years on the police force, it had been an endless stream of murders and mayhem. An individual might change, but a culture which had been taught to ignore the value of life was hard to change.

"Maybe someday we will live in a perfect world," he said.

After a few private moments with Grace, Reese promised to get some sleep after one more stop tonight on the investigation, maybe two, depending on what they found out. He tried to leave her with a smile, but neither of them could put their hearts into any type of levity tonight.

"I promise to get some sleep sometime tonight. Scout's honor," he swore holding up his hand in a three-finger salute.

She smiled. "You were never a scout, I know better than to believe that," she said as they parted.

"Hey, Lady," Reese said, as she started to turn away, "You need to promise me that you will crash out after you finally get off shift, too. Really."

Grace nodded, waved, then turned and walked away.

Reese caught up with Charlie talking to one of the jail guards near the door to the ward. He stood apart and waited for a minute for Charlie to break away from his conversation.

Charlie looked like he was thoroughly disgusted with the world when he joined Reese a moment later. "The police have already been pestering the staff for up to date reports on Kindred James' condition," he said, "And you will never guess who has been the loudest?"

"Captain Andrew Baldwin."

"Correct for the million-dollar prize," Charlie said, waving his hand over his head in a mock salute. "That man has his thumb down hard on every aspect of this investigation."

"Because he has a lot to lose," Reese added.

"He's going to have a lot more to lose if the police chief gets wind of his interference. The chief is walking a tightrope right now; it's not to Baldwin's advantage to piss the boss off. That is exactly what is going to happen when the chief finds out about his attempts to interfere in our investigation."

"Maybe he thinks it's worth the effort," Reese said, which brought a steely nod from the veteran detective.

"He does," Charlie said. "If he is thinking at all."

The two detectives walked to the elevator and headed for the ground floor exit.

"You suppose Baldwin is aware of our suspicions about James' possible innocence?" Charlie asked, rather sarcastically. "Or is he just striving to deflect any criticism of his role in the mismanaged takedown?"

"Any claim he might have made about believing Kindred James was guilty of killing Carver should have gone out the window, prior to the shooting, when I informed him our investigation had placed James as a person of interest, rather than a suspect in the killing," Reese said. "He was aware that we wanted to question James as a potential witness and not as a perpetrator."

Charlie chose to drive when they reached the car parked in a dark corner of the lot outside the main entrance.

"You've got to question why the police chief refused to change the threat level. He had talked with and knew evidence was building that he was not the killer." The pair were approaching their parked police car.

"I would be wondering the same thing," said a voice in the nearby shadows.

Both men reached for their weapons as Pepper Jackson walked into the light near the detectives. He held his hands so they could be seen.

"Sorry, you guys,"

"We are too tired for any games, Jackson," Charlie growled. "You just nearly bought a bullet."

"Might be true if it was someone else in the department, but I know you two better than that, I think," Pepper continued without a pause, "You think there may be some shenanigans going on in the upper levels of the police department that the public needs to know about?"

Reese and his partner were both taken aback by the intrusion into their conversation. An aggressive newspaper journalist, Pepper Jackson had proved to be a pain in the side in several previous investigations, but he was not known for sensationalism. Nor was he noted for hiding in the shadows, unless he had no other way of getting the story. The police ban on identifying officers involved in a shooting incident, for however long the police chief chose to shield his officers from public scrutiny, was being effective. If Jackson had not been able to ferret them out, and he was resorting to stalking detectives in dark parking lots, the cone of silence must be complete.

"Why aren't you out there chasing Baldwin, if you want a story?" Charlie Dent asked.

Unfazed, Pepper Jackson, smiled. "I have been, and he's willing to spill the beans about everything. I'm thinking that his version might be heavily personal biased, because what he seems to be saying is just not adding up," the reporter said. "It does me absolutely no good to get a story if I don't have any way of confirming it. Right now, Baldwin is the only one I hear singing his little tune. Maybe you guys could sing me a few bars of a different tune? Maybe help me out with my dilemma?"

"Not likely," Charlie said, "Besides, right now, I don't think anyone would believe anything we might say either."

"Would you care to amplify your previous indiscreet statement?" Pepper asked, flipping open a small recording device and holding it up to the pair. "I already have it on record that you don't agree with the line of bull Baldwin in putting out there."

"What if I just arrest you for interfering in a police investigation?" Charlie Dent asked, making a grab toward the recording device.

Pepper danced backwards.

"Whoa, whoa, whoa," he yelped, putting a little distance between them. "I'll keep your dirty little secret for the moment, but you and I both know that eventually the truth will come out. Don't you think it would be better if you have someone like me on your side?"

"I've read your column and I'm not sure that having you on our side will be much of an advantage," Charlie said.

Reese, who knew the old detective better than anyone, couldn't tell if his partner was serious or just posturing.

The reporter grabbed at his chest.

"Oh, you've wounded me to my heart," he said. "What's really going on here? Is there some sort of a police cover-up?"

"I'm not at liberty …"

"…to comment on an ongoing investigation, yeah, yeah, I got that," the reporter cut Charlie off. "But we both know that there is a lot more to the story."

Reese chose to respond to that comment, "That depends a lot on what you believe, now doesn't it?"

"I only know what a little birdie is telling me and I'll admit he's chirping plenty," Pepper said. "He's got most of the cops on the force believing that Kindred James was attempting to attack the police with a pipe wrench. He's even thrown out a few hints that a pair of homicide detectives rushed into his crime scene, for some obscure reason, and maybe even moved some of the evidence to taint the investigation."

"Are you referring to our official investigation or Captain Baldwin's shadow investigation?" Charlie asked.

Pepper shrugged. "I didn't know there was a difference, sorry. He says he's investigating the shooting. That's all I know." He ran an index finger across his cheek, which was covered with stubble. "I thought police shootings were investigated by internal affairs," he said, feigning he was perplexed. "How come I've stumbled across not only a second investigation, but a third? Right now, it seems none of these squads involved are co-operating with each other."

Reese knew enough to keep silent and let Charlie respond to the bait that Pepper had thrown out.

"Internal affairs are investigating the police shooting, while we are still working on solving the Carver murder."

"Well, I would venture that Baldwin's investigation is intended to drag you two before internal affairs on charges of conduct unbecoming of police officers," Pepper Jackson replied. "Now," he hesitated, "Do I talk with you or with Baldwin?"

"How about you take what you believe to public affairs?" Reese asked.

"Dude," Pepper fired back, "Those guys don't like me."

"And you think we do?"

Pepper twisted his face in a pained expression.

"Right now, apparently not-so-much," he admitted.

"Don't forget it," Charlie said, opening the car door, allowing light to spill out in an intimate circle. The senior detective hoisted himself into the driver's seat. "Whatever we tell you must be completely off the record."

"How do you expect me to get a story out of that?" Pepper said, seemingly reluctant to abide by the terms put forth by the senior detective.

"You know as well as I do that the truth will eventually come out, and then you will know how to use it," Charlie said. "I hope you choose wisely."

"Did I forget to tell you that Detective Richard Carver was Captain Baldwin's partner when they were both on the streets?" Pepper said, pushing Charlie's door closed. "That is a bit of free information."

Charlie revealed nothing, looking straight ahead for several seconds.

Reese climbed into the car, leaving the newsman standing alone in the parking lot. He had his doubts about the privilege Charlie had just handed out to the journalist, but he trusted his partner. He hoped Charlie was right. A premature release of insider information on this case could lead to a catastrophic disaster for the city. The bombshell that Carver and Baldwin had partnered added a whole new dimension to what was happening. In some ways being a partner was a closer relationship than marriage to most policemen. He wondered just how far the Captain would go and how many was he willing to sacrifice to avenge Carver's death.

"Did we tell Pepper too much?" asked Reese as they cleared the parking lot, and headed across town toward the Garland industrial area off Jupiter Road.

"I'm not sure we told him anything he hadn't already figured out for himself," Charlie said.

Pepper Jackson was a bit of a throwback. He was an investigative reporter, who hit the bricks and checked the sources. With the assistance of Captain Andrew Baldwin, the writer could possibly know more about the police involvement than they did.

"Let's check out the machine shop before calling it a day," Charlie said. "If they can alibi Kindred James out of the Carver murder, it's going to play 'Whaley' with the Captain's excuses."

"Won't the body cameras on the police officers and the dash camera on Baldwin's car shed light on what really happened?" asked Reese.

Charlie Dent's response was chilling. "We have already discovered that data often has ways of disappearing or being altered before it's scrubbed for consumption by the public. If the record is there, it may or may not be true by the time it's released."

"The record on our car couldn't have been altered," Reese protested.

"We need to secure a copy of that tape and put it into a safe location, because while it was not a priority with public affairs, Baldwin will remember we were there and he will be after that recording sooner or later. I don't feel like he can afford to leave it out here in the open."

CHAPTER 18

Lincoln's Machine Shop occupied a corner space in a major complex just off Jupiter and Kingsley. The shop took up about sixteen thousand square feet of a block long building on a side road. A small sign led to a single glass door at the front of the building leading into an office area. Several overhead garage doors along the length of the shop were open to the night air for ventilation.

Approaching the door, Reese and Charlie were instantly assailed by loud, piercing noise.

"Sounds a little like our squad room just after roll call," Reese said as an attempt at levity. "Can you imagine working in this atmosphere every shift?"

"It reminds me of your snoring when we are on stakeout," Charlie said.

The front door was locked and no response came to their knocking so they skirted around the building. The pair entered one of the open bay doors into the shop area. Proximity brought the noise level to a shrill whine and the temperature rose into an uncomfortable range.

"How can people work in noise this loud?" Reese asked his partner.

"Huh?" Charlie replied, cupping a hand to his ear. "I can't hear you," he shouted.

Reese waved him off and they stepped into the shop, circling an idle manual lathe to reach a central aisle. Footing was unsure as they crunched across a bed of metal shavings. Ahead of them he could see a man heading away from them with his hands around the cable controls of an overhead crane. The pair approached the man from the rear and Reese tapped him on the shoulder.

The man, dressed in heavy steel-toes shoes, dirty blue jeans and tattered T-shirt, released the button on the control column which allowed the crane to coast to a stop a few feet further down the overhead rails. He reached up and removed a pair of earphones.

"Sorry, I didn't hear you come in," he said.

A pair of machinists poked their heads out into the aisle, gave them the once over, and disappeared back out of sight.

"What can I do to help you?" The crane operator asked.

"We need to speak to whoever is in charge," Charlie said.

The man shrugged.

"That would be Paul. Follow me," he said, re-engaging the overhead crane and moving toward the rear of the shop.

Reese felt like he was in a parade as he fell into step behind the crane operator. Occasionally, a head would pop out from between the line of equipment, stare for a second and disappear. A little over halfway to the rear of the shop, the operator stopped and pointed toward a group of three men crowded around a CNC milling center.

A wiry man, about fifty, with dirty, sandy hair, a full beard, grease stained clothes, which seemed to be the unofficial uniform of the crew, separated himself from the trio as they approached.

"You guys cops?" he asked and when Charlie nodded, he continued, "Heard ya'll was nosing around the shop earlier today. Don't know what I can tell you that you probably haven't already heard."

Raising his voice above the background noise, Charlie shouted, "You got a quieter place we can talk?"

The shop supervisor motioned toward the front office and led the way. He extracted a ring of keys from his pocket to unlock the door between the office and the shop.

"We normally leave this open, but we are rather scattered in this shop and you never know what or who might wander in from the street," he said, after they entered he closed the door behind them. He didn't bother to lock it.

"Did you talk to the police earlier today?" Charlie asked.

"We got word of the shooting from the day shift when we came in tonight, but we arrived after they were gone," said the foreman, who identified himself as Paul Godfrey. He motioned them toward a pair of chairs in the open office. "Take a load off your feet." The foreman took a nearby chair and faced the detectives.

"I'm afraid we have been pretty well isolated from the news lately, so this whole thing came as a complete shock to us. Kindred James has worked for us off and on for four years during the summers, but never in a million years would I have believed he could have killed someone," he said. "And then get shot down like that," he shook his head. "I just don't get it."

"So, you don't believe he was capable of killing the policeman?" Reese asked.

"That's what I don't understand. The police that came by the shop earlier said he shot a detective during a robbery at a grocery store Monday night, but he was here in the shop all that night."

Reese felt a hollowness forming in the pit of his stomach. "You got any proof that he was here?" he asked.

"That's another thing, the cops that came by today said the time sheets for my crew was evidence and they took them. I don't have any written proof that he was here, but that was the night he borrowed a pipe wrench from Gator Martin to fix his mother's plumbing."

"We've been teasing Kindred all week about fixing her plumbing.

Kindred kept saying he hadn't gotten around to it. Gator kept pestering him about getting his pipe wrench back, while Kindred kept telling him, he forgot to bring it. Gator asked him how he could forget a tool that resembled a augh—well you know." Godfrey looked almost apologetic. "Things get a little raunchy around a machine shop at times."

"Kindred got back at him though, when he said that the wrench didn't resemble that at all; twelve inches was too short." Godfrey laughed and slapped his leg, "First time I ever saw Gator blush about anything."

When he had finished laughing, Godfrey did an about face and grew deadly serious. "Anyway, I had to make out a new timesheet for the shift, but that wasn't all that difficult. You don't get to be a foreman around here if you can't keep track of who's on the floor. I know he was here at the time of the shooting."

"Would the rest of the shift be willing to swear that Kindred James was here all that night?" Reese asked.

Beside him, Charlie was scribbling like crazy in his little notebook.

The foreman didn't hesitate, "Sure. We only have twelve guys on this shift. Every one of them has known the kid for years. They will all have the same story. He was here from eleven o'clock, and was still here when we left at eight a.m. He put in a few hours of overtime Tuesday morning, and one of the office girls dropped him off at his apartment on her way to a dentist appointment."

Godfrey readily agreed to allow each of the men to be questioned separately about that night, but by the second interview it had become obvious that the crew was willing to confirm Kindred James' alibi. The versions told by the crew were varied enough that Reese and Charlie knew they were not rehearsed as to what to say. Other details came out about the suspect, including, while he was not in sight every minute, he was never gone long enough to have gotten across town and back.

"Maybe, he went for a chow run or something?" Charlie suggested to an older machinist, identified as Elmer Wright.

"Ain't likely," he said, spitting a stream of tobacco juice into a strategically placed coffee can near the desk. "Kindred didn't have a license and didn't know crap about driving a car. He was a whirlwind on the forklift, but that old machine wouldn't get him far. He would never leave the shop, and especially not now, when we got all this overtime available. These have been some pretty lean times lately."

"What do ya'll do here?" Reese asked.

"Mostly, oil field," he said. "With the oil business in the crapper, orders for new equipment are bottoming out, but the oil companies still must have parts, you see. They are digging through their scrap yards and bringing in old sections of Christmas trees, casing heads, valves, tubing-head bodies and other crap. We refit them, cut new 'O' rings, redo the pipe threads, polish the flange surfaces, paint them, pressure test them and send them out of the shop as good as new at maybe half the price. Kindred was hired to clean up the metal shavings, driving the forklift, and keeping the shop clean. Since we have been slammed, Paul has been using him some on the Cincinnati drill press. Paul said if the kid came back next summer, he was going to try him out on one of the CNC machines."

"Have you known Kindred James long?" Charlie had asked.

"Hell, yeah," Wright answered. "He came wandering into the shop maybe four years ago, a tall skinny black kid, a bit out of place, if you know what I mean, but Paul gave him a chance and he blended right in with the rest of the shift. I thought he would put in a couple weeks before deciding it was too much work for too little money and scram, but he never did. Heck, we are probably the only Sooner Nation shop in the state of Texas."

An hour later, the detectives left the machine shop in total mental confusion, torn between emotions. Reese didn't know how to characterize them, outrage at the waste of the promising life of an innocent man, or guilt that he had been too late to stop the slaughter.

He slid into the passenger seat of the cruiser and stared ahead as Charlie, apparently feeling the same conflict of emotions, sat silently behind the steering wheel.

Charlie was the first to break the silence between the two men.

"You know," he said in slow measured words, "That all hell is going to break loose when he's cleared of suspicion, you know. I for one don't want to be in the center of the firestorm."

"What's going to happen?" Reese asked, like a robot in rote. From the sickening pain in the pit of his stomach, he felt sure that he already knew the answer.

"A lot is going to depend on how far the police chief is willing to go to suppress the actions taken by his fair-haired boy. Even with all we have, there is a chance that the chief is going to side with Captain Baldwin, that it was a justified shoot."

"Is that even possible with all the evidence we have collected?" Reese asked.

Charlie looked annoyed. "Reese, you've been a police officer too long not to know that the good guy doesn't always win and get the girl before riding off into the sunset. A cover up has already started, you know that. The first step was when the status of Kindred James shifted from person of interest back to major suspect, armed and dangerous. That change could only come from the highest level of the police department. Plus, unidentified officers have been bird-dogging our investigation since the shooting, riling witnesses, stealing evidence, and spreading rumors."

"What can we do?" Reese asked.

"We need to co-ordinate with Mattie to try to get the tag of suspected cop killer removed from Kindred James and dismissed as a possible suspect or person of interest," the senior detective said.

"We'll know really quick how far the department will go to contain that information."

"Do you think they will go that far?" Reese asked.

"I don't know who's conducting the shadow investigation, but I certainly don't believe it is internal affairs. They wouldn't be concentrating on proving James guilty of the murder. Captain Baldwin has plenty to lose if it's determined he led an attack to kill an innocent man out of revenge for his former partner's death. At this point, there is no evidence that the department was behind any cover-up."

The old detective appeared indecisive as he stared at Reese. "I wish there was some way of dropping you from this investigation, but too many people know you were involved," he said.

"You think it's going to go bad?" Reese asked, anticipating the answer.

Charlie nodded. "Depending who lines up against us, they have a lot bigger guns than we do. If Baldwin and whoever is supporting him comes after us, there is a good chance we are going to be discredited, maybe even dismissed from the force on trumped up charges. If it comes to that, I can take early retirement and keep my pension, but you have a lot more to lose."

Reese protested, "But we have proof of James' innocence and evidence that Baldwin ignored our investigation to target him."

Charlie started the car and spun gravel as he left the parking lot.

"We have diddly-squat," he growled. "We have no evidence that Baldwin deliberately overrode our classification of James as a person of interest. And I'm betting those vest cameras and the dash camera on his car are going to be malfunctioning or show nothing conclusive. He was closer to the bus stop and approaching at a slightly different angle which may have hid a direct line of vision to the suspect. I'm sure that other officers saw the placement of the pipe wrench well out of the reach of James, but have you heard anyone disputing that rhetoric Baldwin is feeding to the media?"

"We still have the camera on our car," Reese countered.

"Yeah," Charlie said as he turned south on I-635 and headed south to I-30 toward downtown. "But we have to submit them to internal affairs and we lose control of that evidence."

"Then what do we do?"

"We will copy the tape, like I said, and keep it out of reach. Then, until they get around to pulling us off the case, we continue to search for evidence in the killing of Detective Richard Carver."

"And you think they will allow that?"

"Don't know," Charlie indicated, "They really wanted us to come up with evidence that James was the murderer. Baldwin's actions made it almost imperative that he was the one, but if we start looking elsewhere, the black community is going to know and they are already planning to bring this department to its knees."

"How much time to we have?"

"Carver's funeral is scheduled for Monday afternoon and I don't think anything will happen before then if James is alive. If he dies, all bets are off. From what I saw at the hospital, the activists are waiting to see what happens next."

"Should we be digging into the relationship between Baldwin and Carver?" Reese asked.

"That one we can't touch," Charlie exclaimed. "We are going to have to leave that one to the boys in public affairs, not to say we can't plant a few bugs in their ears, but if we pursue that investigation, it will look like we are targeting the Captain. Of course, he would like nothing better than to use that as justification of his statements about our interference in the case."

"I suddenly feel like we are involved in a game of Chess," Reese said.

"We are, my friend, and we are very insignificant pawns."

CHAPTER 19

"This remains an ongoing dynamic incident that limits the release of more detailed information until further investigation is completed."

That was the complete statement issued by the Dallas Police Chief at his Monday morning press conference when questioned about possible discrepancies arising from statements being hinted by an unnamed police official. The chief refused to make any further statement, even though several reporters shouted out questions across the meeting room in police headquarters. He waved for silence, and when it was not forthcoming, he walked off the small stage, refusing to acknowledge anyone.

Charlie Dent and Reese Barrett, who were not invited to the press conference, were filled in on the short spectacle by Pepper Jackson in the squad room. Jackson had posed the question which disrupted the press conference.

"I don't think the man is going to cover up what happened, but he is going to slow it down and let it take its course," Pepper said. "He appears ready to stall this thing out and hope the citizens of Dallas forget it ever occurred."

Charlie and Reese were given that impression when they contacted Lieutenant Mattie Reynolds after leaving the Lincoln

Machine Shop early Saturday morning. Mattie had set them down for the weekend.

"I don't want to hear one word of either of you stepping outside your homes, or answering the phone before reporting to me Monday morning. I've got to deal with this and it would be easier if you are not available for comment."

"Pepper, you are still a person 'non-gratis' on our investigation until it's settled. You'd best slip out of here before the lieutenant sees you with us, or she will be hanging you right alongside us," Charlie said, dismissing the reporter.

The team of detectives had not spoken to the lieutenant, yet, this morning and Reese could only deduce that she was still in a meeting with the chief and his staff.

Charlie sat stoically across from Reese looking every bit the part of the condemned man. Finally, he looked back toward Reese, "What is the latest you've heard on the kid?"

Reese sighed, "He's still alive. They got the bleeding stopped, but they are keeping him in a medically induced coma because of the head injury. Grace says one of the bullets chipped bones in the spine, but they don't know how severely the spinal column was damaged. He's in restraints so that he's not allowed to as much as twitch a muscle. If he ever walks again, it's going to be after years of therapy."

"You read the newspaper this morning?" Charlie asked.

"No."

"Then let me enlighten you," Charlie indicated, picking up the newspaper from the corner of his desk. "Police should be praised for the swift justice meted out to accused cop killer Kindred James, who was shot in a battle with officers attempting to arrest him Friday night. According to an unnamed Police source, the apprehension of the fugitive, executed with the co-operation of neighborhood watch officers and area patrolmen, was both timely and swift.

Police Detective Richard Carver will be buried Monday afternoon. Several thousand law enforcement personnel from across the state and representatives from departments across the nation are expected to honor the fallen hero."

Charlie looked up from the reading and stared over the top of his glasses toward Reese. He lowered the paper to the desk and slammed his fist down on it.

"Did he actually use the word execute?" Reese asked incredulously.

Charlie glanced back at the story. "Yes, he did, unless it's just Pepper's way of embellishing the story."

"Would you go to that extreme for me, partner?"

"Not likely," Charlie said. "I might stick around after your funeral to make sure the dirt is packed tight enough that you couldn't wiggle out."

The two detectives were still bickering when Lt. Mattie Reynolds, came into the squad room and motioned for them to come to her office. She closed the door behind them and closed the blinds.

"You want a cup of coffee?" Reese asked.

Reynolds glared at him.

"We don't have time for coffee this morning," she said, crossing to her desk. "I've been in conference with the chief and he's very, let's use the word 'upset', although that is way too mild to describe his actual reactions about the recent turn of events. However, he's afraid to move forward until the investigation has run its course."

"Then he is not going after Captain Baldwin?" Charlie asked.

"Right now, it's a question of whether he is going after Baldwin or you two, depending on which will have the least impact on maintaining the peace in our city. If you prematurely release the information that James has been cleared in the murder of Richard Carver, he expects the sky to fall, and he's going to make it his last duty to bury the both of you where you'll never be found. He won't fire you, but he can demote you to pooper patrol at the city dog park. And he will."

"No good deed ever goes unpunished," Charlie said, bring a harsher glare from the squad leader. "Well, what does he expect us to do? Lie on our backs and beg for belly rubs or what? Or are we expected to lick his hand for a pat on the head?"

"You are on dangerous ground, Mister," Reynolds snapped back.

"Tell me something I don't know," Charlie said. "I only care that I do my job right, and that the guilty are caught, and the innocent go free. I don't know how to play this political game where the guilty get a free ride because if they don't, it's going to cause problems in the city. Just give me a road map of what we are supposed to do and we will get out of your hair."

"I don't believe that for a moment, Mr. Charlie Dent, but I'm warning you: tread lightly. Stay on your investigation into the murder of Carver, but keep it quiet. Tell no one what you suspect, because if even a whisper of this gets back to the chief, I can't protect you. I want the killer found, and until you are pushing him through central booking, Kindred James remains a viable suspect as far as this department is concerned."

"So far, the only ones we've talked to were you and that 'super cop' Baldwin," Charlie responded. "That didn't work out so well."

"How about that noisy reporter, Pepper Jackson?" she asked.

"He's been snooping around, but we haven't given him even a nibble," he said.

"It might be best if you viewed him like kryptonite for a while. He already has someone talking in his ear and the chief is aware of who it is. That might work in your favor." She dismissed them without further instructions.

Walking back to their desks, the detectives slumped into their chairs.

"Now I know what it feels like to be on the outside," Reese said.

Charlie mumbled, "Get used to it. We have just been cut off from communicating with the rest of the department. We are on our own."

"I've never been in quite this situation; where do we go from here?" Reese asked.

"Today, we do what everyone else in the department is doing. We honor a fallen comrade with the respect he and his family deserve. And whatever we do, we keep as far away from Captain Baldwin as possible." Charlie suddenly looked very old. "We don't need to do anything which might get him pointing fingers again. I intend to stay on the fringe of the crowd, close enough to be noticed, but definitely out of Baldwin's sight."

Shortly after two o'clock, the funeral service for Detective Sergeant Richard K. Carver was held in one of the larger downtown churches with an overflow crowd numbering in the thousands. The police chief gave a recitation of the highlights of the fallen policeman's career, mentioning his military service in the Desert Storm campaign, and listing the honors awarded to him in both careers.

Reese moved uncomfortably, standing at the rear of the auditorium, when Captain Andrew Baldwin took center stage and offered a eulogy for his former partner. It should have been a speech of respect for the deceased policeman, but to Reese it came across to him that the detective was a lesser appendage to the captain. The junior detective felt somewhat uneasy as he slipped out of the auditorium before the procession. He decided not to join the pageantry as a convoy of hundreds of police cars were expected to escort the hearse to the national cemetery for burial. He had shown his respects.

The detective returned to the police headquarters and made his way through a skeleton force of officers still on duty. Charlie was alone in the homicide squad room. The contents of an evidence box spread out across his desk, spilling over onto Reese's side of the abutting desks.

Charlie glanced up as Reese approached.

"Funeral over already?" he asked, lifting a folder from the evidence box and flipping through several pages of notes. "I decided at the last second to avoid the spectacle."

Reese stared, dubiously, "My bet is you couldn't get a parking space within three blocks of the church, and you didn't want to walk," Reese replied.

Charlie gave a half-hearted grin, but then his face grew pensive.

"Well, there was that, too, but I really don't like all the pageantry and ceremony that goes with dying," he said. Charlie glanced down, but for the briefest second Reese could have sworn that the old detective was misty eyed. Mumbling, Charlie added, "When my turn comes to die I want to go quietly, just dig a hole and cover me over."

Slightly surprised by the depression which seemed to have settled over his partner, Reese was at a loss of words. There was silence between the two for a few seconds before Reese asked quietly, "You thinking about your own mortality?"

Sighing deeply, the old man continued to arrange the different pieces of evidence on the desk.

"Some cases get to you worse than others and you just have to think it through," Charlie said. "Last week Richard Carver, whom I've known for nearly thirty years, was alive. He stopped at a store for a quart of milk and a toothbrush and met his death. A few days later, Kindred James stepped out of a bus stop shelter and was riddled with bullets. Everyone around them had their lives changed forever in the space of those few seconds. We had nothing to do with either incident, other than trying to investigate; just doing our jobs. Now either both you and I are going down for telling the truth, or a career Police Captain is going down for telling a lie. And to top it off, in the name of justice, I'm digging through files and evidence boxes to destroy another man and his family," he sighed, sadly, as he dropped a file beside the box. "Death affects the lives of everyone that meets it. Like dominoes all lined up, push the first one, and they just keep falling over. They hit the next one and fall over and it just keeps falling over."

Reese slumped into his chair. "What are you? Some sort of bard of doom or something?"

The old man grinned, "Maybe the 'or something.'"

Charlie handed a file to Reese. "You going to help me, or do I have to finish this mass destruction all by myself?"

Reese took the file and leaned back in his chair. He opened it slowly, almost as if he was expecting something to jump out at him. "What are we looking for specifically?"

"With Kindred James no longer being a viable suspect in the murder, even if only the pair of us believes it, we need to move on to another suspect. I nominate the old grocer, Duc Tran. You got anybody in mind to nominate, or you want to second mine?"

"Nope," Reese stated. "He's fine with me. I don't see anyone else in the picture."

"All right, this time we build an air-tight case, then we bring him in."

Reese raised an eyebrow. "It's going to be hard to prove he killed Carver with the evidence we have so far."

"Well, we are just going to have to go back on the streets and get some more, then, aren't we?" Charlie winked and reached for a cup of coffee sitting on the corner of the desk. "We have to make a case God can't break."

He took a sip from the cup, made a face and handed the cup

across to Reese. "I made a pot about an hour ago, but this is colder than a witch in a brass bra. Warm it up for me, will you?"

Reese wasn't sure he liked being relegated to the role of gofer, but the old man had already buried his head in a file. He walked to the coffee pot, sniffed the coffee, and decided that it was still drinkable, barely. He filled two cups with black coffee, and returned to his desk. He placed Charlie's cup in front of him, which he ignored, still studying the file.

"Do you think you are going to find anything in the witness statements that Mattie took the night of the murder?" Reese broke the silence.

"You can never tell," Charlie said, glancing up from a page he had been studying. "There is a park in Arkansas, the Crater of Diamonds State Park, where you can pay a fee and search all day for diamonds. Supposedly, the diamonds have been pushed to the surface from an extinct volcano. Occasionally, park people plow the ground and people pick through the loose dirt. If you are extremely lucky and know what you are looking for, you can come up with a real gem. Some people have picked up rough diamonds worth thousands of dollars and tossed them because they don't know what they found. You and I are going to search through the dirt, and when we find that diamond, I hope we will know what we've found."

"What are the odds?" Reese asked.

"I used to check through the list of horses for a race and pick which one would win. This was back when I was a kid. Anyway, I picked in every race, every day for a couple of weeks. I figured out one thing. I don't know beans about picking the right horse, so I am not the right guy to figure the odds. I'd say they are probably not very good, but we are going to plow the ground repeatedly until we find something. This," Charlie said pointing a finger in the middle of the mess on the two desks, "is where we start."

The senior detective noticed the coffee cup, brought it up to his lips and sipped.

"Uh, thanks, Partner."

They spent the next couple of hours re-reading interview notes. They began a list of neighborhood witnesses who were close enough that they should have heard something; already knowing many would refuse to get involved. Again, Reese remembered that Charlie had emphasized that what they didn't find was often as important as what they did. The notes from lieutenant's and other detectives working the case that night had been well vented. By five o'clock, Reese begged off.

"I promised Grace that I would meet her for supper before she goes back on shift at the hospital and I don't want to disappoint her again," Reese said, closing another file. "I'm too bleary eyed to see anything anyway."

"Now you are making excuses for the little lady," Charlie said. "Didn't Grace get enough of your ugly face over the weekend?"

"She had to work one of those nights," said Reese. "She's still shook up about the night of the shooting."

"I can understand that," Charlie replied. He started repacking the evidence box. "Twyla gave me fits when I told her I drove the car between police on one side and the suspect on the other. You wouldn't believe some of the words that little woman threw at me. She has a saucy mouth on her when she gets angry or scared."

"It finally hit Grace that if the patrolmen hadn't recognized us when we jumped the curb, we could have very easily been killed."

Charlie nodded as he finished packing the box. "Twyla picked up on that immediately, but then she didn't have to go through the shock of actually seeing all those officers blazing away at James."

Reese remembered the instant Kindred James ceased to be a suspect in his mind and became something more. That moment when he was pressing hard enough on the kid's chest to break ribs to slow the bleeding, and Grace was sitting there covered in blood, her finger plunged deep inside another hole in the victim to clamp off a bleeder was the defining moment. He was moving in that direction even earlier, but he couldn't define the moment. He didn't have an emotional tie before that moment.

Sometimes the evidence lies, but the character does not. Looking through the yearbooks, reading the potential the young man had, contradicted what he was accused of committing.

"Did you find us a starting point?" Reese asked.

"I want another talk with that Thompson kid, LeVartis. I think there is more there than he's told us so far. It may be thin, but I sensed we developed a layer of trust with that kid when we let him go the other day. He knows we could have made it a lot rougher on him than we did."

CHAPTER 20

Tuesday morning newspaper headlines carried a full tribute to the life of Detective Richard Carver, complete with a photograph of the funeral procession to his grave site. A sideline story, written by Pepper Jackson, questioned the validity of Kindred James' apprehension, shooting, and arrest for Carver's murder.

When Reese picked Charlie up at his small house just south of Forest Lane, the old man was as gruff as Reese had ever seen him.

"Who in hell is feeding Jackson information about this investigation," Charlie asked, glancing toward his junior partner.

"Well, it certainly isn't me," Reese declared.

The police radio band was crowded with calls for more officers to control traffic at the site where James had been shot down. A memorial service was being held there, and the crowd was estimated at several hundred. There were reports of hundreds of demonstrators pouring into the area to protest the violent manner of his take down. The calm which had pervaded the last two days had the potential of erupting into violence.

"I don't think it has, yet, Rookie, but this whole thing has me nervous," Charlie said. "Whenever you mix cops looking for trouble and a group that already feels restricted, there is a chance of an explosion."

"Maybe you shouldn't have eaten breakfast," Reese said.

"Well, I knew I wouldn't have an appetite after reading this," Charlie said, dropping the paper between them on the bench seat of their squad car. "Besides, that wife of mine is trying to make me go caffeine free. Do you know caffeine free coffee tastes a lot like, well … It ain't meant for human consumption."

Reese wasn't sure, being a caffeine junkie, what decaf tasted like, but knowing his partner, he used his imagination. "I'll find us a coffee shop and maybe pick up a couple of donuts, too."

"Are you trying to augment the stereotype of the police force? Better get them in a plain brown wrapper," Charlie snorted.

"Where do we start today?" Reese asked.

"Well, we certainly are not going to the riot. That would make us a bigger target than we already are. Nor would I advise going near police headquarters. Pepper Jackson is out there somewhere and he's looking to pick us up, I'm sure. He's already started a fire; we don't need to give him more gas to feed the flames."

"You still thinking we need to find LeVartis Thompson?"

"Yep," Charlie pointed toward a corner convenience store. "Start right there, though."

Reese made good on his promise of coffee with caffeine and donuts, and then he drove toward the grocery store where Carver had been killed.

Arriving, they found the parking lot empty; the crime tape was gone. One of the large glass windows to the left of the door had been shattered. Iron burglar bars blocked any entry, but the door had been jimmied, and stood slightly ajar.

Charlie growled, "I'll call it in, you check inside."

Reese pulled the door open and stepped inside; broken glass crunched under his feet. Most of the light fixtures had been broken. Enough light filtered into the store from outside to show the littered floor, littered with crushed food cans, glass, and trash. Graffiti had been spray painted on the walls, and the shelves were nearly empty.

He walked around the store, noting that it had been stripped of anything of value. Even the toilet tissue that he and Charlie had joked about being recycled was gone. The coolers lining the back wall had been emptied of beer and drinks. The small office in back had been ransacked, and a small toilet next to it smelled strong with urine and feces. The toilet bowl had been broken.

Reese clinched his teeth in exasperation. As he started back toward the front, Charlie came in the door and stopped by the front counter. Calling out to him, Reese said, "I think I've figured out why he kept such late hours. It was the only way he could protect the store. How can anyone live in a neighborhood like this one?"

"The vultures didn't waste any time, did they?" Charlie replied. "I've got the crime scene team on the way, but what can they do? We can't arrest everyone and this looks like a free-for-all. It looks like they took everything but the wall paper."

"You are right, they just painted over it," Reese said, indicating the graffiti.

Charlie kicked a broken bottle aside and turned back toward the exit. "Let's go pay a visit with our little rock throwing buddy," he said. "The crime scene guys will make sure the building is secure when they finish."

Reese joined Charlie outside a minute later.

"Do you think LeVartis was in on this?"

"Hell, I don't know," Charlie indicated, "I would have thought we scared him enough the last time that he wouldn't come near this place, but if he wasn't in on the looting, he likely knows who was."

"I wonder why we didn't get a police report on the break-in. This burglary was maybe a couple of days ago, but no one filed a report."

"Weekend lull? Cut back in police patrols? I don't know," Charlie shrugged the suggestion off. "No one else has ties to the store, and with the old man gone, I guess nobody cared one way or the other. I can only say there must have been a lot of people in on this."

Following the car's Navigator, they located the home of the Thompson family. They were surprised to find that it was only a few doors down from the house owned by Duc Tran. This house was in a worse state of repair than Duc Tran's, however. The roof sagged, the floor of the rotted porch was nearly impassible, and the screen door had most of the screen torn out. Another door was open, and the loud canned laughter from a game show was blaring from a large flat-screened TV which was visible by the detectives through the open doorway. The two heard no conversation from anyone within the structure.

Reese mounted the porch and stepped gingerly to the door. The porch swayed under his weight and gave him a slight sense of vertigo. He rapped on the door frame loudly enough, he hoped, that the noise would carry over the sound of the TV. Through the door, he could make out the back of the head of a man sprawled out in a recliner facing the TV. The game show hostess reached up and spun a wheel. The man did not respond to the knock.

Charlie had joined Reese beside the doorway, and he grabbed the screen door, slamming it shut a couple of times. The man peered over his shoulder, and, although it was apparent that he spotted the two detectives, he made no move to get up.

"LeVartis!" Charlie shouted, stretching the name into three extremely loud syllables. "Get your rear in gear and answer the door."

"Or just wave us in, for Pete's sake," Reese added.

The man motioned for them to come inside.

Eyeing Reese and Charlie as they came toward him, he spoke for the first time. "If you guys are from the probation department, I still have my monitor on," he said, raising a leg to display the heavy bracelet around his ankle. "If you're selling Bibles, I ain't interested."

The man's words were slightly slurred and as they got closer, Reese was slammed with the odor of a rather large, unwashed body, and the man's breath, which smelled somewhere between a brewery and an outhouse. "That kid is never where he's supposed to be."

Charlie reached out and cut off the TV.

"Now why did you go and do that for? I was watching that show," he said, trying to climb out of the chair.

Reese reached out and touched his shoulder and pushed him back down.

"Are you LeVartis' father?" he asked.

The man in the chair relaxed upon discovering the attention was not pointed his direction.

"Ain't, no way. That little puke is my girlfriend's bastard," he said. "You must be cops. What has the little SOB done this time?"

"If you two are not related, it isn't any of your business," Charlie, who had moved to face the man, replied. "Could I get your name? I'm Detective Dent and the man at your other shoulder is Detective Barrett."

The drunken man attempted to lock into a brief staring contest with Charlie, but lost, looking away.

"Roscoe Love," he finally admitted. Love was maybe medium height, difficult to really judge in his reclining position, somewhere between 35 and 40, packing at least three hundred fifty pounds. Almost every inch of his exposed skin was covered with crude prison tats, including his shaved head. Most of his face was hidden behind an unruly beard soaked in beer and spotted with bits of cupcakes.

Charlie stared soberly down at the reclining man. "Mr. Love, we've already seen enough parole violations to earn you an all-expense paid trip back to the big house."

"What did I do?" Love protested.

"Let's start with drinking," Charlie said, pointing out several beer bottles scattered around the chair. A half empty bottle of a regional beer rested on a small table beside the man.

"You can't come in here and accuse me of drinking," Love said. "This is my house and there is nothing in my parole about having a bottle."

"You invited us in," the detective replied. "If you are going to break probation, you really should be a little more discrete with who you let in *your* house. Do you own it, or do you pay the rent?"

"Hell, no, I just live here. My girlfriend owns it," Love stated.

"Since you live here, do you have any knowledge of LeVartis' whereabouts?" Reese queried.

"Uh, no," Love replied. ""I don't know where that little snot got off to, but his mama is going to tan his hide when he comes back."

"Uh-huh," Charlie grunted.

"Don't go blaming anything on me that punk did," the parolee said.

"We need information on the burglary of Duc Tran's grocery a few blocks over."

"This is just a lot of bull," he protested. "You ain't going to turn me in for this."

Charlie and Reese stood silently, waiting.

"That little Vietcong, he had it coming, anyway," Love said.

"Maybe," the senior detective said, "But it wasn't your decision to make. What about Mr. Tran makes you think he deserved to lose everything he had?"

Love stopped. "I never went in the store, but I've seen him around the neighborhood. He just doesn't fit in. You know what I mean, he just didn't belong here."

Reese wondered if Roscoe Love, who appeared to have spent more time in prison than out, believed he himself fit in the community. A nod from Charlie told him that he was thinking along the same lines.

"If you never went in the store, the crime scene team now

investigating the burglary there will not turn up any fingerprints for you, will they?" the junior detective asked.

Love backtracked very quickly. "This monitor allows me to travel a short distance from the house. I may have been there once or twice, but I didn't take part in any burglary."

"Are you aware those bracelets have GPS tracking technology in them?" Reese asked, watching the parolee carefully to see his response to this revelation. "I bet if the probation department checked their records over the last day or so, they are going to paint a set of prison bars across your near future."

The ex-con's mouth opened and closed a couple of times like a big mouth bass out of water. "The door was open, I was only looking for a little beer," he said. "Besides, the old man wasn't there."

Reese backed up a couple of steps and glanced toward the open door leading into the kitchen. At least twenty-six packs were spread out on the kitchen counter and stacked on the floor near the refrigerator. Either Love had gotten there early in burglary or he had some very generous accomplices.

He glanced at Charlie, gave a half grin, and then pointed to the half empty bottle of beer. He spoke to Love, "I think you had better drink up. Where you are going, it will be a long time before you get another one."

Charlie walked to the kitchen door, then turned, pulling out his handcuffs.

"Aw, crap!" Love stated as he slowly stood up from the recliner and placed his hands behind his back.

The three stepped through the open front door, and as they moved toward the porch steps, Reese reached back to close the door, and the parolee spoke one last time.

"Thanks, Detective, better make sure it's locked, or all the people peeking out through their windows at us will suddenly decide they need a new television set. Locking the door is going to leave that snotty kid locked out until his mama gets home."

Reese decided that being locked out of that home wasn't such a bad deal.

Later, downtown, Roscoe Love was persuaded to give up the names of five others present when the grocery store was burglarized. He denied the kid was part of the raid on the store. He, also, vehemently denied breaking the door lock or spray painting any of the graffiti. Reese silently wished him good luck on the first claim when the case went to a jury. He seriously doubted the petty crook had enough talent to do the graffiti.

Reese was frustrated as he left the interrogation room and joined Charlie in the viewing room next door.

"This guy is a real piece of work," he said to his partner, who was studying the suspect through the one-way glass. "One second he's all but admitting a felony, and the next he's denying a simple misdemeanor. I can't tell when he's lying or when he's telling the truth. I don't think he knows either."

Charlie agreed, turning from the glass and slumping in a nearby chair.

"I know it's our collar, but I think it's best if we hand him off to burglary detail," he said. "Even if Duc Tran was half blind there is no way he would have mistaken James for this fat slob. Pursuing this angle is not going to get us any closer to the killer."

Reese readily agreed that there was little use in pursuing this line as part of a murder case. Burglary detail was equipped to handle Love a lot more efficiently.

Mumbling under his breath, the younger detective said, "Maybe Tran had a good reason to be scared in that neighborhood."

"Don't worry about losing the bust," Charlie said, probably noting a bit of disappointment from his junior partner. "In this business, what goes around comes around and a case this size will earn you a lot of brownie points with burglary detail. After all, Carver was one of theirs, and I'm betting there is a lot of pinned up rage there. They are not going to miss anything, and they are going to be in a giving mood toward us which will come in handy later." He punctuated his statement with a light tap on Reese's chest with his index finger.

Reese was in a considerably better mood as he returned to the squad room. Charlie called downstairs and contacted his buddy in burglary. By the time Charlie had filled in his contact on the suspect and turned the case over, Reese had begun building a plan.

First, he contacted the Texas Department of Human Services and requested a home visit and investigation into the welfare of one LeVartis Thompson. Even if his mother was not involved in the break-in, she certainly wasn't doing anything to protect her son. Even foster home care was a better alternative to the situation in which he was living now. Charlie would probably say he was going all mushy on him, but Reese felt the kid at least needed a chance.

Next, he laid out a grid of pawn shops and gun shops within three miles of the grocery. The junior detective felt it likely that if Duc Tran possessed a gun, he would not have gone too far from the neighborhood to purchase it. By the same reasoning, it was unlikely he would have sought a source within a mile of the store, because there was a chance he might have been recognized.

If he had purchased a weapon, there was still a chance that he had purchased it from an individual. However, Reese decided that since Tran held an innate distrust of everyone, he would have felt safer purchasing a gun from a store.

Since the Texas government had come down solidly behind gun possession, the state was quickly becoming a battle ground. Even policemen were looking over their shoulders as they did their duties. This was especially true since an officer had been nearly killed by a gun toting neighbor of a suspect. The man had opened fire when the officer was attempting to apprehend the shooter's neighbor, hitting the policeman numerous times.

Reese was sitting back in his chair, eyes closed, head back, and mouth gaped open when Charlie returned a few minutes later. The old detective stifled a snicker as he sat down heavily in his chair. When that failed to elicit the desired response from his partner, he slammed his hands down loud enough that other detectives in the room stopped what they were doing and glanced toward Charlie and Reese.

Reese flopped forward and stared at his partner.

"Sorry, I was thinking about the case," he apologized.

"Does that sound effect, like a nest of hornets, always occur when you're thinking or was that just the little gears in your mind switching tracks?" he asked. "Because, if you're thinking processor makes that much noise, you need to get it repaired."

Reese shook off the fog clogging his mind.

"Sorry, I guess this case is getting to me, I'm exhausted." He attempted a weak smile.

"Next time, keep your mouth shut, you were scaring the natives and these guys don't scare easy," Charlie said with a wink. "Does Grace know you snore like that?"

"I'm not sure that is any of your business," Reese replied.

"Don't worry about it, Partner, if I really wanted to know, I would have asked my wife. Have you noticed that whatever one woman finds out, they all know? If you snore like that around Grace, I'm sure half the people you know already are aware."

For some maternal reason, Twyla had adopted a motherly role in Grace's life, so Reese didn't attempt to deny Charlie's statement. If Grace knew, Twyla knew and one thing the partners had discovered was that Charlie's wife always told everything she knew. Reese wondered if that could have something to do with the old detective's morose attitude over the past couple of weeks. Charlie would have been unable to vent his frustrations for fear vital information on the case might leak out.

"Sorry, Charlie," he said.

The senior detective seemed to be reading Reese's mind because he did nothing to clarify his statement. He sighed and glanced at the notes Reese had lying out on his desk.

"Working on something?" he asked.

Reese shifted back into business mode.

"The department got nowhere into checking for a gun purchase by Kindred James, but, if he didn't kill Carver in a botched robbery, then we need to check into a purchase by the next suspect."

"Well, I'm fairly sure you are not talking about that slob back there," Charlie said, jabbing a thumb back in the general direction of the interrogation room. "So, I assume you are talking about our shrinking violet shopkeeper. I've been thinking about that too," he indicated, reaching out and drawing one of the notes Reese had made toward him. Glancing at the page, he looked back to Reese. "What is this, some sort of secret code? Can you read your own chicken scratching?"

"It's a list of pawn shops and gun shops within three miles of Duc Tran's store," Reese said.

"That's a lot of territory," Charlie said, sliding the list back across the table. "Did you know Dallas has more gun dealers than gas stations? Fact is, you can probably buy a gun at most gas stations if you ask the right person. Most of them are not very exact about following the law on gun sales, either. You can buy anything from a midnight special to a fully automatic assault rifle on the streets, if you know who to ask."

"Somehow, I can't picture Tran being one of those in the know," Reese said. "Maybe I'm profiling him wrong, but I can't see him going anywhere but to a legitimate gun dealer. I don't think he would go very far, either. You know, not too close, not too far."

Charlie pursed his lips, "Makes sense to me. What have you found so far?"

The question was rhetorical and Reese knew it.

He furrowed his brow, "I've checked maybe a third of the possible dealers within three miles and I have a list of thirteen so far. If we check them all, it's going to be a lot of footwork."

Sighing, Charlie groaned, "My poor feet. Couldn't you have thought of this when we had cooperation on this investigation?"

"Tran wasn't a suspect at that time," Reese said.

"That's where you are wrong, Rookie, you need to learn to suspect everyone," the senior detective concluded.

CHAPTER 21

The laws of chance have a way of being cruel. Two days and dozens of stops had produced no results on the search for a weapon, other than a constant dialogue about aching feet from Charlie. Reese was beginning to understand Nero, who fiddled as Rome burned.

The demonstration against the vicious takedown of Kindred James had erupted into violence after a police cruiser accidently struck a child in the street near a north Dallas bus stop. The child was not seriously hurt, but in retaliation, two police cars were burned. Then police reacted with tear gas grenades, which resulted in nearly a dozen injuries as people scattered to escape the gas.

Police headquarters was under siege from activists requesting the release of vest camera footage taken during the shooting, but unknown to the public, the camera footage had been *lost*. Police officials' excuse for refusing to release the tapes was that they were intricate to the investigation. Secretly, the chief had opened an internal investigation into the evidence's disappearance.

Reese was torn about releasing their dash cam footage, but Charlie was adamant that it not be turned in immediately.

"Until the police administration does a little house cleaning, if we turn over the tape, it will disappear just as quickly as the other tapes," he explained to his partner.

Reese wasn't sure the senior detective was right, but he kept silent, yielding to Charlie's position. Reese felt like he was caught in the middle, knowing the unofficial rumors associated with the police shooting were wrong, but aware there were people in the department willing to sacrifice him and his partner to maintain the lie. So far, no move had been made toward them, but the implied threat hung like a cloud over their heads.

The only thing holding the city together in an uneasy peace was the belief that more than likely James was guilty, even though an undercurrent of opinion was forming that James had an unimpeachable alibi.

The thirty-seventh gun dealer Reese and Charlie visited was a small hole in the wall pawn shop, which advertised cheap firearms on a tattered sign in their front window.

"I wonder how long this sale has been going on," Reese commented as he stepped from the police car.

Charlie, who was driving, got out and mounted the crumbling sidewalk in front of the narrow store. Chained, rusting bicycles lined the entry, and weed whackers, campsite lanterns, and cheap watches cluttered the sole display counter visible from the street behind the dirty display window.

"Looks like surplus junk from Noah's Ark," he said, pushing open the heavy door which set off a bell attached to the frame.

An emaciated man, covered in tattoos, looking the part of an anti-drug educational program, seemingly floated from the small office in the rear of the shop. He established a position behind the counter, complete with signs reading 'Cash Only', 'IDs required on all gun sales' and 'We ain't interested in fishing equipment.'

"Are you cops?" he asked. Without waiting for an answer, he said, "Our records are up to date and we don't deal in stolen goods."

"Are we that obvious?" Charlie asked, flashing his shield.

He asked the man's name, who reluctantly stated that he was Lewis Brogan, and that he owned the pawn shop. Charlie filed the name away in his mind as someone they might have to revisit.

"One can never be too careful," the thin man said, attempting a smile, which came across as a sneer. He had several teeth missing, and the few remaining lower teeth were stained nearly black with nicotine. Charlie glanced at the man's hands, and noted the nicotine stains permeating the man's fingertips. He imagined that the man's lungs would look much the same.

"Sold any handguns in the last couple of months?" Charlie asked, pointing toward a heavy locked case behind the counter.

"I take it, you are not in the mood to buy a back-up piece," the living skeleton said as he erupted into a coughing fit. Regaining his breath, barely, he continued, "I've got a very nice Berretta, two shot, which weighs next to nothing, very easy to conceal. I can let you have it at a fraction above cost."

"Uh huh. What's wrong with it?"

"Trigger pull is a real bitch," the pawn shop clerk said, chuckling. "Takes a lot of pressure to fire the dang thing, and most people fear the blast. Sounds like a cannon going off, and it kicks back like a bucking bronco. Most of my customers don't want to do that much work."

"What kind of work? You mean like going to the bother of filling out the paperwork to get it registered? Or maybe they don't have the strength to even pull the trigger, right?" Reese asked.

"Hey, don't look at me," the clerk said, waving a hand in front of his face in denial. "All my transactions are perfectly legit."

"Then you shouldn't have any trouble showing me your records about the sale of a .38 caliber knockoff within the last two months."

"I don't remember selling one, but I don't deal in cheap crap. That Berretta I offered you comes with a $500 sticker price, not counting the customary policeman's discount. I might have sold a slick Browning, which might fit your request, but nothing else. I have the records to prove it."

"I'll bet you do," Charlie said. When Brogan hesitated, the senior detective spoke again, "Well, can we see them?"

Brogan gave him a look of indifference as he searched through several books of records behind the counter. He pulled out a dog-eared journal. "It's a little ragged from all you policemen thumbing through it, but it's all here."

Reese, who had watched the exchange from a few feet away, noted a stealthy look of doubt from his partner. The laws made them keep the records, but they didn't require them to make them legible. Charlie cringed as if looking thorough the ledger was a task on par with dumpster diving.

"You want to handle this rookie," he said, handing the book to Reese.

Reese thought about mouthing a silent no, but held his peace. Charlie's eyesight wasn't what it once was, and it wasn't unusual for him to turn over mundane paperwork to him. Reese had an aversion to paperwork. The old man was still better in spotting key errors and omissions. Maybe Charlie believed Reese, whose handwriting he referred to as chicken scratching, was better able to read the jumbled record. Reese wondered what the old man would say if he knew the junior detective had difficulty reading his own notes.

Reese reached out and took the ledger. Moving down the counter, he found a space on which to work that was clear of clutter. Charlie continued to engage Brogan in conversation, but he could sense the pawn shop owner's repeated glance in his direction. Yeah, he's got something to hide, Reese thought.

As he suspected, when he opened the ledger, he was confronted by a mess which a forensic scientist would spend a week to decipher. For someone running a hole-in-the-wall pawn shop, Brogan was doing a bustling business in guns. A quick estimate showed the number to be close to fifty transactions per month, most with other dealers, but a surprising amount with individuals. Reese, felt he probably shouldn't be surprised, with the new gun laws passed by the state legislature, and the National Rifle Association's pro-gun campaign; gun violence incidents for Texas were near the top of the nation. Even many of the timidest citizens of the state had begun to feel it necessary to arm themselves, fearing police were no longer able to protect them.

The ledger he held recorded only transactions. Records of compliance must be in a separate and probably equally obscure ledger.

The transaction ledger was sketchy at best. Even if recorded, the nature of the transaction was, in several cases, open to interpretation. An entry listed a date, seller, and purchasing customer, but in some cases, the description of the weapon sold was hard to determine. A sale might describe a sale of a weapon, but fail to note manufacturer, caliber of weapon, or model number. Hopefully, the serial numbers were accurate. The only way to piece the information together was through recollections of Brogan, but Reese suspected he had developed a very poor memory about those transactions over time.

Reese was frustrated. Trying to determine the caliber of the weapons sold using sketchy information at best was beginning to push the wrong buttons. One entry stood out, the sale of a Bersa Thunder 380 CC about three months earlier. He couldn't be sure, but it looked like the transaction was recorded out of sequence. The buyer was listed as a gun shop over on Grand Avenue. He called Brogan over to him and pointed out the entry. "What's this?"

Brogan sneered. "Bersa Thunder is the brand name of an Argentinean gun maker. The 380 is self-explanatory," he said, without further elaboration.

"And the CC?"

"Concealed carry," Brogan said. "Compact little semi-automatic, no front sight, easy to conceal, deadly at close range. Not particularly high tech, but popular for self-defense."

Reese felt a little queasy. The pawn shop owner felt comfortable in dealing with weapons designed with one purpose in mind: killing people. The weapon obviously had no use in sports shooting or hunting.

"Did you by chance test fire any of your weapons, like maybe for a bit of insurance?" Charlie asked Brogan. "I'm sure your customers wanted to make sure their investments were functional and clear of any, shall we say, interest by the police."

"You guys are a pain in the ass," Brogan said. "I'm glad we are regulated by ATF, they leave us alone. All my customers met the three-day waiting period for the background check."

"Alcohol, Tobacco and Firearms won't leave you alone if we question a few of these sales," the senior detective indicated. "ATF can be a lot more thorough in digging through your records, and with the mess I've seen so far, you would be explaining for a long time."

"What do I have to do to make all this go away?" Brogan asked, maintaining the façade that he was in control of the situation. "I'm sure we can reach some sort of agreement."

Charlie turned to Reese. "That sounds a whole lot like a bribe, Partner. Do you think he intended to offer a policeman a bribe?"

"Sounded a bit like it, didn't it? I wonder if he knows the penalty for attempting to bribe a public official. Maybe you should ask him?" Reese said, looking at the pawn shop owner, who had suddenly lost part of his bravado.

Before Charlie could speak again, they were interrupted.

The bell over the door clanged, drawing their attention toward the customer entering, a Hispanic man in his early thirties, shaggy haired, with a plethora of tattoos covering his bare arms and shoulders. The newcomer quickly sized up the situation, turned and slipped back out of the front door.

"I hope we are not costing you any of your business," Charlie said. "The sooner you start answering our questions, the quicker you can get back to doing whatever it is that you do here. Otherwise, we may have to take you in for questioning and that is bound to have some effect on business."

Brogan flung his arms out in a gesture of mock surrender. "You misunderstood me, Officers. I'll give you whatever you need."

Reese nodded, looking back at the ledger. "Was this sale on the .38 the only transaction you did on this caliber in the past several months? Do you sell a lot to other gun dealers?"

"Dealers and collectors," he said. "Your first-time buyer normally goes to Gun City or one of the other big dealers. As you probably know, we deal in only secondhand guns."

'The ones harder to trace,' Reese thought. In most instances, a weapon manufactured a century earlier was still operational if there was a source of ammunition. Gun registration might work well on paper, but once the weapon hit the street, in a lot of cases it was impossible to trace back to the current owner without a major investigation, which most departments were not prepared to make. Sometimes records got lost, or doctored, as the gun passed from one hand to another. The junior detective wondered if Brogan was a loser or a doctor.

"Are there any other, let's say, questionable transactions for this caliber weapon that my partner might be interested in?" Charlie asked.

The divided attention of the shop owner was beginning to have the desired effect, but he recovered quickly. "There is nothing questionable about that deal. They had a customer for a pistol in that price range, which they didn't have in stock, so they called me and I sent it over. We split the profit. The customer got his gun, they made money, I made money, and everyone is happy. End of story."

"In that case, I'm not going to find a signature for a buyer, am I?" Reese asked.

"I didn't sell the gun, they did. It's not my concern whether they have the proper records or signatures."

"I wonder if they are going to say the same thing about you," Charlie said. The senior detective wrote down the relevant information in his pad. Tapping the closed pad as he slipped it into his shirt pocket, he made eye contact with Brogan. "If we don't find out what we need, we will be back."

Reese dropped the ledger back on the counter, sliding it toward the gun shop owner. "If I were you, I'd put some effort into getting your ledgers in order."

They left the pawnshop dissatisfied with the information acquired. Reese climbed into the passenger side of the squad car, slumped in the front seat, and adjusted the air vent from the AC to flow across his face.

"Do you think we are on to something?" he asked his partner.

Charlie's face was covered with sweat and he appeared to be in some discomfort. He did not answer immediately.

"Probably not," he sighed, finally. "There are dozens of transactions like this one going on every day of the week. Maybe it was totally legit, I don't know. It was interesting that customer doing a quick exit when he discovered us there."

"Think he made us as cops?"

"Well, duh," Charlie said. "Even more interesting was that he was a cop, too, and he didn't want to be seen with us."

"Undercover? Really?"

"Call it an educated guess. He avoided us, but he was slick about getting out quickly without drawing too much attention from Brogan. Our little pawnshop seems to have drawn interest from another quarter. I would speculate that Brogan is in for a nasty surprise."

"What's the penalty for illegal transfer of weapons?"

"Depends on what agency our undercover agent is working out of. If he's fed, Brogan could be looking forward to a lengthy stretch in a federal pen. If he's with the state agencies, the governor will probably give him an *Atta boy* pat on the back and a certificate of endorsement from the NRA. It's a screwed-up world we live in."

Reese had to agree. He glanced at his wrist watch. The time was a few minutes until five o'clock. Even though they were parked over a mile off the Interstate, the sound of rush hour traffic as already was blanking out other sounds from the city.

"I suggest we wait until morning before visiting the Grand Avenue gun shop," Reese suggested. "Grace had an unusual day-shift at the hospital and I sort of promised to meet her after work at the hospital."

"She still assigned to that prisoner ward?" Charlie asked.

"Yeah."

"How's Kindred James doing?"

"He's showing signs of improvement and they are bringing him out of that induced coma sometime today," Reese said. "He's breathing on his own. The paralysis in his legs is still prevalent. He may never walk again."

"Well, there are some in the police department that are wishing he never comes out of the coma. I'll bet you even money that Captain Baldwin will crap his pants if James starts talking."

"They may get their wish about him not talking, from what Grace told me. That head wound he received may have scrambled his brains. He might not remember the night he got shot down."

Charlie pushed the air vent away from him and reached for the buckle of his seatbelt, drawing the belt across him, and snapping it in place. "That could explain why they haven't released the information which exonerates him in the cop killing. First, they wanted him dead, and when that didn't work, they hoped he had been effectively muzzled. Imagine how they are going to react if he awakens and start telling his side of the story."

Now that he had time to think about all the implications, Reese felt a moment of panic. "Do you think Baldwin will try to kill him, again?" he asked. Now that the thought which had plagued them both had been broached, his partner appeared sad.

"I don't know, Rookie." Charlie bowed his head almost touching the steering column. Dent appeared in the strong daylight to have been drained of anything positive, reflecting only the evil which seemed to surround the whole sordid affair. His words were dripping with timidity as he tried to grasp the implications his answer might bring.

"I can't imagine that much evil from any man, but when he thought James had killed his former partner, he wasn't rational. Right now, if James starts talking and we have the evidence to back up his words, Baldwin is going to be forced to acknowledge his attack was deliberate and was directed toward the wrong man.

"Personally, I don't think he has the guts to admit he was wrong, especially since it means a long prison term. I sense Baldwin is still harboring the hope that James will die and he will be able to cover the murder up. If not, I fear he will carry this bloody farce to the bitter end. By extension, if he was willing to cover up the murder, he isn't going to hesitate to add the names of a pair of troublesome detectives to his death wish list."

CHAPTER 22

Reese Barrett arrived at Dallas Southwest Regional Hospital about an hour before shift change, and made his way to the county jail ward. News that they were bringing Kindred James out of the induced coma had already spread to the media. This information release was a courtesy to the community leaders seeking the opportunity of stepping in front of a camera to berate the city administration and the police department as a bunch of racists.

The young detective believed they were wrong. Evidence was mounting that Captain Andrew Baldwin was an equal opportunity hater, striking out as a matter of revenge, not color. Tremendous pressure had to be building within the captain making him unstable. He might strike out in any direction.

Extra police had been assigned to guard the ward from the pressing crowd which had spilled out of the waiting room into the hallway. Many more were outside the hospital, being held behind a police barricade.

Reese squeezed through the crowd, uttering no comment into the microphones shoved into his face. Several he recognized, including Pepper Jackson, who was holding court with one of the officers at the door to the ward.

"Hey, Barrett! We just heard James was going to make it," he shouted over the noise of the crowd. "How does the department feel about that?"

Reese shoved passed the newsman, "Since when did you decide I speak for the department on anything?"

Jackson laughed. "I'm not even sure they are talking to you."

Inside a small alcove, a deputy sheriff assumed custody of Reese's gun before allowing him to enter the general population of the ward. The prison ward was divided into small bays with beds lining both walls to the side of a central walkway. Each bay had permanent walls on the sides and a sliding partition across the front. Prisoners were clearly visible to the guards and hospital staff from the central walkway. Reese could see Grace in one of the far cubicles, but he was looking for the cubicle holding Kindred James. It was about a third of the way down on the left side.

James had changed a lot in appearance in the six days since Reese had seen him at the bus stop. His head was heavily bandaged from the crease across his forehead, where he had escaped death by a micro-fraction of a second.

If he had not begun to turn as the bullet was fired it would have drilled a hole between his eyes. The shot was not police academy trained, which instructed the cadets to aim for the central body mass, where the emphasis was in neutralizing a threat as quickly as possible. The head shot, although extremely effective, was a high risk shot and was normally reserved for specially trained squads, like SWAT or snipers where the kill shot was necessary to protect innocent people. Normally, firing three quick rounds into the chest cavity was taught. Even a close miss would take the shooter out of action.

The head shot did not fit the agenda of neutralizing an opponent, where a slight turn of the head could lead to a miss, and a still active shooter. If Baldwin had fired that first shot, it was a well-aimed attempt to kill James instantly. Although it was obvious to

Reese that murder was intended, most of the department was not ready to accept that belief.

Reese counted off the wounds on the bedfast man. A second bullet had penetrated the upper chest, missing most of the vital organs, but damaging a major blood vein leading into the heart which required two surgeries to close. That had to have been the wound Grace had stanched.

Another bullet, where Reese had tried to plug the hole, had entered between the lower ribs and penetrated to the spine. This bullet could cause paralysis.

Additionally, Kindred James had been wounded in his upper right arm, left thigh, and the rear calf of his left leg. He had twisted as he fell and his quick descent to the concrete floor of the bus stop had probably saved his life as most of the shots went high. Nearly fifty shots struck either him or the shelter in the five seconds or so before Charlie had climbed the curb with the squad car blocking off the police from their target.

The prisoner was asleep and appeared to be resting calmly. A lot of the medical equipment that had been cocooned around him had been disconnected and moved aside. Communication with the patient was still barred by the physicians, which was a plus for Reese. If he remained silent, no one had access to the victim. He and Charlie counted on conducting the investigation unimpeded.

However, Reese had a pipeline to Kindred James through Grace Evans. He had felt compelled to get word to the victim, to assure him that he was not alone. He knew that would be small comfort to Kindred, but he needed let him know, for Reese's own selfish reasons. The kid had almost been killed, and, without intervention, Baldwin would complete the destruction. His media campaign to paint James as a vicious murderer, who had attacked the police to avoid capture, was playing daily on the news.

Still trying to put the pieces of the puzzle together, he did not notice when Grace approached him. She walked up beside him and tapped him on the shoulder.

"What, you ignoring me now?" She asked playfully.

For a second, Reese felt like he was shifting gears as he fought the emotions raging inside of him. From rage at the injustice inflicted on James to the love he felt toward Grace was like opposite ends of the universe.

"Sorry, I didn't see you coming," he finally squeezed the excuse out.

Grace smiled. "I'm not sure if I were you I would have admitted that."

Reese's mind switched into search mode before realizing his excuse could be taken quite awkwardly.

"I was temporarily blinded in awe, my lady," he said in his best Shakespearean tone. "Perchance I did not have the ability to speak."

Grace laughed. "Perchance you speaketh too much."

"I'll shut up now," Reese said, bowing slightly.

"Good idea," Grace said. "I get off in about ten minutes. I'm hungry enough to eat a whole cow."

Lately, their dinner dates had not gone very well. They seemed to run the gambit between cold food and murder scenes.

"It's not going to have a good start if that mob outside sees us together," Reese said. "I'm going to fight my way out of here and you join me outside the emergency entrance when you can. I think they will leave you alone." He wasn't sure why he hadn't thought to call her and have her meet him outside the hospital, but he had also wanted to see Kindred James. "I'll have the engine running."

Reese wanted to kiss her, but, while two might keep a secret, a dozen can't, and there were too many eyes around the open bay. He was forced to settle for a caress of her arm before heading for the ward exit.

His escape did not go smoothly. The media crowded in on him, shouting questions, jousting for positions with their cameras. Reese realized it had been a mistake to come to the hospital. There was no covering up the fact he was here to see the suspected cop killer.

He tossed out a couple of *no comments* to the crowd as the security burrowed him a passageway past the waiting room. Angry eyes glared at him as he edged past the protesters. Pepper Jackson was waiting in ambush at the end of the hallway near the elevators.

"The word is out that Kindred James was unarmed when the arrest was made," he said without preamble. "Black leaders are planning a major march in downtown to police headquarters tomorrow. Rumor has it they are bussing in thousands from out of state."

Reese had expected it to come to a head soon, but still held out hope that it would be much later. The sudden rush to judgment was not allowing enough time for investigation.

"I try to avoid dealing in rumors," Reese said, shoving the argument aside.

Jackson stepped in front of him to block him from the elevator. "You might want to start. I heard that the time sheet for James has found its way to the chief and rumors are flying that police are pressuring certain witnesses to change their statements about where he was that night."

"Sounds like someone is worried," Reese replied.

"Yeah, and rumor has it, he is worried about you and your partner. My little birdie told me that officers are dogging your every move, and Captain Baldwin is considering filing a complaint against you for insubordination at the arrest site," Pepper Jackson said. "How much longer can you keep what you know a secret?"

"That's a good one," Reese said. "First, he claims we were not close enough to see what was occurring and now he claims we interfered?"

"May I quote you on that?" Pepper asked, poised with a pad and pen.

Reese reached for the elevator button. "My official word is still no comment."

Fifteen minutes later, when Grace arrived, he had the air conditioner turned as low as possible and had cooled the interior of the car down to a tolerable level. Even in the shadows of the seventeen-story building, heat had topped out at over a hundred, and less than an hour after the high point of the day, temperatures were still in the high nineties.

Grace was panting from the heat as she slid into the passenger seat beside him. "I'm casting my vote for snow right now," she said, while repositioning all the vents to blow on her face. Global warming sucks." She sat there for a full minute with her nose pressed within inches of one of the vents, breathing deeply, and making pleasurable moaning sounds. After a minute, she leaned back against the headrest and brushed her hair back.

"I didn't make any specific plans for tonight. What would you like?" Reese asked.

Still breathing deeply, Grace sighed. "I don't care, long as it's cold and wet, preferably both, in a tall glass, with ice."

"You don't drink," Reese reminder her.

"Well, after a day like today, I just might start," she said. "Remind me again why I volunteered for day shift. I've never been so busy in my life."

Reese back the car out of the parking space and headed out of the parking lot, heading to a dinner theater they had attended a couple of times before. The theater served a full menu and the movie was usually a popular first run. The major selling point now was that neither would have to move an inch from their seats, while dining and watching in cool, air conditioned comfort. Grace had leaned back and closed her eyes.

"Were you busy with the shooting suspect?" he asked, heading north.

Grace's eyes fluttered. "Partially," she admitted. "They brought him out of his induced coma about ten o'clock this morning and Dr. Reynolds had me assisting since I had experience upstairs in the hospital's coma ward. That went pretty much routine, but there is just so many things you do to stabilize the patient. Once you stop the propyl drip that keeps him under, it only takes a minute for the drug to be out of his system."

"He came out okay?"

"Textbook recovery, but I wasn't prepared for the pain he had coming out. I hope he wasn't in that much pain while in the coma. He was fighting the breathing tube and we had to take it out, but he fought like a banshee."

"And of course, you've seen a banshee fight?" he asked, hoping to distract her from the scene of abhorrence she was projecting with body language.

Grace shook her head. "Don't tease me, Reese Barrett, you know what I mean. The doctors were not willing to take the respirator out until they checked his lung function. Imagine waking up and not being able to breathe. They had his arms handcuffed to the bed rails and I thought he was going to tear them off. He was fighting for his very life. If he hadn't been restrained, he could have seriously hurt himself or someone else—meaning me."

"I guess that would cause a panic reaction."

"He was in a panic, but he was so weak that in a matter of a few seconds he had calmed all the way down," she said. "Once we got him stabilized and the doctors were satisfied he could breathe on his own, it was okay."

"Did he say anything after you got the respirator out?"

Grace seemed to relax, almost as if coming out of the experience herself.

"No, he was asleep by then. But all those reporters outside bothered us all day. They almost got in the ward once by sheer numbers. We were nearly afraid to leave the ward because of the questions and someone sticking a mike or camera in our face. Then the police tried to question Kindred James, but the doctors turned them back."

Reese went on immediate alert. "Did they talk to him at all?"

"No, the doctors wouldn't allow it. I told them that only Detectives Charlie Dent and Reese Barrett were authorized to speak with him once they give their clearance because you were conducting the investigation."

"And they believed that?"

Grace smiled. "They were so upset by that rude policeman that whether official or not, they are not willing to allow anyone to talk to him."

"Rude policeman?"

"Yeah, he was in plain clothes when he came in today, but I recognized him as the other officer riding with Captain Baldwin the night of the shooting." Grace was no longer smiling. "He was so insistent that it was almost an ugly scene. From his reaction to the mention of your name, you might want to cross him off your Christmas card list."

CHAPTER 23

Charlie Dent was in a complete rage when Reese briefed him about what happened at the hospital the day before.

"Every step we have taken in this case has Baldwin running interference," he said. His face had gone splotchy red and his fists were clinched so tightly that the whiteness of his knuckles stood out in sharp relief. He slumped into his chair in the squad room and leaned forward over his desk. "If he's coming after us, I think it is time to go on the offensive. No more Mister Nice Guy."

Reese had seen him madder and he had enough sense to duck then, but not now.

"It sounds to me like he's trying to cover all bases to deflect blame for this mess from him on to us."

"Maybe," Charlie said, "But the fool made one very bad mistake, well two actually. First, he dared to tangle with me, and secondly, he leaked to the press that we were not present at the takedown, therefore undermining his own case that we interfered with his orders. What orders? Commands that officers under his command open fire on an unarmed suspect? I think it is time to release the dashcam photos to the police shooting team."

The police have a way of making those tapes disappear," Reese said, "What about rumors that the tapes, taken from the vest cameras, were inadvertently misplaced?"

Charlie's reaction was completely opposite to what Reese expected as he broke out in a broad smile.

"I'm betting those tapes are miraculously resurrected when our footage appears on the news," he said.

Reese felt his heart stop. "They will crucify us for releasing the film outside of the department."

The senior detective's grin disappeared and a stern tooth clinching cloud came across his face.

"That's why I want you to step back from this, Reese. This could be a career ender and I don't see any need for both of us to go down. Call in sick, take some time off, do whatever you need to put some distance between you and this investigation. I've got enough time in that I can retire with full pension, but there is no need for you to throw your career away."

"I thought we are partners," Reese said. "I'm not going to back down if you're not. I refuse to allow office politics to dictate what's happening to us." While Reese had to suppress the desire to take the escape route out that Charlie was offering him and the pending consequences made him physically sick, he was resolved not to flee. "We may go down, but we will go down together."

"Fine words, Reese, but you could be throwing your whole career away," Charlie said, solemnly. "You could lose more than Baldwin in the end game."

"I'm not going to be railroaded into allowing his bloodlust to condemn an innocent man to a lethal injection," Reese said, refusing to back away. "Let's do this."

By now, they realized that even Baldwin must have known that camera evidence existed which would contradict the statements he had been leaking to the press. Maybe the captain had a large enough ego to believe if nothing had surfaced so far in the investigation that he was home free. So far, no photo evidence had appeared, he had managed to steal the alibi evidence, intimidate witnesses, and had waged a campaign to discredit any statements the two detectives assigned to the original murder case might release.

Revealing what they knew now had other inherent dangers. Demonstrators were already gathering in the plaza below them. Word of the shooting of an unarmed black man by police would almost certainly result in a riot situation. Especially if word slipped out that certain people in the police department had attempted to cover it up. Reese and his partner were going to be under heavy scrutiny for not revealing evidence pertaining to doubts on Kindred James' guilt.

Their priority was to escape from headquarters without being cornered by the gathering protest outside. Second priority was to get a copy of the film into a trusted media source and as much as either detective hated to admit it, Pepper Jackson was the best source.

Most of the crowd was gathering in the plaza so they slipped out through parking in the rear of headquarters. Charlie drove, while Reese put in a call to the newspaper, which connected him with Pepper. The News reporter agreed to meet them at a location a short distance from the newspaper's office.

"I hope you understand why we can't bring the film to your office," Reese said.

"You want to call it plausible deniability?" Jackson asked.

"We are going to have a hard time ignoring this one, Pepper. It's evidence and we can't allow it out of our possession. Everyone is going to know where it came from; we just don't want them to know how it came to be in your possession."

"Then I'll bring a recorder and duplicate the film. If asked, I say it was given to me by someone in high authority," he said. "That always stops them cold. They are usually afraid the finger is going to be pointed at them or that someone higher up is out to get them."

Jackson met us about twenty minutes later and ushered us into the back room of an uptown dining destination for the elite.

"A friend of mine owns this place and he doesn't mind me holding my confidential meetings here. They only open for the evening meal, so no one is around at this hour that might see us," he indicated.

He had brought a media specialist, who removed the film quickly and ushered it into the back room. It took him only a few minutes to duplicate the tape.

"Have you seen the tape?" Pepper asked.

"Don't have to, we were there," Charlie said. "All that we ask is that you hold the tape until we call you and inform you we have turned the original over to Luther Nichols, who's heading up the shooting team."

"Hold it?" Pepper complained. "What am I supposed to do in the meantime?"

"Do whatever you need to do to get it ready for release, just give us a little time to distance ourselves from it," Charlie said. "The fallout could be devastating, so it might not be a good idea to make this release an exclusive."

"If what's on this tape what I believe I believe it is, it's going to be too hot to sit on very long," Pepper indicated, taking the duplicate tape from his media man and holding it aloft as if that act would give him insight. "The rumor on the street is that Captain Baldwin plans to file a report against you two sometime today to not only get you off this investigation, but off the police force."

"Hopefully, this tape will vindicate us," Reese said.

The detectives departed the restaurant after eliciting a promise from the columnist to delay the film's airing until the early nightly news. Reaching the squad car, Charlie looked at Reese with sadness in his eyes.

"I'm sorry I asked you to wait in releasing the film," he said. "Baldwin has a reputation of not always following the rules, but

I never suspected he was willing to throw a fellow cop under the wheels of a bus to save his own neck."

"You must have suspected something," Reese said, as he slid into the passenger seat.

Charlie hesitated a long thirty seconds before answering.

"Dashcam has been around long enough that people tend to overlook it. To be honest, the cam didn't occur to me until after the event so I never thought to turn it over to the shooting team. Forgetting was probably a good thing because it might have disappeared with the body cams from the officers at the scene and we would have little to counter his accusations. Subconsciously, maybe in the back of my mind, I felt we needed an edge. You saw how Baldwin acted that night. He felt vindicated in his own mind that he had done the right thing. I think he truly believed that James was guilty of murdering his former partner and that he was justified in his actions to bring the victim to his own perverted sense of justice."

Reese had gone beyond the point where he could think of Kindred James as a suspected killer. "Should we tell the Lieutenant what we are planning?"

"Not unless you want your head handed to you in a hand-basket," Charlie replied. "It's better if she doesn't know. She's the one that may need plausible deniability. We are beyond that stage."

After the drive, back to police headquarters, delivering the tape to Luther Nichols had been easy enough. Although he didn't say anything which might indicate his state of mind, the internal affairs officer seemed to be waiting for them. He rose from his position behind his desk as Charlie reached out and handed the film over without hesitation. The two veteran police officers locked gazes for several seconds, before Charlie released his grip on the tape.

"If there is any fallout over not surrendering the film

immediately after the shooting, it rests entirely on my shoulders," Charlie informed Nichols, "My partner had nothing to do with this."

Reese started to object, but was stopped by Lt. Nichols, who turned away.

"It's best if you don't say anything," he said, taking the film. "There may be repercussions and your partner is wise to try to keep you out of this." He turned the film case over in his hand. "Who else has seen this tape?" he asked.

"As far as I am aware, no one," Charlie said.

It was a stretch, but Reese calculated Jackson had not had enough time to return to his office and view the tape. It was a matter of semantics, but his partner had not technically lied.

Nichols dismissed them with a flourish, seeming satisfied for the moment with obtaining another piece of the puzzle.

"I'll get back to you on this later," he said.

Reese could feel the eyes of the internal affairs officer boring into his back as he and Charlie left the office. They chose to bypass checking in to the squad room, choosing to return to the streets. Although neither man said anything, Charlie headed their squad car back to the store where all of this had started.

Reese sat in stunned silence. He had contemplated how his career would end many times, but he had never imagined this scenario. When he put on the uniform, he was aware that he could be killed at any time, but life was uncertain at best. All men die, but he thought he was living a life of purpose, seeking justice, and protecting all those who can't protect themselves. In all his thoughts, he had never felt that he might be the one needing justice. He was sure Charlie's statement to Nichols had ended his career.

When they pulled into the grocery store parking lot about thirty minutes later, it was evident that the city had done a thorough job of securing the door into Tran's store. Every piece of glass behind the burglar bars had been broken out, however. Vandalism was probably courtesy of LeVartis Thompson or some of his buddies. Charlie parked the car, got out and walked slowly down the length of the storefront surveying the damage. Glass crunched under his feet and he kicked a piece of broken brick back toward the street.

Reese joined him near the rusting ice cabinet where they had questioned the old Vietnamese clerk the night of the murder.

"I doubt if Tran carried insurance," he said. "He's out of business."

"There are going to be no winners in this case," Charlie said, leaning his bulk against the ledge beneath the missing window. He picked up pieces of glass from the ledge and dropped them to the pavement beneath his feet. The old cop looked toward the sky, as if seeking answers there, and puffed out a deep sigh between pursed lips. "No winners at all."

Despite the late summer heat, Reese shivered from a sudden chill, which had no origin.

"Let's go check Tran's house to see if he has returned," he suggested.

Charlie was slow to respond, finally nodding and starting toward the car. "By now, Nichols has seen the tape and has called in the police chief, maybe even the mayor, and all of them are running around trying to cover their asses and find someone—anyone— to take blame for this. The activists are celebrating because they are going to get the riot they want. Carver's family is going to be in shock over the atrocity committed in an act of revenge, some policemen are contemplating suicide, and all they must do to stop everything is cover it up. They might even consider that possibility until the evening news," the old detective said. "The only heroes in this whole drama are you and Grace trying to save a man's life."

"You were a part of it, too," Reese said, to mollify his partner.

"I'm no hero," Charlie said. "I saw this firestorm shaping up before it happened, but I could not figure a way out. I've known Baldwin for years and I knew what kind of idiot he was. I could have kept you out of this."

"What can we do now?"

"We still have our guns and our shields," Charlie replied. "We are cops and cops solve crimes, so we keep going." The old detective almost broke into tears before he turned away and started the car. "Reese, I wish I had a better answer."

He drove by Tran's house on the shady lane a couple of blocks away. The house was still locked up and there was no evidence anyone had attempted entry. The mailbox near the front door was overflowing. A cursory inspection revealed a cornucopia of bills and advertisements, but nothing of a personal nature. One envelope caught Reese's eye, however.

The printed envelope bore a return address, but no company name. The name of the recipient appeared through a plastic window. Reese turned it over and noticed a bank logo on the flap.

"Did we check into the possibility that Tran had a bank debit card or credit card?" he asked Charlie.

"Nothing local, but I don't see how he could have done business without some sort of banking system," Charlie said. "I'm sure all his retail business was in cash. I didn't see one of those swipe machines in the store, but I don't see how he could work with suppliers without a credit card."

"If he's in hiding, he must have some source of funds," Reese stated the obvious. "We should be able to trace where and when he's using it."

"Good idea," the old detective said. "I'll call it in to the lieutenant and see if we can get a warrant issued for that information. Meanwhile," Charlie said, taking the envelope from Reese's hands and flipping it over to the flap. "Look at this, will you? It appears someone has already opened it." He slipped a fingernail under a corner of the flap and pulled it outward. "I think maybe we ought to inventory the contents to see if anything was stolen, don't you?"

The envelope contained a detailed page of charges and payments against the card, including a monthly minimum payment, which staggered both detectives. Evidentially, the old shopkeeper hadn't gotten a very good percentage rate, and he had run up quite a tab. Currently a lot more money was coming out of the account than was going in. He estimated it would not be very long before the credit card company shut him off.

The billing date was prior to the disappearance of Tran.

"This bill is not going to help us find him," Reese said.

"The next one will," Charlie said. "I think we can get a partial billing with a warrant."

He fished his cell phone out of his pocket and called Mattie Reynolds.

Not enough time passed to spread the word that their heads were wanted on a silver platter, so the lieutenant listened. He told her about finding the *torn* envelope on Tran's porch beneath the mailbox. Charlie gave her the account information and requested information on any local banking accounts the old Vietnamese grocer may have had.

Charlie listened gravely to the lieutenant for almost a minute before hanging up. Sighing, Charlie slipped the phone back into his pocket.

"She said she would get right on it, but indicated it may be slightly delayed. The demonstration is just shy of a full-blown riot at police plaza and the chief has ordered officers in riot gear to form a barricade around HQ. Things are getting dicey down there."

"Police in riot gear is like pouring gasoline on a fire," Reese said. "They already had barricades and extra officers at the hospital. No riot gear yet, though."

"It's going to be nothing compared to the bomb we planted in the chief's office this morning," the old detective indicated. "When that goes off, the whole town might go up in flames."

"Were we right?" Reese asked, feeling the sickness creeping back into his stomach. With this amount of stress, he was beginning to understand why old time officers like his partner suffered from alcoholism or stomach ulcers. "I mean were we right to sacrifice the city for one man; one who is very much out of it anyway."

"First," Charlie said, as they walked back to the car, "We didn't do it. The demonstration was inevitable from the second Captain Andrew Baldwin decided to make this takedown his opportunity to exact revenge for the killing of his ex-partner. Then, he made even more mistakes by trying to cover it up when he realized he had shot the wrong man. Our bomb was the truth and truth almost always wins out."

Reese was still skeptical. It felt like the lie was winning.

CHAPTER 24

The two detectives drove by the home where LeVartis Thompson had lived until their encounter with Roscoe Love. The house was dark and locked up, which they took as an indication the kid had been found. The boy's mother had been rounded up in a dragnet which had swept up a large segment of offenders from the store burglary. Reese Barrett made note to check on the welfare of the little vandal.

Charlie's buddy in burglary had been giddy when the round-up had been described to him.

"It's true; there is no honor among thieves. They turned on each other like a pack of sharks; when one's injured they all want a bite. Every one of them was willing to incriminate his buddies to cut a deal. We may be clearing cases for a month," the burglary detective had said.

Less than a mile of driving later, Charlie steered the car into a left turn into the parking lot of the E. Grand Avenue gun shop. It was in the middle of a block about half way between South Barry and South Haskell Avenues facing the west. The shade of the building sliced across the glare of the midmorning sun, temporarily blinding Reese until his eyes readjusted.

The Grand Gun and Ammo Shop was a sizeable store with a high volume of clientele. Four men were looking at various weapons displays and clerks were handling them as quickly as possible. From the murmur of conversations the detectives picked up, purchasing the correct gun was a time consuming endeavor.

The sound of muffled gunfire could be heard coming from the rear of the store. Signage advertised the indoor shooting range and several people seemed to be taking advantage, even on what Reese thought would be a slow Thursday morning. The range was between a payday loan company and a title loan company. Shops on that side of the avenue had fronts solidly reinforced with burglar bars. The rest of the block was vacant so it was unlikely anyone could hear the firing from the range outside the small grouping of buildings.

The sales counter was about two-thirds of the way back a few feet away from the right wall. A clerk behind the register noted their entry and waved for them to come back to him.

"Sorry, I couldn't greet you at the door, officers," he said with a smile as Charlie and Reese approached, "We've got quite a crowd in here this morning and our rules state that someone must be behind the counter at all times, so that's me."

"Are you afraid of being robbed?" Charlie asked.

The uniformed clerk laughed, pointing to a second shelf beneath the rim of the counter. Several pistols, undoubtedly, Reese decided, loaded and within an easy reach.

"Only a fool would try something like that. We are well prepared."

"And knowing we are police officers, I guess, is part of the training." Charlie said.

"We have all types of people walk through that door. With the type of merchandise, we carry, we learn to read people rather quickly. Call it profiling if you like, but, in your case, I caught a glimpse of your disguised emergency flashers before you got out of the car."

If the clerk had a good profile on them, Reese was having a difficult time pegging the clerk to a type. He was absent the tattoos, body piercings, B.O., and the creepy feeling of sleaze he had experienced in most of the other shops they had hit during the last week. He appeared to be intelligent, young, maybe twenty-four or five, slender build, and well-dressed. If it wasn't for the fact he was standing behind a gun store counter, Reese would have profiled him as a police officer.

As if understanding the problem Reese was having, the clerk motioned for him to look beneath the counter where the clerk flipped open a billfold to display a miniature ATF shield.

"In a second, I'll take you back and show you the gun range," he said, closing the wallet and stuffing it into his pocket before bring his hands back to the top of the counter. "I'll get one of the other clerks to fill in for me for a couple minutes," he said, hand signaling to a beefy middle aged man, just finishing with a pair of shoppers, who were moving toward the door.

"Willie, can you sit the counter for a few minutes. I'll be right back."

Willie was somewhere between Reese's and Charlie's age with graying hair cut very short in a military buzz. He walked with a limp and Reese noticed he had no bend in his ankle when he came toward them, either as the results of an ankle fusion, or an artificial leg.

"Got you covered, but you'd better get back quick," Willie said, "I got me a couple of hot ones looking to buy that sharp deer rifle up by the front window. Don't think either has been on a deer hunt in their life, but they got themselves a deer lease out in West Texas. Just didn't have enough money on them to lock up the deal. Told them I would hold the .357 until four o'clock, but I had other people interested in it. They will be back."

Charlie and Reese followed the clerk through a rear door into a hallway with windows on one side looking out on several dividers along the range firing line. Despite the double pane glass, the noise from the weapons was deafening. The clerk used pantomime to lead them to a small office at the end of the hall, which held an array of disinfectants and hearing protectors. When they entered, the clerk closed the door and eliminated maybe ninety percent of the noise. Reese yawned, trying to achieve equilibrium again. Charlie was doing the same.

"Kind of loud isn't it?" the employee asked.

"Let's just say our qualifying ranges are a lot better sound proofed," Reese said.

"Ours, too."

"We are not messing up an undercover assignment, are we?" Charlie asked.

"No, I've already given this place a clean bill, but working here gives me access to some of the other gun dealers and some of them are not clean," he said. "This is the only spot in this store which is not under surveillance from cameras and I defy anyone to understand anything recorded in this racket. So, we can talk freely."

"I meant yesterday, when you popped into Brogan's Pawn Shop and disappeared rather hastily," Charlie said.

"Oh, you caught that," the agent said, laughing, identifying himself as agent Leonard Snow. "Good eye, but to answer your question, Brogan would have been suspicious if I had reacted any other way. We've got a deal cooking on a couple of assault rifles which, you might say, are definitely not kosher."

"We are interested in a questionable transaction between Brogan and Grand Avenue a couple months back," Charlie said.

"That's a little before my time," said Snow. "But, I might be able to point you in the right direction."

"We are trying to trace the purchase of a .38 used to kill a police officer a week ago," Charlie said. "The weapon was not recovered, date of purchase, or location is unknown. Our suspect probably couldn't have purchased a weapon legally. He's a legal immigrant entering the country as a political refugee, but he never took U.S. citizenship."

Agent Snow frowned. "That's not going to narrow it down very much. Anyone who wants a gun can purchase one legally or illegally. There is a whole industry trafficking in stolen weapons, most ending up in the hands of collectors, but a surprising number of them moving in private sales."

The young agent sized up Charlie, "Remember, as a kid, putting aspirin in a Coke and shaking it up. That's what the ATF is attempting to do now, with these sting operations. If we can build cases against crooked gun dealers, maybe we can slow the sales on illegal weapons. We've had some success in putting a cap back on the bottle without getting soaked." He looked away, "If that's all you got, however, I'll warn you now, it will be next to impossible to trace the weapon. These guys have more angles than geometry."

Reese interrupted Snow. "Humor us for a moment," he said, quickly laying out the sketchy details on the sale of the Bersa Thunder 380 about three months prior. "Brogan said it was a split deal with both him and Grand Avenue co-operating as dealers, but that Grand handled the transfer transaction. Any way you can determine where the gun went?"

Snow closed his eyes and tilted his head toward the ceiling. "Give me a day or so, and I'll let you know."

Reese gave him a business card with their office number and cell phone numbers on the front. "You are not in any danger if you get caught in contact with the local police, are you?"

"We can't be distrustful of everyone," Snow indicated. "Those under the table gun sales are taking food from these guys' mouths. They get a commission on every gun they sell. Hell, most of them would probably jump in and help you find the gun if it was sold illegally."

Reese felt his mind shift into high gear and the fine hairs on the back of his neck stood out like spikes in a dog collar. If they were making extra money to move weapons, it also seemed logical to him that the chance for a bigger paycheck by simply looking the other way on a questionable background check also provided an incentive of another type. He wondered if Snow was taking that possibility into his assessment.

A quick check of his partner disclosed a stern frozen face of doubt on the usually stoic face. Too many times in law enforcement they had seen even the best of good intentions twisted to a corrupt pathway. In that brief second of eye contact Reese and Charlie dismissed Snow's statement as highly unlikely.

"Just do the best you can," Charlie said, "We may not have more than a day to wrap up this investigation." Charlie did not elaborate for the ATF agent, leaving Snow perplexed by the old detective's last words.

Reese was worried about his partner. When, as a rookie detective, he had been partnered with the gruff old veteran homicide detective, Reese had been overwhelmed by the knowledge and understanding of human nature that Charlie displayed. He had quickly learned that the old man's bark was a lot worse than his bite, at least toward him. Even his outbursts of temper seemed to be carefully measured to get the right impact on witnesses and suspects they dealt with daily.

In the last few months, Reese had noted with dismay a change coming over the old man. He seemed unable or unwilling to cloak his feelings of anger or frustration at perceived wrongs. The partner he got back from the hospital stay was not the same one who checked in, unknowingly close to death. Being close to dying and realizing, maybe for the first time, that he was mortal seemed to have left Charlie with no time for what he referred to as "B.S."

"Just tell me like it is or get out of my face," had replaced the *"Let's*

wait and see what happens" attitude that Charlie was known for, and at times it appeared to be evolving into something less pleasant, less tolerant. While Reese agreed with much of what Charlie did or said, it was with a mixed note of apprehension what he accepted with this new Charlie. The old man seemed to be slipping, and Reese didn't like it one bit.

"Can you believe how naïve some people can be?" Charlie asked when they reached the street. "Getting co-operation from those guys is a lot like dealing with a skunk," he mumbled. "Squeezing information out is next to impossible, and there is always going to be one hell-of-a stink involved."

Charlie wasn't known for pessimism so the impression he emitted was disconcerting for Reese.

"Maybe we need to step back from the investigation for a while," Reese said, not really believing the old homicide detective would agree to back down at this point, but Reese wanted to judge his response.

Charlie opened the car door and slid behind the wheel. Starting the car, he basked in the cool breeze from the air conditioner. Temperatures were already in the high eighties, headed for one hundred and three by four o'clock.

"Nothing in this world would give me greater pleasure than to run away and hide," the old detective said. He glanced at the wrist watch on his left arm and sighed. "Less than an hour from now, Pepper Jackson, if he's stuck to our agreement, will broadcast the dash cam video. Knowing him, he probably has a nationwide linkup so everyone in the country between the ages of three and ninety are going to know what happened here.

"There is no doubt in my mind that Captain Baldwin was behind the theft of the time sheets which would have verified Kindred James' innocence. His footprints are all over this case and the dash cam tape should show the world just what type of man he is, but don't expect justice out of this case Reese. What's justice for one is an injustice for another. If we hadn't interfered, I have no doubts James would have died, and Baldwin would have pushed for an end of the investigation. James, if he survives, is likely to be horribly crippled for the rest of his life. There can be no justice for him, ever. We violated a half dozen police procedures by revealing that film to the public so I don't expect it to end well for us either," he said. Charlie slammed down on the steering wheel in frustration and anger.

"If you understand anything at all about the relationship between police and the courts, Baldwin is the only one who has a chance of walking away from this mess scot free. In the meantime, we still have a murderer out there on the streets, whose investigation is being overshadowed by the very thing which caused the spotlight to be cast in the first place."

Still an hour away from the breaking news event, Reese suggested checking back in with Lt. Mattie Reynolds to see if their credit card inquiry had raised any red flags. Reese called, catching her eating a light lunch at her desk.

"We got a hit on the card and it's as you suspected. It was in Oklahoma City earlier this morning. The Bethany Police have already spotted where he is staying, and they are going to pick him up shortly. Now, you two are in a bit of hot water with the chief. Somewhere in all the venom he was spitting out, he was raving about two rogue detectives not following the chain of command in releasing evidence. He saw the tape you left, and was wondering why he was not made aware of it until six days after the shooting."

"Tell him its newly discovered evidence," Charlie said gruffly. "We were rather wrapped up in trying to save the life of a kid who looked like a sieve, and the thought that our dash cam could have caught the events closest to the action just did not enter our minds. Right now, we could use an order to pick up Mr. Duc Tran from

Oklahoma. Do you think the department could wrangle the paperwork? Oh, and you could cut us orders to go get him if you are not too busy now. We are a little concerned at who might be sent if we don't get the orders first."

Lt. Reynolds laughed loud enough that Reese could hear it from the other side of the car.

"I should shut you two cowboys down on this one. The chief is biting nails of the ten-penny variety. You have put him in quite a spot."

"Then we need to make an arrest of the real murderer before he does something stupid, don't you agree?"

"What if your suspect decides to fight extradition? That is possible, you know?"

"He's accused of killing a cop," Charlie said, "No way are they going to hinder us bringing him back to justice. But we need to go now, before the chief steps in and delays our investigation."

Reynolds sounded unconvinced by Charlie's logic, but the senior detective reminded her that they had kept her informed every step of the way and had access to the same evidence they had in arriving at this point in the case. He made no mention of the copied tape which was in the hands of the media. Reese speculated that the old detective was having second thoughts about turning over the film to Pepper Jackson. Even without the knowledge of the tape, the chief was madder than a wet hen, the verdict of which side he was going to come down on was still undecided.

"Just go," Reynolds relented. "I'll fax a warrant to the Bethany police. Just get him back here in the next twenty-four hours or you won't have to worry about what the chief is going to do to you. I'll strangle you with my own bare hands," she said. "I am not going to answer for the screw-ups in this investigation all by myself. You get me!"

After Charlie completed the call, Reese spoke up. "It sounds like she's pretty angry at us, too."

Charlie shrugged it off as he pointed the car north. "She's not angry at us, just scared."

"You think she's worried about her involvement in this case?"

Scoffing, Charlie picked up I-30 and headed for the mix-master to catch northbound I-35E.

"The lieutenant is bullet-proof in this case, you poor, dumb rookie. Can't you even tell when someone is worried for you?"

CHAPTER 25

Reese felt they were running away from a fire storm which they had helped create. By the time he and Charlie had reached Denton, the snippets of film displaying the one-sided shootout in Dallas were on national news. Broadcasters were warning viewers about the graphic violence on the tape.

A major riot was brewing at Dallas Police Headquarters between several hundred angry people protesting of police brutality and not enough uniformed cops attempting riot control. More police officers, some off duty, and reserves had been called and were hastily reporting in to the main headquarters to be routed as needed. Some moved to help control the expected riot, some to South Oak Cliff to control looters, and a few to traffic control. In South Oak Cliff looters were taking advantage of the situation and the community was under siege from the looters and from arsonists. At least two looters had reportedly been shot by shop owners. Officers were reporting sporadic gun fire in areas they could not control. The Fire Department was moving to keep the fires from getting out of control as well. Even the 911 Call Station beefed up the number of operators.

Charlie and Reese were probably the last two people in the nation which viewed the violence on film, but it seemed every major television network and radio station in the country broke away from regular programming with a breaking news bulletin.

"Turn it off, Reese," Charlie said, after they had listened to several minutes of the news story on the radio. "We don't need to hear what is happening. There is going to be a lot of violence, a lot of posturing, and accusations flying between the two sides for several days before someone comes to their senses. That is not our fault. This was set in motion when Captain Baldwin shoved us aside, took 'control' and started his little vendetta."

The detectives stopped in Ardmore, Oklahoma, just long enough to stretch their legs, gas up, and grab a quick sandwich from a fast food restaurant. Reese planned to take over as driver for the final leg of the trip, which they estimated to be another hundred and twenty miles. It was nearly three-thirty when they made their next stop. Checking the distance, Reese figured it would be well after office hours before they reached Bethany. They would then have to locate the local jail. They might also find, after their arrival at the jail, that Tran had already been transferred to the county lockup.

The restaurant was nearly empty, but an overhead television in a corner was turned to a news channel which was showing the shooting in Dallas. Reese looked up to see him and Grace attempting to stop the flow of blood. Grace's face was recognizable, but all that was visible of Reese was his rear end.

Charlie nudged him in the side.

"Look, they got a picture of your best side," he said, smiling. "That rear is probably one of the most broadcast derrieres in the world."

"I did not want to hear that," Reese said.

"Then, Rookie, you should have arranged to be looking at the camera if you wanted your face in the news. After this, you are going to have to turn around when someone asks for your identification."

Charlie was laughing so hard at his joke that he started coughing. "Just think, my partner the a-a-a …"

"Don't say it," Reese interrupted. "And you need to hush before you cough yourself into an early grave, or I shoot you, whichever comes first."

"Think of it, your rear end may get as much publicity as Janet Jackson's wardrobe malfunction. It could become a catch phrase like that. Like, uh, let me think."

"Charlie, I am going to do you a great deal of harm if you don't stifle it."

In a corner of the camera's field, it showed the figure of Charlie Dent carefully picking up the pipe wrench with a gloved hand and bringing it to the shattered front of the bus stop shelter. The two detectives froze in place, glanced at each other, and then grinned.

"Well, that should dispel any statements Baldwin has made about the suspect being armed when he moved to the front of the shelter toward the police," Charlie was smiling. "Damn, I didn't realize that my finding the wrench was on the tape. That is a game changing bonus."

"Yes, it is, Partner," Reese clapped a hand on the older man's shoulder.

Turning slightly to find the source of hushed voices, he began to feel very exposed. One of the waitresses was talking in hushed tones and she made a gesture, pointing up toward the small, flat-screened TV set.

"Let's just grab the sandwiches and eat on the road," he said. "We are drawing attention."

"Don't worry about it, Rookie. Unless you flash your rear, no one is going to recognize you. I, on the other hand, am a star."

They settled for cheeseburgers, fries, and colas. Charlie had eyed a burger loaded with jalapeños, bacon, and dripping with habanera sauce, but for once he took the smart road and backed away, choosing the plain old-fashioned cheeseburger. Reese was sure Charlie's diet had been what put the old detective in the hospital for a week, three months earlier. A bit of fear that his junior partner might tattle to his wife, may have played a factor in Charlie's final decision as well. Probably even more than the fear of a repeat visit to the hospital and the discomfort he had endured after the operation to repair his damaged stomach. There was almost pain in the old man's face as he opted for the generic burger.

They got back on the highway shortly after four in the afternoon, and, twenty miles farther north, they were slowed by torrential rain. *El Nino* appeared to have caught up with them on the north face of the Arbuckle Mountains. Reese slowed because the highway was difficult to see. Behind him, coming off a long grade which ran maybe five miles, eighteen-wheelers dropped off the mountain, pushing eighty miles an hour and burying the squad car under a continuous assault of bow waves that threatened to wash them off the road.

"Where is a cop when you need one?" Charlie muttered, darting a sharp glance at the rear of each truck as it sped passed them.

They were forced off the road by the rain for nearly an hour in Pauls Valley. They pulled into a restaurant just off the Interstate and watched the storm for nearly an hour through a large plate glass window. Most of the other traffic had been forced off the road as well, and many opted to join other travelers in the store. As a result, the window seats were at a real premium. On the other hand, the trucks appeared to be taking the storm as just another obstacle in a Grand Prix event.

As Reese returned from the ice cream counter with a dip of chocolate mint and another of Maple Nut in plastic cups, he glanced at his watch.

"You know we are going to be well after hours when they release the prisoner to us, don't you? Later than they are going to want to."

"I'm more concerned about it being Friday night," Charlie said. "What if we can't get him out until Monday morning?"

Reese had considered that, deciding he preferred to be in Oklahoma City than Dallas right at this moment. The Dallas mayor and police chief had scheduled a press conference at seven tonight.

"Grace and I had two whole days off and had planned some getting to know each other time," Reese lamented. The sweet, creamy ice cream eased some of his pain. "It's been nearly three weeks since we had significant time off at the same time."

Charlie chuckled, "Twyla had me penciled in to mow the grass this weekend. I think I won't miss that if we don't get back to Dallas."

By five o'clock, the rain had let up enough that Reese and Charlie could get back on the road again. Since they were unfamiliar with the Oklahoma City area and its traffic, and with the added havoc of the weather of a windy, rainy Friday night, it was almost eight o'clock when they passed the sign marking the Bethany city limits.

They found the police station, which was in the 6700 block of North West 35th Street, a few minutes later. The parking lot was nearly empty in front of the building. Reese pulled into a slot as close to the main entrance as possible, hoping to minimize being soaked by the persistent rain, which alternated between misty showers and sudden downpours.

It was misting when the two detectives stepped out of their vehicle and began running for the door; but before they stepped onto the sidewalk, a sudden downpour soaked them to the skin. The rain stopped almost immediately after they reached the sheltering overhang.

"Well, that's a fine howdy-do," Charlie grunted, stopping to sling some of the water off his head and face. "It appears everyone is trying to get into the act of dumping on us today." Charlie brushed at the water, but to little avail.

"You think the big guy is joining in with everyone else?" Reese asked; brushing off some of the water, but having no more success than his partner.

Charlie finished with his water shaking dance and looked at his junior partner.

"Other than Twyla, Grace, and maybe Lieutenant Reynolds, I think maybe he is the only one in our corner," he said. "Don't jinx it, Rookie." Lately Charlie had taken to calling him Rookie again as a mild rebuke. Charlie was open about being religious, and the "Rookie" designation was his way of telling Reese to be more respectful of the higher power.

Entering the station, they quickly determined their negative luck was holding. Only a pair of 911 operators in a small office and a rather bored desk sergeant stretched out behind a desk. The officer stumbled to his feet when they came in and greeted them.

"What brought you out tonight in all this rain?" he asked.

Charlie and Reese flipped out their shields.

"We're here to pick up a prisoner for transport back to Dallas. You guys picked him up on a warrant for us earlier today," Charlie said.

"Well, I hate that you made the trip tonight with all the rain going on, but he was transferred several hours earlier to the county lockup in Oklahoma City," he said. "I have the paperwork your department sent, but you're not likely to find a judge to sign off on it this time of night. Heck, with tomorrow being the weekend, you might not be able to get him out of there tomorrow either." The desk sergeant fumbled around on the desk for several seconds before retrieving the fax Dallas PD had sent out. "What is he wanted for in Texas?"

Charlie took the papers and quickly scanned them to make sure everything he needed was there before handing them to Reese.

"Murdering a cop," the senior detective said to the sergeant.

Solemnly, the sergeant paused as he made the connection. His jovial manner turned deadly serious. "This related to that riot going on down there in Dallas?"

"Yeah," Charlie replied. "The guy ya'll captured pointed out the wrong guy as the shooter, and almost got the kid killed."

"I heard about that on the news, but I didn't make the connection," the sergeant said. "I heard the police down there dropped the murder and attempted armed robbery charges against the kid, but are still investigating him for resisting arrest and threatening police when they attempted to question him."

Reese joined the discussion, "If I was you, I wouldn't believe everything they are telling you," he said. "They are trying to cover their own asses. Next they will probably be saying the shooting occurred because the suspect didn't cooperate with police."

"How come they are not saying what you are saying?" the Bethany cop asked.

"Maybe, because they were not there, and we were," Charlie said.

The sergeant took a close look at the pair and Reese felt like a microbe in a Petri dish. Sudden recognition lit up the face of the Bethany cop. "I remember now. Your face was all over the news in that dashcam film," he said, speaking to Charlie. He glanced at Reese, but was drawing a blank until Charlie pointed behind the junior detective. He circled the desk and looked behind Reese as it dawned on him what he was seeing. "My wife claimed that was the prettiest ass she has ever seen on a cop before."

Reese felt his face reddening, as reflected in the broad grin which covered Charlie's face. Charlie wasn't going to let him live this down for a long time.

"Just wait until I tell the guys tomorrow that I met a couple of celebrities in the station tonight," the desk sergeant said. "Think maybe I could get an autograph for my wife?" he asked.

"From me or the cute ass?" Charlie said, grin still in place. He and the sergeant laughed; Reese didn't.

Ten minutes later, after they had made their escape from the police station, the pair decided to drive close to downtown Oklahoma City and rent a motel room for the night. They planned an early start in the morning. Charlie finally relented and took pity on his partner, backing off the jokes somewhat and concentrating on the case.

In some ways, Reese was relieved, but in others, he was not. His partner had been almost morose since his return to active duty after the long layoff following his hospital stay. It felt good that Charlie had regained some of his humor. On the other hand, Reese worried that the pendulum had swung too far. Some of Charlie's reactions were boarding on hysteria. Anxiety seemed to seep out of every pore on the old man. It was a sobering reaction to realize that whatever they accomplished on this murder investigation could lead to an undesirable outcome for their careers.

CHAPTER 26

They checked into a motel room complete with two double beds, clean sheets, a hundred fifty television channels. An inhouse valet service promised if the two of them would leave their wet clothes outside the door, they would be returned the next morning, laundered or dry cleaned, and pressed.

"We are going to feel very foolish if we look out in the morning and our clothes are not there," Charlie said.

"I'm willing to take the chance," Reese said. "This suit is soaked and beginning to smell."

Charlie took a sniff at his suit, curled up his upper lip, and turned his face away, holding the offending clothes at arm's length.

"Same here," he said.

Charlie found a folder which listed several sources for food delivery in addition to room service, checked the time to see if it was within listed times, and then called a pizza parlor. He ordered something called a 'humongous meat pizza' which claimed to contained every type of meat ever found on a pizza plus onions, mushrooms, bell peppers, black olives, and three types of cheese on a tossed pizza crust. He also ordered a dozen wings, mixed, and a couple of two liter colas. The price matched the large size. As an after thought he asked for jalapeño peppers on the side.

Reese was on his cell phone with the Oklahoma County

Sheriff's Office to start the process to get Duc Tran released to them for the trip back to Dallas. He seemed to be on permanent hold.

"I hope you are hungry," Charlie said.

Reese ignored him. He had turned the TV on earlier, but muted it so they could make their calls. The senior detective was apparently attempting to run through the whole viewing menu.

Cupping his hand over the receiver, Reese said, "Did you remember to put some jalapeños on the side?"

"Yes," Charlie grunted, shook his head, "And if Twyla finds out she will kill me."

Reese grinned, "If the pizza doesn't kill you first."

Reese returned to the elevator music playing on the phone.

Charlie's paused his channel surfing on a news station.

The infamous shooting scene in Dallas was showing, with a broad disclaimer at the top of the screen warning it was too graphic for viewing by children. Even with the sound muted, Reese had no problem reliving that night as he watched. The station showed a full two minutes of action, starting with police, weapons drawn, suddenly opening fire when Kindred James poked his head out of the shelter. The bus stop shelter had shattered under the barrage, and then the squad car sped in and blocked the shooters from the victim.

As the young detective watched the silent version playing out before him, realization struck him like a blow in the stomach. Suddenly, Reese remembered he had fully expected to be struck by bullets before the firing ceased. He shook violently as the knowledge that Grace could have also been killed filtered into his consciousness.

Sitting in the front passenger seat, Grace had been the closest to the dying man, and she would have seen everything. Later, at the hospital, Grace had been visibly shaken by the violence, but, like the TV, she remained mute about the fear she must have felt in those few seconds. She had been the first to react when the car hit the curb, bailing out and running to the shelter even as policemen with raised weapons closed in on the scene.

Charlie had grabbed the handle of Reese's door, nearly before the car stopped rolling, before moving to the front of the unit to stand between the armed police and their target as Reese raced after Grace. Charlie stood like a statue between them glaring toward the officers before they lowered their weapons. The old detective was framed in profile, and his face was obscured in darkness, but Reese didn't need to see his face to understand Charlie's defiant stance; he had seen it before.

After the clip, they cut away to a picture of a press conference with the mayor, police chief, and several other high ranking police officials standing behind a podium with the U.S. flag hanging overhead. The camera panned to the crowd. Every available chair in the room was occupied. A battery of cameras lined the walls of the long room and dozens of microphones clung to the podium like a grasshopper invasion on a corn plant.

Charlie wished Reese was off the phone so he could turn the sound back on. He watched in silence as the mayor made a brief statement, while framed in the glaring lights from the cameras. Several people were waving, trying to get his attention for follow-up questions, but the mayor stepped back, placing the Dallas Police Chief into the spotlight.

Noticeably absent from the chief's entourage was Captain Andrew Baldwin, who normally stood slightly behind the chief, beaming out with a Gomer Pyle type open-mouthed grin, nodding in agreement at everything his leader said. Baldwin had developed a bit of notoriety by always being present whenever there was a photo opportunity.

Baldwin's absence could mean that either he was falling out of favor with police administration, or that he was being kept out of the public eye until the investigation was complete. Neither detective particularly cared which scenario was being displayed, they were just tired of looking at that slack-jawed gawker hogging the limelight, and were enjoying his obvious absence from the scenario. Reese finished his call about the same time the news conference ended.

"We are all set for in the morning, unless Duc Tran suddenly chooses to fight extradition back to Texas," Reese commented, as he reached for the channel changer lying beside him on the bed. "They haven't informed him, yet, that he has that option and he hasn't requested an attorney, so a judge should sign off on the custody exchange quickly. Now, where is the pizza?"

Glancing at his wristwatch, Charlie said, "They promise a thirty-five to forty minute delivery because of the extra cooking time due to the extra ingredients, so they have about maybe fifteen more minutes and I can't see them getting it here early."

Charlie was grumbling again. "I should have taken you up on that second dip of ice cream in that little hick town we stopped at during the rain storm."

"Pauls Valley."

"Huh?"

"Pauls Valley, you know the town we stopped in."

"Yeah, yeah, yeah," Charlie said, shaking his head. "What time was that? Maybe four or five o'clock? It's after nine o'clock now so it's been several hours since I ate and I am starving. My stomach is biting at me, partner, and I hope there is enough pizza so you can have some too, because I ain't sharing my part."

Charlie talks a big game, but with the rabbit diet Twyla had kept him on for the last few months, he had lost fifty pounds. With the weight loss, the old detective had also lost a large portion of his appetite. He might eat his way through a couple of slices of pizza, so Reese wasn't worried.

"I would think that the shooting clip would be old news by now. I figured they would at least have shortened it by now." Reese said, changing the subject.

"The Dallas shooting clip and the news conference that followed."

"We hadn't seen the news conference, why didn't you turn up the sound?"

"One, you were on the phone, and, two, you were talking. I didn't want those jailers to think we were having too much fun. Then I noticed you staring at it earlier, so I decided not to give you another reason to shoot me."

Keying the sound, the pair listened to what Charlie called the talking heads, in a summary of what people had just heard in the press conference. Reese discovered he hadn't missed much by not being able to hear. It was mostly a rehash of things they already knew.

"Did you ever notice that those who know the least are the ones that talk the loudest?" Charlie asked. "It doesn't sound like they know any more than the rest of us have already deduced."

"Maybe they just like to hear their heads rattle," Reese suggested. "That guy sounds like he's trying to fill dead air space between commercial breaks."

They did learn a couple of things, however. Rain had moved into north Texas and had disrupted the protests, rioting, burning, and looting. Rains were expected to last until midday Monday, so the city was getting a brief respite. Also, the chief had not pointed a finger at them and gone into some type of voodoo ritual, so as improbable as it sounded, they hadn't been horse collared by the department just yet.

Pizza arrived minutes later. Contrary to Reese's belief, there were ample jalapeño peppers, which made Charlie very happy. True to the junior partner's belief, the old detective only managed two slices and four of the wings before surrendering. Charlie headed to take a shower while Reese finished eating. When the older man came out, Reese traded places. While Charlie put the rest of the pizza and wings in a small refrigerator in the room, Reese grabbed towels and entered the bathroom.

When he came out fifteen minutes later, feeling almost human, he found the old man asleep with his wet clothes laid out at the foot of the bed. Reese took the effort to make sure their clothes were placed outside their room, and called the motel valet to pick them up, then he called Grace.

They talked until nearly midnight before Reese broke the connection, pleading exhaustion. Grace did inform him that Kindred James was awake and other than a severe headache appeared to have no brain injury. He had almost no feeling in his legs so whether he would ever be able to walk again was still in debate by the medical staff.

Charlie had cut the sound off the TV before passing out, so while he was unable to sleep, Reese stared blankly at the screen. It was nearly an hour before sleep overcame him. Even though it had been only ten hours since the shooting tape had been released, the scene revealed by the dashcam was already the hot subject of the late-night talk shows.

Reese awoke the next morning to find his clothes lying on the foot of his bed. Charlie was sitting up on the other bed, gnawing on a piece of cold pizza.

"They offer a free continental breakfast downstairs," Reese reminded him, as he attempted to sit up.

"Cold pizza is better," Charlie said. "I always prefer breakfast in bed, so I can still be in my underwear."

The image did not sit well with Reese. "What does Twyla say about that?"

"She says no to the breakfast in bed, but she hasn't stated an opinion about wearing underwear to breakfast. She gives me some stern looks on occasions, but she hasn't kicked me out of the house so far.

Somehow, the image of Charlie wandering around the house in his underwear wasn't that appealing to Reese either. He opted for a slice of cold pizza, but popped a few of the wings into a small apartment sized microwave oven to warm them up. Cold pizza was good, cold wings, not so much.

Charlie and Reese arrived at the county lock-up about eight-thirty, and after going through the preliminaries, they were allowed into the inner sanctum. A deputy sheriff in charge of the facility met the detectives at the entry to the jail.

"We have him in a single lockup under suicide watch, and we got a judge coming in about ten o'clock this morning to hold an extradition hearing. Hopefully we will have you on your way before noon," he said.

The deputy stood about six foot two, solidly built, broad shouldered, and was humorless. He had a pair of dark eyes, which seemed to dart around taking in every detail around him at once. Reese decided the man was well suited for his role in law enforcement as a jailor.

"If he really did finger the wrong man for the murder of that policeman in Dallas, we don't want to inconvenience you any more than is absolutely necessary."

Charlie agreed. "We have some people in Dallas who want to talk to Mr. Tran about the murder of a police officer. Since we have some time before the judge arrives, could we see the prisoner?"

"You can see him, but he doesn't speak enough English to be coherent," the deputy said.

"Bull," Charlie said. "He's lived in this country for forty years. He probably speaks English as good as we do, but with a Cajun accent. He pulled that stunt with us, too."

"Well, we hope you nail him to the wall," the deputy said. "We are kind of fond of Oklahoma Sooner football in these parts and they had Kindred James penciled in as a future All-American. Your Mr. Tran is not welcome in these parts."

"I'm not sure he's going to be all that welcome back in Dallas, either," Charlie said. "He's just our mess to clean up."

The guard directed Charlie and Reese to a visitation room while the deputy disappeared into the bowels of the jail, returning in a few minutes with the little Vietnamese grocer, dressed in a jumper suit with 'prisoner' placed in prominent letters across the front and back.

The last two weeks on the run had not been kind to the fugitive. He was small before, but now he seemed to slowly be dwindling into nothing. The jump suit hung on his narrow shoulders and thin legs. The suit legs had been rolled up so he could walk and grotesquely skinny arms hung like shriveled vines from the sleeves. Gone from his eyes was any sense of defiance, surrendering now to a pathetic look akin to a frightened child, or an animal that had been repeatedly beaten into submission. He looked across the table at Charlie and Reese as if he expected a physical blow to come at any time.

Reese glanced at his partner, noticing Charlie had assumed an expressionless mask, but beneath the table his fists were clinched. It wasn't difficult for Reese to comprehend that punching out the little man was exactly what Charlie wanted to do right now.

Instead, the older detective broke out in a tense smile, but his fists remained clenched.

"Mr. Tran, I am sorry that we had to meet again under these circumstances, but we need to get you back to Dallas to answer some more questions about the robbery. Remember when we told you there would be follow-up questions and that we needed you to stay available for our investigation?"

Tran glanced up, but averted his eyes. "I am in much trouble?"

Reese knew enough about Charlie's interrogation methods to stay out of the conversation until his senior partner invited him in. He resisted an impulse to tell the little man just how much trouble he was in.

Charlie cleared his throat.

"I'm not going to lie to you, Mr. Tran. It would have been a lot better if you had not left the area. We really need the information which you alone can provide. We are going to give you a ride back to Dallas so you can tell your story to the proper people. You should be able to get on with your life quickly after that."

Like living the rest of your life in prison, Reese thought.

The young detective watched as Tran dropped his shoulders and began to visibly relax. Obviously, he had not had access to the news the last couple of days. If the little shopkeeper had seen the news, the local officials might have had an even more justifiable reason to keep him on suicide watch.

While Charlie hadn't exactly lied about anything, he had tip-toed along the edges of the truth, more across the line than inside. Technically, Mr. Tran had not yet been charged for the murder of Detective Carver, nor did the pair intend to make an arrest until they had him safely in custody in a Dallas Police Interrogation Room. Until then, Charlie and Reese would be walking a tightrope to maintain an atmosphere of mutual co-operation between Tran and the Police.

Calculating the time was right, Reese spoke up.

"Can I get you a cup of coffee?" he asked Tran. "It's likely to be a couple of hours before we take you back to Dallas. Sorry, we have to keep the handcuffs on you, because of police procedures, but we will make you as comfortable as possible for the return trip."

Reese glanced at his senior partner and caught a nod of approval. His was a timed response which served a dual purpose.

Subconsciously, it planted in Tran's mind the seed that going back to Dallas wasn't going to be too bad; but also, it suggested that going back was not avoidable.

The last thing either detective wanted was for Tran to fight extradition back to the state of Texas. If Tran stood before the judge and stated he was not going to fight extradition, they might still make the noon departure time. Reese was thinking he might salvage Sunday for a day with Grace. While he had been able to talk to her nearly two hours last night, it was not the same as being able to see her; to be able to smell her, and touch her. Reese sensed that Charlie felt the same way about Twyla, and if they wrapped this up today the old detective might even happily mow his grass.

Reese started toward the door, then stopped and looked back at the man sitting handcuffed behind the metal conference desk in the dingy room.

"You want sugar or cream with your coffee, or do you just want it black?"

Tran looked startled by the gesture Reese was making, a reaction which he probably did not expect from police officers. The young detective wondered if the little man even remembered that he and Charlie had questioned him at some length only two weeks earlier.

"Maybe, black?" the shopkeeper said in a hesitant voice, as his eyes glanced around like those of a caged animal looking for an escape. "Or, or, or a little cream, but if you do that I need sugar—lots of sugar."

Finally, someone who knows his own mind, Reese thought sarcastically.

"Okay, one black coffee coming up, with or without cream, but with cream you will want lots of sugar. I got it."

Tran looked confused, but Reese repeated the order as closely as possible. He didn't believe that Tran realized what he was saying until it was repeated back to him. Reese was also slightly mystified that the halted English the Vietnamese shop owner had used that first night had all but disappeared. Evidentially, the accented speech and trouble understanding English was something which came into play when the old man felt threatened.

The scenario reminded Reese of the time he had walked into a Puerto Rican bar where no one understood English, that is, until he flashed some money. Then, suddenly, everyone spoke and understood the language. Maybe it was a motivation factor. It didn't matter to him, but it did indicate that Mr. Tran could understand even the most remote nuances of the language.

Unless the detectives actually placed the Vietnamese grocer under arrest, they were not required to read him his Miranda Rights, warning him of self-incrimination, but more importantly, that he could not be questioned if he invoked his right to counsel. Reese dreaded the complications if, at the last minute, Tran asked for a lawyer, who would file a ton of worthless motions with the Oklahoma courts, delaying his return to Texas. Sometimes it felt like the laws to protect the accused worked in the opposite direction, delaying justice for the victim.

Reese compromised by bringing back a full Styrofoam cup, with a handful of creamers and packets of sugar. Let him fix his coffee any way he wanted. The detective was willing to do everything necessary to keep the smile on the face of the little man.

For the next thirty minutes, the Dallas detectives spent their time convincing the suspect it was in his best interest to go along with the plan to return him to Dallas to answer more questions about the armed robbery in his store.

By the time the Judge arrived to approve or disapprove of the extradition they had convinced the little man that it was his idea that he return to Dallas. Wavering Oklahoma's hold on Tran was little more than a formality.

The judge arrived in his golfing attire minus the cleats. He indicated there was a break in the rain coming up, and that he had a golf starting time scheduled in less than an hour. He was unwilling to cater to any delays.

Reese silently wished him luck. The rains which had plagued them yesterday had moved on earlier this morning, but they had dumped enough moisture that the water hazards had probably doubled in size. It was obvious the judge wanted no complications in determining that for himself; he cut short the normal legal review of the case, and signed off on the extradition. The process took less than fifteen minutes. It was apparent that the state of Oklahoma had absolutely no interest in keeping the Vietnamese grocer in the state any longer than was necessary. Duc Tran was listed as a material witness on the request.

They cleared the courts by eleven o'clock, and were underway back to Dallas with their prisoner before noon. Overnight rains had cooled the state, but the mid-August temperatures were already climbing toward the one-hundred-degree mark by the time they reached the car. Oklahoma County deputies escorted Duc Tran out and stuffed him into the back seat.

"Sorry, but departmental policies require us to transport you in handcuffs, but we will make you as comfortable as possible," Reese told him again, crossing to the other side and sliding into the front passenger seat.

Charlie took over behind the wheel as they headed south out of the city.

Duc Tran sat unmoving in the rear seat staring out the window. Reese thought he might finally be realizing the situation he was in, but the detective could not generate any sympathy toward the grocer's dilemma. The detective thought about James battling for life, Grace covered with blood, and he and Charlie contemplating the ends of their careers. Even if Tran had not committed the murder, he had lied to them. That had led to a riot gripping the city and an innocent man left forever maimed. He failed to generate even the least bit of sympathy for the man in their rear seat.

"Let's drive straight through," Charlie suggested as they picked up I-35 headed south. "I don't intend to stop until we cross the Red River."

Reese agreed even though it meant an uncomfortable five-hour trip. Like Charlie, he was anxious to get Duc Tran back in Dallas. This time he would be questioned as a suspect rather than a witness. The questions would be a lot harder.

Other than a bathroom break in Gainesville, a quick burger and refueling the car, they stayed on the road making the trip in a little over five hours. They were slowed by the rains, which they caught up with shortly after crossing the state line south of Thackerville, Oklahoma. Thackerville, home of the world's largest casino, was a major destination for a lot of North Texans, but today it was nearly hidden by rain.

Charlie, who had surrendered the wheel to Reese in Gainesville, called ahead to Lieutenant Mattie Reynolds and requested that she meet them at Police Headquarters. Despite it being after hours on a Saturday afternoon, it appeared the whole department was still on alert when they pulled into the parking lot. As they took the manacled suspect out of the car he showed fear for the first time. He walked through the lot into the building with leaden feet.

Police stared at them as they made their way to the elevator and rode up to the homicide squad room. Somehow word had gotten out to the rank and file that a suspect in the killing of detective Carver was being brought in for questioning.

The lieutenant met them at the doorway and directed them to take the prisoner to interrogation room A, the same room where Charlie had questioned him that first night.

CHAPTER 27

"Charlie, take him in," said Lt. Reynolds. "Reese, I need to see you for a minute."

Reese followed the homicide squad leader down the hallway and around a corner, entering a darkened room adjacent to the interrogation room. Through the one-way glass on the connecting wall, they could see Charlie enter the bare room with the little grocer, still in handcuffs. The senior detective motioned for the little Vietnamese suspect to take a seat on one side of a metal table, bolted to the floor. Other than the table, the only furniture in the room was two chairs. Charlie pulled out a handcuff key and freed his wrists.

The lieutenant turned on a camera to record the interrogation and adjusted the volume on the sound system, checking the needles on a control panel for maximum clarity. Satisfied, she stepped back and turned toward Reese.

"I sincerely hope you and Charlie have a way of breaking this guy because the chief is about ready to bust you two to bicycle patrol on the Interstate," she said.

"I never learned to ride a bicycle," Reese said.

"So much the better for his purposes," she stated.

Reese had suspected as much. "At least he's not talking about termination, is he?"

"Not yet," she said. "His current plan is to keep you two around so he can make your lives a living hell."

The junior detective cringed inside.

"I take it that he wasn't very happy about the media getting access to the dashcam tape, was he?"

"No, he wasn't and neither was I," she said, "What were you two thinking? Don't you Yahoos know that I have your backs?"

Reese dropped into a chair facing the window. "Too much of the evidence was disappearing."

"Yeah, but things have a way of coming out. Two missing body cams worn the night of the takedown have mysteriously reappeared," she said. She didn't indicate they told a different story so Reese assumed they sustained the validity of the dashcam.

"These two tapes appeared when? After the dash cam footage was aired to the public, right?"

Lt. Reynolds plastered on a face which reminded him of someone caught with a hand in the cookie jar.

"Well, there is that," she admitted. "I think that's why the police chief isn't parading around the plaza with your heads on a pole. Reese, you and Charlie made the chief look real bad. He has a memory like an elephant; he's not going to forget this any time soon."

"I appreciate you warning us, but why aren't you talking to Charlie about this?"

Mattie sighed, "Charlie already knows," she said, dropping into a chair beside him. "I'm surprised he let you get involved in the politics of this case."

"Charlie tried to keep me out," Reese said. "I wasn't going to let him take the fall alone."

"Well, he certainly didn't do you any favor," she sighed. "The chief's mood is at a critical point, and I need for you to impress on Charlie that speed is absolutely necessary. That rain outside will be gone by tomorrow and the marchers will be back on the street. We need answers now."

"Then, I'd better get back with Charlie," Reese said as he started to rise from his chair.

"No, wait," the lieutenant said. "You've probably noticed that Tran is a lot more comfortable when talking to Charlie and sort of gravitates to him when you are in the room. I noticed his body language the night of the murder. I'll get you back in there at the proper time, but wait until Charlie has developed a good rapport with him. For some reason your suspect seems to view Charlie as a sympathetic authority figure."

"And I'm chopped liver?"

"Exactly," she exclaimed. "Maybe it's the age factor. Some cultures have a lot more respect for their elders."

"Tran is probably ten years older than Charlie," Reese said incredulously. "What could they have in common?"

Reynolds sighed deeply. "Well, they fought the same war."

Reese had to laugh at that one. "Charlie was too young to have fought in Viet Nam," he said.

The lieutenant stared closely at the face of her lead detective through the one-way glass.

"Well, Tran doesn't have any way of knowing that. Right now, he is reaching out to Charlie Dent as an ally."

Reese had noticed the body language before, but now he really concentrated on the little grocer. Tran was leaning toward Charlie, seemingly hanging on every motion and gesture the senior detective made. The younger man wondered why he hadn't noticed that attraction before. Maybe it was because from the beginning he had felt a twinge of animosity toward the little man. It was normal, even expected, that the senior partner would take the lead in the questioning of a suspect. Reese had stepped aside, as was customary, and allowed Charlie to assume the leadership role from the beginning. Now that the younger detective was out of the room, he could readily see that Tran appeared to be a bit more co-operative with the dialogue.

"When Charlie gets Tran's tongue loosened up, I'll send you in to sober him up a bit. If you two can get him thinking in two different directions, he should make mistakes," she concluded.

Reese watched as Charlie sat across from the suspect and flipped through a folder, grunting, nodding, and moving from one page to another as if satisfying himself about certain details before addressing Tran. After a couple of minutes, he closed the folder and peered over his glasses toward Tran. He removed his glasses and wiped them on the tail of his shirt.

Slipping them back on, he cleared his throat. "I suppose you are aware that certain doubts about the suspect identification the night of the robbery and murder are causing us some problems. Can you clarify what you saw that night? Start with when Police Detective Richard Carver walked into your store." There was an undertone of edginess to his voice which could very easily be overlooked unless you knew Charlie Dent well.

Tran pursed his lips and a crease appeared between his eyes, indicating that he was thinking hard before speaking. Charlie did not let the silence linger.

"Did you know Carver? He lived only a few blocks away and was probably headed home after a long day. Did he come into your store very often?" Charlie asked in shotgun fashion, broadcasting the questions and speculations out without giving the little man time to answer. When he stopped, the room grew very quiet, once again.

The tension building in Duc Tran was obvious. He darted his eyes around the room as the silence grew. Charlie continued to look at him expectantly waiting for an answer. Silence leaves a void which must be filled, and it was obvious that, this time, the detective was not going to continue until Tran responded.

"He had never been in my store before. I did not know who he was," Tran said.

To Reese he looked like a little puppy waiting for approval after performing a trick.

"What time did Richard Carver come into the store?"

Richard Carver, Richard Carver, Richard Carver. That name was going to be repeated dozens of times in that room. Calling the victim by name humanized him; made him real. Reese knew the drill. After a while, the repetition would drive a pang of guilt into Tran's heart, regardless of how he tried to avoid what he had done. For now, he was still under the illusion that he was being questioned only as a witness.

Tran was unable to give a specific answer as to the exact time.

"It was late, that's all I know."

"Did he speak to you before going to the back of the store?" Charlie asked.

"No."

"Did you see him when he came in to the store?"

"I don't think so."

"You know Tran, you either did see him or you didn't." Charlie made a notation in his notebook, closed it, and then looked again at his witness. "When did the robber come into the store? It must not have been more than a minute or so after Richard Carver. You saw him enter, right? What was the first thing he did?"

"He came to the front counter and asked for cigarettes," Tran said in stilted English. "The first man was at the back of the store."

"Then you did see Richard Carver enter the store, didn't you?" Charlie frowned and poised his pen over his notebook. He shook his head, wrote in it again, then placed the pen across the page, as a marker, and flipped the book closed. The pen and notebook routine was a distraction tool Charlie was using to break up Tran's concentration.

"Details like this are extremely important to us," Charlie said, shaking his head from side to side, like admonishing a child. "A second ago, you couldn't remember. Please think about these questions and answer them as truthfully as you can. Why didn't you say anything about the guy that shot Detective Carver speaking to you when he came in to the store? Did you get the cigarettes for him? Do you remember what brand he asked for?" Charlie asked sharply before dropping off into silence.

The sudden silence was unnerving the little storekeeper. This time he realized the gap in his story.

"I was just so scared," he stammered. "I didn't remember until right now."

"Were you scared because he was pointing a gun at you when he came in the store?"

Tran lunged at the explanation as if it was a lifeboat slipping away from a drowning man.

"Yes," he nodded, "He was pointing the gun at me when he entered the store."

Charlie placed his hand on his notebook on the table. He leaned forward toward the small Vietnamese storekeeper.

"There are a few things here that I don't exactly understand," he said calmly, spreading his fingers out as he placed both his hands on the table. "You are saying a man came into the store to rob you of a pack of cigarettes, right? Were you aware that Kindred James, the man you pointed out as the man who killed Richard Carver, didn't smoke?"

Reese chuckled. The detectives didn't know whether James smoked or not, but neither would Tran. Charlie's statement was sending him into a quandary to find a rational answer.

"I didn't know," he answered after a pregnant pause.

"What brand of cigarettes did he ask for?" Charlie asked.

"I don't remember," Tran said.

Charlie cleared his throat, opened the notebook, picked up the pen, and made another notation in his pad.

"Mr. Tran, I'm finding it troubling that your memory is failing. Have you considered checking with a doctor to see if you have dementia or something? How could you not remember what he asked for in this situation?"

While waiting for an answer, Charlie made yet another notation, setting the notebook aside.

"I mean how are you expecting to comply with the demands of a gunman pointing a gun at you if you can't remember what he said?"

The eyes on the little shopkeeper had grown watery, but now they were tinged with defiance. His body had gone rigid, probably with fright. By now, Reese was aware of the pressure his partner was slowly applying to their supposedly cooperating witness. For the moment, unsure of how to answer without digging himself into a deeper trap, Duc Tran remained a silent witness.

Charlie appeared to grow tired of waiting.

"I mean if it were me and I was in that situation, the one thing I would remember is what the man wanted. I'd be scared he would shoot me if I asked him to repeat himself. It was a man, wasn't it? With your memory problem, there was a possibility you could forget that detail, also, right?"

"It was a young black man," Tran said, flatly. "He asked for a pack of cigarettes."

"A polite killer who only wanted a pack of cigarettes," Charlie mused. "If he had a gun, I would have thought he wouldn't have to be polite. And only one pack? I'm surprised he didn't demand a whole carton of them, or, heck, all of the cigarettes on the shelf."

Duc Tran was retreating into silence.

Charlie appeared uninterested in his state of mind.

"Mr. Tran, you still haven't told me what the cop killer was wearing," he said. "I mean was he dressed in blue jeans and t-shirt, or was he wearing a pair of those droopy drawers which kept falling down around his knees, showing his '*tighty-whities*,' or lack thereof? Maybe he had a hoodie, even though it was very hot out that night. You need to give me something to work with here," the senior detective indicated. "At least give us some idea, because your first identification didn't work out very well. An innocent man got shot all to hell." Charlie's last words came as a vicious assault which seemed to stagger Tran mentally.

But, knowing you have done something wrong and being contrite enough to admit it are two entirely different things. Charlie's last words had stunned him, but the grocer quickly rallied, attempting to find some type of level footing. His face quickly flashed from signs of grief and defiance, to denial of any wrong doing in the aftermath of his bogus identification.

Lt. Reynolds, who had been watching the interrogation quietly beside Reese, sighed.

"I thought Charlie was going to flip him that time. Maybe it's time you make an appearance; see if you can give Tran some pucker power."

"I know just the thing," Reese nodded. He rose and headed to the interrogation room. "I'll be right back."

Charlie called it dropping a bomb. It didn't matter whether it was true or not, or if it even hit the target. If it was close enough to the truth and close enough to the suspect, the effects were the same as if you made a direct hit.

Reese knocked on the door and entered without waiting for Charlie to respond. He poked his head around the door frame and focused on Charlie.

"We got a hit on the weapon and we should have identification rather quickly," he said. "Lab jumped right on it."

Closing the door, Reese returned to the observation room. Apparently, during the minute it had taken him to return to the room, nothing had transpired, but, at the same time, a lot had changed.

Charlie had gotten to his feet and was glaring down at the little shopkeeper, who had shrunk to an even smaller size.

"This is going to change everything," Charlie said, after waiting at least another minute, allowing Tran to absorb the full impact of Reese's statement.

The detective continued, "A lot of people have found ways of purchasing unregistered weapons. One way is to purchase them at gun shows, which allows transfer without a background check. Some people do it through private sales between individuals. Others have found a way of combining the methods to get their hands on an untraceable gun, but you know what? The law is going after those weapons dealers, making them responsible for any crime committed with those unregistered weapons they pass on. These gun sellers have started to develop their own bargaining chip with police, by keeping clandestine records of those transactions. They are keeping records of their own ballistics tests, too, and once we match ballistics with a gun they sold, we will find the owner."

Charlie smiled. "With or without your help, we should soon know who purchased the weapon that killed Detective Richard Carver," he said. "When we do, we are going to shoot the bastard down like the coward he is. A fitting justice, don't you agree Mr. Tran?"

The grocer sat, head bowed, silently.

In the observation room, Lt. Mattie Reynolds stirred restlessly.

"Is he threatening Mr. Tran with physical violence?"

Reese looked over at her.

"Tran is still holding to the belief that we haven't seen through his charade that a robber killed Carver. Even his mind is not twisted enough to believe we are threatening him."

The lieutenant seemed concerned.

"Well, he certainly has me convinced. Do you have any evidence on the weapon used to kill detective Carver?"

Reese shook his head. "Nothing specific," he said. "We got an undercover ATF agent checking out a lead for us, but we haven't heard back from him."

"Well, good luck with that one," Reynolds said, rather sarcastically. "Those guys are not famous for sharing information with local police."

"They are when the victim is a policeman," Reese said. "We ran into him while he was working undercover and helped him, so he should help us."

Meanwhile, Charlie had regained his seat and his notepad.

"Mr. Tran, I'm still waiting on some type of description on what the suspect was wearing. Can you enlighten me just a little bit?"

"It was two weeks ago," the little Vietnamese man said. He voice had climbed nearly an octave and a half, and he was bordering on hysteria, something which Charlie had to have noticed. "What difference would it make now?"

"Oh, I'm sure he's changed clothes, but people are creatures of habit. While they will change the clothes, they are often reluctant to change their styles. I'm betting when we find the shooter, he will be wearing clothing nearly identical to what he was wearing the night of the shooting. You know, same shirt—different color, similar pants and almost no one looks at the shoes. Did you see the robber's shoes that night? Forensics indicate you would have been standing less than a yard from where the fatal shot was fired. Surely, you had to have seen something that would help us."

The pair in the observation room was quick to note that Duc Tran was dressed almost identically to the night of the shooting.

"Oh, I forgot, forensics said the gunman would have been bent almost doubled over, backwards over the front counter when the fatal shot was fired. If you reached out, you could have touched him." Charlie stared at Tran for a long second. "I wonder why the robber, who was standing close enough that you could have reached out and touched him, felt safe enough to turn his back on you while gunning down a man coming up an aisle with his arms full of groceries. Were you too much of a coward to even try to save the first man's life?" Charlie asked, harshly.

The senior detective did not give the little grocer time to answer.

"You still haven't told me what the man was wearing or anything about the gun," he peered into Tran's puffy, watery eyes. "You do know guns don't you Mr. Tran? I mean you were ex-military and all. Shoot, you probably know more about guns than I do. What can you tell me about the gun used to kill Detective Richard Carver? Hopefully, more than just 'it was a big gun' because, Mr. Tran, we know the gun wasn't all that large. Now don't we?"

"You don't know anything about me?" Tran whispered.

Charlie flipped back through his notes. "We take a special interest in witnesses, especially ones who decide to leave town and hide out, hoping the situation solves itself while they are absent," he said. "Ah, here it is," he scanned down a page in his notes. "You were a captain in the Vietnamese army, a well-respected negotiator, awarded several medals for bravery, defender of Saigon in the later part of the war. Seems you were married with six children, but you made sure you had a seat on one of the first helicopters to leave when the capital fell. What about your wife and children, Mr. Tran? Did you choose to leave them behind?"

Reynolds gasped. The lieutenant had been instrumental in building the profile on the little grocer, but knowing the facts was

different than having them shoved in your face. Charlie's accusation was raw, naked, and piercing. As a high, ranking officer in the
Vietnamese army, Tran had the power to rescue his family, but his
first inclination had been to facilitate his own escape rather than to
protect his family. As the impact of the accusation sank in, Reese
watched as any sympathy his homicide squad supervisor might
have been feeling for the little man evaporated instantly in a blazing
flash of revulsion.

Turning ashen faced toward Reese, she said, "He really did
that, didn't he?"

"Later records showed that his family tried to flee the country
by boat, but no country had any record of them being picked up and
they were assumed to have been lost at sea," Reese nodded as he
spoke. "I'm betting if we had more detailed records we would find
Duc Tran using his fleeting power to throw women and children off
the helicopter to make room for his sorry, skinny rear end."

"Do we have anything on the gun used in the killing? I'm beginning to believe he is quite capable of killing our detective and
attempt pinning the crime on someone else," she said. She had
stood, and was very close to the glass separating the two rooms.
She was glaring at the suspect.

"The only lead we have is a very thin one," Reese said, apologetically. "Right now, we don't have anything solid that we can
build a case on."

"His character indicates he is quite capable of killing, and, also,
of attempting to frame someone else," she said. "But what prompted
him to turn killer in the first place, and why frame Kindred James
for the murder?"

"We pressured him before he had a chance to come up with a
credible lie about the shooter. James was just extremely unlucky to
have his face pop up on the tape when everyone was pressing hard

to get an ID. I can't imagine why Tran would knowingly set out to kill someone. What could he hope to accomplish?"

"Have you Mirandized Tran yet?" the lieutenant asked.

"No," Reese said, "He hasn't been charged with any crime, yet."

Mattie Reynolds' face had grown stone cold.

"I want him properly read his Miranda Rights. Get him to sign a statement that he has been read those rights. Then do your best to get an attorney waver, to legally keep those blood sucking lawyers out of this. I want his ass nailed to the wall before those protesters hit the streets in the morning."

Reese left the room and walked slowly to the interrogation room, knocked and waited for Charlie to come to the door.

"Mattie says to put him under arrest."

Grim-faced, Charlie nodded, turning toward Tran. He fixed his eyes on the former military officer.

"Duc Tran, you are under arrest for the murder of Police Detective Richard Carver. You are also under investigation for making false statements which resulted in the shooting of Kindred James."

CHAPTER 28

Charlie filed back into the squad room and plopped into his chair across from Reese. Staring at his partner and at Lt. Mattie Reynolds, who was standing beside Reese's desk, he sighed.

"As soon as we hit the Miranda, Tran clammed up tighter than Fort Knox," he said. "He has refused to say another word."

"Do you think we have enough evidence to make a case against him?" the lieutenant asked.

"Likely, on the perjury, but who knows, he might stick to the black man, but just that he was pressured into making a false identification," Charlie said.

It was evident the old detective was exhausted, enough so that, after the grueling session in the interrogation room, he sounded like he had lost the passion of the crime.

"Most of the rest of it is circumstantial evidence. I like our theory of what happened, but convincing a jury can be a whole other ballgame. We just don't have a smoking gun."

"Well, he doesn't know that," she said. "That gun lead has got to be eating his insides up."

"The gun lead is only a hunch," Reese said. "The odds are likely to pan out to be something totally different than we are hoping. The odds are stacked against an illegal gun sale having anything to do with this case."

Reynolds looked from Charlie to Reese.

"My detectives think they have a lead and then get cold feet. Now you have second thoughts. What is this world coming to anyway? Charlie, I remember when you were younger that if you caught even the scent of blood in the water, you were all over it like a shoal of piranha on a wounded water buffalo. I remember once you told me you had a hunch on a case and you weren't going to let facts get in your way. Remember? You were right then, and you are right now. I am expecting that attitude on this case. I need, you need, the police department needs, and our city needs for you to get this case right," she said. "I believe you are on the right track, so do you, and, furthermore, I expect you to prove it."

Resigned to the fact that nothing more could be accomplished on a late Saturday night, the detectives took Tran to the Lew Sterrett County Jail on Commerce Street for booking. It was after two in the morning on Sunday before they completed this task. Duc Tran had remained silent throughout the ordeal, refusing to answer any question, even when he was asked his name.

Reese was too tired to be angry, but Charlie was angry beyond words as they left the county jail and headed back toward the police station. The plan was to drop Charlie off to pick up his car, and then for both men go home for a good night's sleep, meeting up later in the day to discuss the case, and their next moves.

"If Mattie had stayed out of it for one more minute, I would have gotten a confession," Charlie fumed. "He was either going to confess or I was going to beat the crap out of him."

The rant seemed unusual, coming from Charlie, who was normally the level headed of the pair. More than once, Reese recalled Charlie sitting him down because he became too emotionally involved in a case. Reese could tell that Charlie had gone beyond his self-imposed limits and was threatening to make it a personal affair. Reese surmised the temperament of the senior detective during the final moments of the questioning had been the major factor in the lieutenant pulling the plug on the interrogation. Charlie was working himself into a frenzy which could have led to drastic, rash actions, which would have jeopardized the investigation.

Knowing why did not appease the rage, however. Charlie was wound as tight as a cheap watch and on the verge of exploding, even an hour after leaving the interrogation room. Whatever connection he had cultivated with the suspect had been hopelessly severed.

"I was losing it back there, Rookie. Let this be a lesson to you," Charlie said, uncharacteristically choosing to ride shotgun rather than drive. The senior detective was a bit of a control freak, and it normally took effort to wrestle the steering wheel from his hands. "I didn't say a word which would indicate how I felt about him, but I'm sure he sensed it. You could sense it too, couldn't you? I just wanted to get my hands around that scrawny neck of his and squeeze until he confessed."

"I think the lieutenant was thinking the same thing, only she was afraid you would act on your rash impulses. She called it."

"And you didn't, Partner?"

"No," Reese said, "I knew you had it under control."

"Reese," Charlie paused, "This time you are wrong. I wanted nothing more than to kill that little worm. I was tired, and if I had been watching myself through the glass, I would have called it, too. I think now that I understand some of the rage that was going through Baldwin's mind that night James was shot. Not to say I condone it, but I think I can understand it."

"Would you do that for me?"

"Hell, no, Rookie," Charlie laughed. His humor had returned, but it sounded stilted, and seemed hollow and forced. The old man was mentally and physically exhausted. "You are going to be lucky if I even bother to throw dirt on your grave. You get yourself killed and you are on your own to exact revenge."

Reese and Charlie were both under a lot of stress. Reese thought about the uncomfortable trip back from Oklahoma City, when they had been afraid to speak to Tran; afraid of breaking an unspoken truce between the two sides. For a brief time, there had been an opening when the two men may have felt a bit of sympathy toward Tran, but that time was past.

Reese's partner was suffering, again, because of the smugness displayed by the suspect. And while most of that smugness had been perceived as arrogance, at least by Reese, it was an attitude which had driven Charlie to the edge of rage. Whether the emotion radiating from Tran was real or not, the mixed emotions was what Reese perceived as the reason for Charlie's anger. Lt. Reynolds had been right to pull the plug on the questioning.

"I almost had him," Charlie muttered, almost as an affirmation to himself.

"At least you got to make the arrest," Reese said as they left the Lew Sterrett parking lot.

"Yeah," Charlie said, "But, with what we have so far, I'm not sure he can't beat the rap. And I'm beginning to doubt my ability to communicate further, because I'm starting to think in gibberish."

The senior detective remained locked in his own thoughts as they drove back to police headquarters and Reese dropped him off.

"Go home, Charlie. This day has been too long and neither of us is thinking straight right now," Reese said, as he waited for the old man to switch vehicles. "Heck, I don't think I am capable of thinking at all any more tonight."

Charlie moved slowly, like an old man, seeming to be unsure of where he was going. Reese almost had second thoughts about dropping him off rather than taking him home, but Charlie seemed to rally after a few minutes.

Halting for a moment outside his car, Charlie said, "That was a good touch on that gun. If it checks out, this is going to be the longest long shot I've ever seen in police work. I've got to think this thing out."

"Sleep well, Charlie and don't wake me up before noon."

"We might not have that luxury, Reese. By Monday some sleazy lawyer is going to be screaming the virtues of our poor cop killer, and asking for a personal recognition bond because he's such an upstanding member of the community," Charlie said in parting.

CHAPTER 29

Sunday morning started out hot and was going to get hotter. Temperatures were already in the eighties. In Texas, that is merely a discomfort. The real temperature rise was in the pulse of the community as it prepared for another day of demonstrations against police brutality. Despite his intent to sleep in late, Reese was glued to the television early, watching the day's events unfold.

The police chief, in a bit of damage control, was speaking at one of the local black churches, announcing that the remaining charges against Kindred James had been dropped and proclaiming justice would be served. He called it an ongoing investigation. He used his best political savvy to deflect accusations hurled against the department and his officers, individually, in the current crisis. The chief still skirted around the subject of Captain James Baldwin. True to form, the chief announced that his investigation had led to the apprehension and arrest of another suspect in the death of Detective Richard Carver. Also, true to form, the chief declined to identify the new suspect, which brought catcalls from a disbelieving audience. Reese was not surprised by the reaction.

Questioned concerning the behavior of the arresting officers which had left an innocent man horribly wounded and fighting for his life, brought confirmation from the chief that the incident also was under further investigation, both by his office and by the office of internal affairs, which, he was careful to explain, regularly investigated shooting incidents by the police department.

Determined not to lose the whole weekend, Reese called Grace and got her to agree to a luncheon date, and then contacted Charlie and Twyla inviting them to make it a foursome at a quiet restaurant, removed from the anger and fear gripping the city. Reece picked up Grace at eleven-thirty, and when they arrived at the restaurant, they found Charlie and Twyla had already secured a table for four in a secluded corner, well out of sight of most other patrons.

Shaving nicks from an uneven shave were strong indicators that Charlie had not had a good night, or at least, he was not able to get enough sleep. Although he was attempting to show the more jovial side of his personality, it was very apparent that he had lost the fight with his pillow the previous night. Large purplish bags drooped below his eyes, which were watery and sad.

A waiter arrived seconds later with drinks, ice tea all around, which Charlie had ordered. He spouted off the menu specials for the day, asking if the group needed more time to decide. Reese and Grace settled on the baked salmon while Charlie, under the watchful eye of Twyla, decided on the chef salad with light French dressing and garlic croutons. Twyla chose an appetizer plate, containing mini-egg rolls, baked potato skins, fried cheese sticks, chicken strips, and an assortment of sauces. She relented somewhat and allowed Charlie to sample from her plate, pretending not to notice as he nabbed his choices.

Although the meal was a success, Charlie became more recessive as the clock ticked away. Twyla attempted to cover for her husband, but even her buoyant personality failed to make up for the doleful vibes coming from the old detective.

"Lighten up, partner," Reese advised, only to be greeted by Charlie's icy stare.

Charlie dropped his napkin on the table beside his plate. "I'm sorry, everyone, I'm just not feeling like being very sociable right now. I have too much on my mind."

Although they had agreed not to talk business, Charlie's statement broke the dam, and it was impossible to avoid the topic any longer.

"Charlie and I are going to need to cut this luncheon short," Reese finally admitted. "Somewhere out there is a gun which has already killed one man, and no one else is looking for it. We need to keep after it until we either get a rock-solid indictment, or die trying."

Charlie gave me one of his half grins.

"Carrying it a little far aren't you, Partner?"

"Well it seemed like a good idea a half second ago."

"He's right about one thing," the old detective said. "There are answers out there that we need right now, and no one can get at them but us. Nobody seems to be trying to get at these particular answers but us. Sorry for spoiling lunch, but we are not done with this case, and there are leads we need to follow up on before the chief decides to retire us both."

Reece reluctantly left Grace with Twyla after they had settled the bill, and the two men headed back to east Dallas to check on the progress the ATF agent had made on tracing the weapon on the phony invoice.

Arriving at the gun shop, Charlie stayed in the car while Reese entered. Since the detectives had been seen together only a few days earlier, Charlie and Reese had decided that if the three were seen together again so soon, it might trigger a response from the clerks, which could blow the cover of the agent. The undercover ATF agent they had encountered two days earlier was not on the floor of the shop. Reese approached the clerk the agent had talked to previously.

"I was in here the other day talking to a young guy, who showed me a really sharp Beretta Storm, I believe it was, or something like that."

"Was it a Beretta Px4 Storm SubCompact?"

"I don't really remember," Reese said, playing dumb. "I'm sure he would remember. I told him I would be coming back, I just didn't know what day for sure I would be able to get back here. Is he here today?"

The clerk seemed reluctant to pass on a potential customer, but after a brief hesitation, he flashed a thumb toward the gun range in the rear. "If he's too busy, I'm sure I can help you with selecting a gun," he said.

"I kind of promised him I would ask for him if I was still interested. I mean, if he was here, you know?"

That was a physical blow to the clerk, but not totally an unexpected one. The detectives were already clued in that the clerks got a commission on each gun sale. The reluctance to allow him access to the other clerk was growing awkward.

Finally, sighing, he said, "Grab some ear protection. We have a full house on the range today."

Reese was instantly assailed by ear piercing blasts as he slipped through the door into the hallway running the length of the range. It appeared every station was taken. A short heavy set man, dressed in camouflage stretched to the limits, was popping off groups of shots with a .45 caliber at a paper target about fifteen feet from his stand. Every shot demolished the target. The ATF agent was standing behind the shooter, who seemed to delight in quick fire at a target he couldn't miss, as he wiped out ammo at an unbelievable clip. When he stopped to change targets and clips, Reese caught the attention of the agent. The agent said something to the shooter, turned, and walked back toward Reese into the hallway.

"You have a gun that I might be interested in," Reese shouted over the noise. "Can you get free for a couple of minutes or should I wait?"

The agent pointed to the door leading back into the gun shop. When they were away from the range, both men took off their hearing protectors. Their appearance signaled a lost chance at a commission for the other clerk, who, surrendering, moved toward the front of the store in search of someone else needing help.

"Sorry I didn't contact you back," the agent said. "I didn't get a chance to look at the records we have on the transaction until I opened the shop this morning. I'm still not sure what to make of them or whether they are related to your case." He reached under the counter near the rear of the store, keeping a watchful eye out toward anyone who might approach them. "The whole deal is dirty as hell and I'm still not sure what to make of it. I don't know what good the information will do you. ATF is going to get a good case of dealing in stolen firearms against Brogan, however."

"Can we tie it to our investigation in any way?" Reese asked, unwilling to concede that the clue was leading to a dead end.

"It's still possible," the agent said. "There is no document identifying the buyer, but I did find a notation from an employee here to turn the gun over to the Vietnamese guy. It listed no names for either the buyer or seller. That still leaves you hundreds of suspects, but my gut feeling is there aren't that many ethnic Vietnamese looking to buy unregistered weapons in this neighborhood. You got good instincts. Maybe you should check into a career with us."

Reese had no desire to become a federal agent, but if this case didn't make, he decided it could become a possibility.

"How do we put the gun in Duc Tran's hands?"

The agent shrugged. "Maybe when we raid Brogan's shop, he might be willing to give Tran up for a little consideration on his sentencing."

"You have a date on that yet?"

"Soon; we are seeking the warrants now. Once the warrants are secured, it will go down rather quickly. I don't want to leave that dirt-bag on the street any longer than I must. This sale is not the only one he has made illegally."

By quoting no timetable and extending no invitation to the Dallas Police Department team, he had affectively excluded them from early access to Brogan.

As a detective, Reese knew the limitations under which policemen worked. He was going to be left begging for crumbs. He caught the subtle warning that Brogan was the federal investigation's property. Although no words had been said, he understood that he was going to have to wait until the feds moved and only then would he be allowed sloppy seconds to the gun dealer, maybe. If the feds could build a strong enough case against Brogan and his suppliers, they might even be willing to overlook the needs of the local burglary-murder investigation altogether. Gaining access to information or suspects from the feds was next to impossible, if they decided they didn't want local authorities having a role in their investigation.

"For us, this is a high profile case," Reese said, reminding the agent of what was at stake.

The agent, keeping up the pretenses of his undercover role, removed a small handgun from a locked case and set it on the counter between him and the detective. "This is a really nice weapon, streamlined and easily concealed." Quietly he added, "I'll pass your concerns along, but it's not my call," he said.

Reese recognized the standard copout. Insight into the true meaning of the expression came suddenly to his mind. A *copout* was a means of evading responsibility for what was happening. In the past few weeks, the junior detective had seen too much of this attitude; and to have the attitude named after his profession was a bit painful.

"It never is," he said with a touch of bitterness, "no one is ever responsible."

CHAPTER 30

Charlie Dent was less than enthused by the details of Reese's meeting with the undercover AFT agent. "Those guys move slower than a snail with a migraine headache," the veteran detective exclaimed. "Then, even if Brogan makes a deal with the feds, there is a good chance we will come up empty handed, Partner."

"He did drop us one morsel, however," Reese said. "He let slip that the gun was handed over to a buyer of Vietnamese descent."

"That's an awful skinny morsel, there are probably a thousand men in the metro area which would fit that bill and even then, we are hanging on the slimmest string of a possibility that the particular weapon in the sale had anything to do with our cop killing. Sounds to me like this angle could be a dead end."

"What else do we have?"

"Not a whole damn lot," Charlie admitted. He snickered, suddenly. "Sorry, your backside and Mattie's sudden closing of my interview both just popped into my mind."

"My backside is a closed subject. As for you last night, I think Mattie was afraid you were going to go postal on him."

Charlie smiled, "I seriously thought about it. That little coward was sitting there, refusing to answer my questions, while at the same time poking those pitiful watery eyes of his in my face.

I would have been doing everyone a favor if I had punched his lights out."

"Any chance he could have been sincere?"

"Not in this world. He was playing us from the beginning, and I, for one, am tired of it."

"Do you think he might still have the gun?"

"The odds of that are greater than the odds of the feds turning over useful information to us," Charlie said. "He's had a week and two hundred fifty miles to ditch it. He didn't have it when picked up by the Bethany police. It wasn't in his motel room, and nothing of any value was found in that old car he dumped up there. No, he had enough sense to get rid of it."

They still had to put the murder gun in Duc Tran's hands for a conviction.

"Do you think his friend might shine any light on this situation?" Reese asked.

"Sure, I'm always a sucker for finding needles in haystacks," Charlie said. "Besides, I don't see an alternative unless they let me beat a confession out of him.

*   *   *   *

Charlie Dent and Reese Barrett were waiting outside the doors of Mark Pham Do's law office the next morning before the first secretary arrived to open the firm. They made it known they were there to see the attorney as soon as he came in.

The wait wasn't long. Mark Do was the third person to arrive, breezing into the office, less than fifteen minutes later. He displayed no reaction to the detectives sitting in the reception area.

Turning to a middle-aged secretary, he said, "Amber, get me a pot of coffee and three cups." Shifting his attentions back to the detectives, he said, "Come in gentlemen, I've been expecting you."

The detectives arose and followed him into the office where they were pointed toward a small conversation pit in one corner. The area contained a pair of overstuffed leather couches and a low burnished metal coffee table. Before they were comfortably seated, the secretary returned, poured fresh brewed coffee into three identical cups, each was black porcelain with the name of the law firm embossed in gold letters. Creamer, sugar, and a selection of artificial sweeteners were available in a small bowl beside the cups.

Both detectives ignored the condiments. Charlie picked up a spoon and stirred the cup in front of him before lifting it to his lips and taking a shallow sip. The liquid was still too hot to drink. Setting the cup aside, he nodded to his host.

"If you knew we would come back, you must have a pretty good idea of why we are here." he said.

The attorney, who seemed unfazed by the high temperature of the coffee, took a sip before nodding.

"You are still trying to gather information on Duc Tran. I have been informed that he's been arrested for the murder of the policeman."

"Word travels fast," Reese said.

"Mr. Tran is shopping for an attorney, according to the rumor circulating through the Vietnamese community," Do said. "I don't handle criminal cases, but I was able to make him a good recommendation."

"I won't insult you by asking who you recommended, but we would appreciate the name of Tran's friend," Charlie said.

Do grinned, stood and moved back toward his desk. "I thought you might."

At his desk, he pulled a pad from a desk drawer, wrote several lines of notations on it and tore the top sheet off. Coming back to the conversation pit, he deposited the sheet on the table in front of Charlie.

Charlie glanced at the message as he picked it up, folded, and stuffed it in his pocket. In bold clear handwriting, it contained a name, an address, and a phone number. He digested the information a second before glancing up at the attorney.

"What can you tell me about this man, Ha Minh?"

"Not a lot more than what you have in your hands, I'm afraid. Like Duc Tran, he seems to be one of those fringe characters who never seem to fit in with the rest of the Vietnamese community. I've made a few inquiries around, but haven't been able to find out a whole lot about him. He came around about the same time as Tran so it's a safe bet that he moved here after Hurricane Katrina. It's possible they knew each other in Louisiana, but that would only be conjecture on my part."

"Well, at least we know they were well enough acquainted to exchange favors. I wonder what else they exchanged," Charlie speculated. "At least it gives us something to go on."

"If there is anything else I can do for you, just let me know," Do said, standing and stepping toward the door, a gesture which could only be a sign of dismissal. "If Duc Tran did kill the policeman, it will create a real blight on the reputation of our community, detectives. But, just the suspicion of it being one of ours has the potential for even worse situations. The Vietnamese community will do whatever is necessary to assist you in reaching the truth in this case. We can live with the shame of one of our own being a murderer, but we cannot live with the suspicions."

Charlie and Reese drove immediately to the address the attorney had given them.

Ha Minh proved to be an older version of Duc Tran. He appeared to be in his mid-eighties, bowed by years, peering at the detectives with thick, old style bi-focal glasses. He admitted the detectives into the living room of his home. The room had been converted into a cobbler shop and smelled strongly of leather, tannic acid, shoe polishes, stains, and sweat.

The cobbler shop in his home certainly was not up to code, even in a residential area. The normal complaints from neighbors of heavy foot traffic in and out of the neighborhood did not seem to have been a problem. The house was located less than three blocks from where Tran lived, and was in the same cookie-cutter architectural design. Both houses could have been built by the same builder using the same post World War II blueprints.

"I hope you don't mind if I keep working," he said, politely enough, but he avoided eye contact, keeping his vision firmly affixed to the floor. "I promised to have a pair of shoes resoled by four o'clock, but I wasn't feeling very well this morning, and I am running very late."

The old man appeared to glide across the floor to a work bench located on the far side of the room. He removed his glasses, and put a half-shield over his eyes, which appeared to have high magnification. When he looked back toward Reese, his eyes filled the whole frame of the glasses.

"If you would like to look at my work, feel free to do so while I set this job up."

"I would have thought it cheaper to replace the shoes than to have those repairs," Reese said.

Ha Minh grinned broadly, revealing mahogany colored stained teeth with several gaps set in a thin-lipped mouth.

"If you please, do not tell my customers that or I would be out of business rather quickly," he said.

Unlike Tran, Minh had almost no accent, just the slow southwestern pattern of speech. Evidentially, Minh was quick learner; Reese could detect no New Orleans type speech or hesitation normally found in those speaking English as a second language.

"We are detectives with the Dallas police department and I'm sure you know why we are here," Reese said.

The old man's smile did not fade.

"Yes, I expected you would be coming by," he said, with no note of animosity. "Mr. Tran called me at home late yesterday and asked if I could help him secure an attorney. I'm sure you have talked to Mr. Do, who gave me an excellent recommendation for him."

"What is your relationship to Mr. Tran?"

"He's just a friend," Ha Minh said. "He doesn't have many friends, so he comes by my house maybe once a week and we share gossip of the neighborhood and a few social drinks. He likes to watch old westerns on TV so he comes here."

Reese couldn't recall whether the TV in Tran's house worked or not. It didn't really matter.

"Mr. Tran told us that he has been robbed several times in the past few years," Reese said. "Has he told you anything about the robberies?"

The old cobbler nodded in the affirmative. He had picked up a strip of leather and was industriously shaping it to fit the shoe sole.

"People like Mr. Tran and I are always an easy mark for those who take what they do not earn," he said. "Mr. Tran has been robbed several times, but he is also afraid of the police. He says when they came; they treat him like he had done it himself. He is a prideful man and to be pushed around by the robbers and then the police was hurtful to him."

"Was he a soldier during the Vietnam War," Reese asked. He already knew the answer, but he wanted the conversation to go in another direction. He understood the sense of frustration the old grocer must have felt, being robbed of his labors and finding no recourse with the authorities. It didn't really matter who was at fault. The attitude was what was important.

The old cobbler sighed.

"We all were back then. It was a war of statistics with hundreds and thousands dying every day. Many blamed the Americans, but when they began pulling out of the country, the atrocities grew in number."

The tiny bent man crossed himself with the catholic sign of the cross.

"I could see the end coming and I got my family out of the country in the fall of 1972," the elderly Vietnamese said. "I didn't know Duc Tran then, but I don't think he left the country until Saigon fell three years later."

Charlie had seen the angle Reese was using in the questioning, and had backed off to a corner, close enough to listen to everything said, but far enough away to not become part of the conversation. He busied himself looking at the various leather items around them.

"Tran came out in the final days, didn't he?" Reese asked.

"He told me that the Viet Cong came in so fast that most of the soldiers threw their weapons away and ran, but there was no place to go. Dense smoke covered the city and he said you could smell the dead being burned by the thousands. The crowds were pushing in on the U.S. Embassy, and they were airlifting the staff and high ranking government officials out of the country. If they had stayed, they would have been killed. Tran was airlifted out on one of the final helicopters to leave the capital. His family was trapped outside the city."

"Did they make it out of the country?"

The old cobbler looked up from his work with sad watery eyes.

"He got word that they had joined the boat people fleeing the country, but the Viet Cong sent ships to stop them. Their boat may have gotten through, but thousands who escaped in the boats died at sea at the hands of pirates, who robbed them of what little they had, holed the boats so they would sink. They left the refugees to drown. He never heard from them again, so he really never knew what happened."

The sad story sent shivers of aching pain through Reese. However, while there was no way to condone what happened to Duc Tran, it was not justification for what he had done. It did go a long way toward explaining the mindset of a man who viewed himself as a constant victim. First the war, the loss of his family, the disruption of his life along the gulf, and then more people attempting to take what little he had away from him.

"I suppose Duc Tran killed people during the war, didn't he?"

"He was a soldier."

Those four words needed no further explanation. Reese viewed Tran as a man whose only success in life lay in his abilities as a soldier. Civilian life had not been easy for the old warrior.

"Was Duc Tran angry about what happened to him?"

Ha Minh took the leather he had been forming and moved to what appeared to be a heavy sewing machine. Carefully, he started fitting the leather over the shoe's upper piece to be stitched in place.

"Detective, I don't think any man could undergo the trials he has faced without bitterness," he said. "Tran, at times, was a very bitter man."

Reese knew his next words would shake the old man, but even he was shaken by the response.

"How long has Tran been planning to strike back at those who robbed him?"

The cobbler didn't answer at first. He picked up a cobbler's hammer in one hand and an awl in the other. He lined up the tools over a spot on the edge of the new sole. He struck down hard on the tool, and then inspected the results of his blow.

"The last few months have been the worst. He was robbed last April, and again in early July. The robbers refuse to leave him alone. The last time when he called police, he said the policeman told him that he would have to come to the police station to file a report; but since they only came in the store, grabbed some cigarettes and beer, and then fled, there would be no evidence to find them." Ha Minh sat the tools aside and looked up at Reese. "The policeman wouldn't even come to the store to investigate since Mr. Tran's loss was so small." Continuing to stare, he continued, "When thieves take everything you have, how can they call it small?"

Reese had no answer for that question. He could feel the bile rising in his stomach and he fought to control the nausea. "How did Mr. Tran get the gun he used when the police detective came into his store?"

He had expected a denial from the old cobbler that Tran had been involved in the murder, but Ha Minh was straightforward in his response.

"If you look around my shop, you will see very few shoes. Shoe repair is a dying art in this country. I also work in leather to make billfolds, horse bridles, saddles, belts, and chaps. The past few years, I have begun to build my business by making custom holsters for those wishing to carry a concealed weapon. I have forged a relationship with several gun dealers and they often loan me weapons to use in designing my holsters."

"You loaned one of the guns to your friend?" Reese asked.

The old cobbler nodded. "He said he wanted it for self-defense."

"What happened to the gun?"

"Duc Tran is an honorable man," Ha Minh said. "He returned the gun to me, saying he had no further use for it, a day after the shooting at his store."

"And you returned it to the gun dealer?"

"No," the cobbler said, "Mr. Brogan, the man who loaned the gun to me did not want it back. He said he had arranged to get the gun *off his books* and wanted nothing to do with it again."

Well, Mr. Brogan wasn't going to get what he wanted, Reese suspected.

Charlie, who had watched the exchange came closer and spoke.

"Do you still have the gun?"

The old man bowed his head.

"Yes, I still have it, but I do not know if Tran shot the man in his store. He never told me."

The cobbler got up and shuffled his feet toward the front door, stopping to reach under a makeshift counter just inside the door. He reached down and pulled out a paper bag and handed it to the senior detective. Inside the bag were a pistol and several rounds of ammunition.

"Have you touched the gun?" Charlie asked.

The cobbler shook his head, indicating his answer was negative.

"Not since he brought it back to me that day," he said. "You will not find my fingerprints on the gun, detective. I have always been a cobbler and I know little about guns."

After admonishing Ha Minh not to leave town and not to talk to anyone else about the case, the detectives told him that he could expect further questioning, and that he would have to testify against his friend.

The two detectives left the cobbler, and Reese called in to the lieutenant.

"We believe we have recovered the murder weapon," Reese said.

Charlie had reclaimed his position behind the wheel of the squad car.

"Get it to forensics and get back here. The chief is planning a news conference and he's trying to decide whether to give you an award or hang you from the nearest lamppost."

After signing off, Reese turned to his partner.

Charlie grunted, "I don't know about you, partner, but personally, my money is on option two."

CHAPTER 31

After booking the handgun into evidence, the homicide detectives turned it over to forensics with instructions to expedite fingerprint analysis, and, also, on matching a test fired bullet with the one taken from Detective Richard Carver's chest. Forensics Sergeant Bjorn Halsteen promised to call them the minute the comparisons were complete.

The detective pair then returned to their squad room to face the lieutenant before taking on the chief. Reese didn't know which he disliked worse, being under the eye of Lt. Mattie Reynolds, or having a sit-down discussion with the police chief, who likely would be listing his shortcomings as a police officer, and then imposing punishment. Arriving, he discovered the two events would take place at the same time. He couldn't even use the excuse that he didn't know what was expected of him, because the stern faces around the lieutenant's desk indicated he was about to find out in minute detail.

The chief had commandeered Reynolds desk and looked up solemnly as Charlie and Reese filed into the small office.

"Take a seat, we are going to be running through the highpoints of this investigation rather quickly," he said. "So far, I have found several items which bother me a great deal. I hope you can give me some clarification."

Reese eyed his partner nervously, but the veteran detective had become resigned to his fate, showing none of the stress that Reese felt. In that brief glance, Charlie conveyed to him to keep silent, that he intended to answer the chief.

The chief was thumbing through a stack of reports, evidentially provided by the lieutenant. Pausing, he peered at the detectives.

"When did you decide that Kindred James was a major suspect in the murder of detective Richard Carver?"

"We were given identification by the shopkeeper, Duc Tran, only hours after the shooting, but it took us several days to determine the identity of the suspect," Charlie said, keeping his answers direct, volunteering no other information.

"When did you decide, he was not a major suspect in this case?"

Reese had anticipated this question, but hearing that it was knowledge that they had eliminated him as a likely suspect was encouraging.

"Several hours before he was spotted and apprehended, we decided the likelihood he had committed the offense was very remote. It's very unusual for a person to change his behavior so radically that he would resort to violence, except maybe in a domestic situation. A violent crime did not match the background information we had developed on the suspect while establishing his identity."

"Certainly, that designation was not yours to make," the chief said.

Lt. Reynolds, who had sat quietly through the beginning of the interview, spoke up. "Chief, our job is mainly determining who committed a crime, not only finding the evidence, but eliminating possible suspects. They informed me of their doubts and I chose to designate Kindred James as a person of interest, not as a major suspect. My detectives followed proper protocol."

The chief cleared his throat.

"When did this notification go out to our patrols?" he asked the lieutenant.

"I agreed with their assessment and released that information immediately, which was approximately six hours before Kindred James was spotted."

The lieutenant had developed a bit of fire in her words.

"The information was passed along in time to have been part of the second shift briefing. Everyone in the department should have been aware James was no longer a major suspect in the killing, but was being sought only for questioning."

Appearing ill at ease, the chief flipped several pages of the report, before again glancing up to look toward Charlie Dent.

"Let's skip forward to the night of Kindred James' apprehension, shall we? You and your partner were off duty. What prompted you to go rushing across town to where he was taken down?"

Charlie leaned forward in his chair.

"I'm from the old school, and out of habit I keep a police scanner on most of the time. I heard a report that the cop killer had been spotted at an Abrams' location. Since our investigation had not confirmed another suspect, I felt we needed to investigate. Frankly, I was concerned that the bulletin that James had been downgraded to a person of interest had possibly not been relayed to the officer in charge," he said.

"Are you claiming that Lt. Reynolds did not handle this properly?"

"No sir," Charlie said. "The lieutenant acted properly. We are referring to actions taken by Captain Baldwin for not following departmental procedures which resulted in nearly killing an innocent civilian."

The chief stared at Charlie with a look of unadulterated hate.

"You are aware Captain Baldwin filed a complaint against you and your partner for attempting to interfere in the apprehension of a murder suspect?" the chief asked.

"Person of interest," Charlie said, calmly. "At that point, we had no suspects."

The chief winced like he had been struck in the side of the head.

"I remind you that he was the senior officer on location."

"We were aware," Charlie said. "We were also made aware that your office had not been contacted on this high-profile takedown. Nor was a tactical squad called, which is standard procedure in any anticipated extreme danger arrest."

"To indicate Captain Baldwin did not follow police procedures is a very serious charge," the chief indicated.

"Were you called before this incident went down?" Charlie answered his question with a question. "We had enough time to come from across Dallas to reach the scene to argue our case before Kindred James was shot down. There was no way we knew before we arrived at that location that procedures were not being followed. We were trying to save the life of a man we had every reason to believe was innocent of any crime."

"That's a stiff indictment," the chief said. "If you had the evidence that the takedown did not go the way it was reported, why did you chose to delay to report it at that time?"

"Honestly," Charlie sighed, "Baldwin had already dismissed our concerns, marginalized our protests, and portrayed our arguments as insubordination. He dismissed our protest about what happened and internal affairs did not question us. Then, evidence that we had gathered began to disappear, witnesses intimidated, and records were altered. I am concerned at this point that, if we had thought of the dashcam earlier and turned it in, the footage might have disappeared. We did not consider in the heat of the moment that we probably had caught the whole incident on film. That realization came several days later."

"And you couldn't think of a better way of revealing that tape other than releasing it to the media?" the chief asked, emphasizing it as an accusation.

"I think your investigation will find that the media gained access to the tape only after it was turned over to internal affairs," Charlie bluffed. The old detective was an expert in lying.

"Do you for one second believe my partner would have allowed the release of the tape to the media if either of us was aware it was going to show several minutes of his ass waving in the air?"

A quiver of a smile touched the lips of the police chief.

"That tape does put me in an awkward situation, Detective Dent," he said. "Your delayed actions in turning over the tape may have contributed to the unrest in our city. Since the tape was released, a lot of the wrath pointed toward this department has been deflected from us onto a small number of men involved in the shooting. In the black community, your efforts to save Kindred James' life have been recognized. Some are even calling your efforts to save him a heroic act."

The chief stopped and stared at the detectives for nearly a minute before continuing.

"I am faced with the dilemma of disciplining detectives whose actions saved a man's life, and calmed an angry segment of the city, marking these detectives as heroes among that faction; an action which will likely bring public opinion down around my neck. Despite the consequences, it is imperative that I emphasize to you in some way that you must follow the chain of command."

Reese was aware that if the police chief chose he could dismiss them from the force. Even the police union would have a difficult time defending a case against their firings. All they could do now was to wait for the chief to pass his judgment.

The verdict was not long in coming.

"I cannot allow your actions to go unpunished." The chief

hesitated, studying the faces of the two detectives. "I have decided to retain you, however. I am placing you on a month of restricted duty within police headquarters. Hopefully, under close supervision, you will learn to work as a part of this department. At the end of that period, you will return to full duty and all record of this disciplinary action will be expunged from your records. I cannot emphasis enough the consequences if you withhold information from me again, gentlemen."

Reese exhaled, realizing he had been holding his breath while waiting for the chief to decide their fate.

"Do you want to know how I arrived at this decision?" the chief asked. He did not wait for an answer. He smiled, "It was that stupid image of that ass waving in the air, and the image of my officers going to extremes to save the life of a citizen. That scene started me to questioning everything I had been told about what happened that night. You can't imagine how much this department needs heroes right now.

Coincidentally, I requested Captain Baldwin's resignation this morning. Until this incident, he was a good officer. I will challenge you two men to prove that you are worth the sacrifice I have made by not supporting my friend."

"Do you think Dallas County will indict Baldwin for attempting to kill Kindred James?" Charlie asked, which brought a withering response from the chief.

"Dallas County might indict a policeman for drunk driving, but there is no way the district attorney is going to get a grand jury to indict an officer for attempted murder."

While Reese Barrett and Charlie Dent sat stunned by the chief's decision, Charlie's cell phone rang.

Almost like a robot, he picked it up, identified himself, and listened intently. Reese listened as Charlie added a couple of 'okays', an 'are you positive' and, finally, 'we'll be right there' to the conversation.

Hanging up, he turned to the police chief, "Chief you wanted to be kept informed, so while you normally don't follow our day to day investigations, you might want to see this."

* * * *

An hour later, the police chief, Lieutenant Mattie Reynolds, an assistant district attorney and Detective Reese Barrett sat silently as they stared through a one-way glass into an interview room at Lew Sterrett jail. Duc Tran was escorted into the room wearing a jailhouse jump suit and handcuffs. The old man, only a shell of a man to begin with, now had the appearance of a child as he was led to the table in the center of the room.

His attorney, a fleshy, middle aged man with graying blonde hair, cut in a style that seemed almost retro seventies and detective Charlie Dent were already seated at the table.

The attorney was the first to speak.

"I have advised my client that he does not have to answer your questions," he said.

Charlie shrugged, "He doesn't have to speak, he just needs to listen."

The senior detective began laying out the evidence before them.

"We know there was no attempted robbery in your store when Robbery Detective Richard Carver was killed. We are also aware that you attempted to frame another man for the crime."

The preamble left no room for doubt that Charlie Dent was in control of the situation.

Tran continued to stare at him with angry, watery eyes.

Charlie talked about the life the defendant had lived, bringing his personal history up to the point of his relocation in Dallas after Hurricane Katrina.

"If you ever had any friends, you left them all behind when you came here. It must have been extremely lonely. People didn't show you any respect; you didn't even get the respect that comes with age in your native land, did you?" he asked, not waiting for an answer. "When you were treated with disrespect long enough, you struck out in anger."

"The only friend you had left in the whole world even turned against you, Duc Tran," Charlie said, reaching down to a satchel beside him on the floor and lifted a paper bag out and put on the table in front of him. "Ha Minh said you returned this to him the day after the shooting in your store. It's the weapon that was used to kill a police officer and it has your prints all over it. We have matched the slug shot into Detective Carver's chest with one test fired from this weapon. There is no doubt that you fired that slug into his chest, but I want to know why," Charlie rose to his feet and stood staring down at the manacled prisoner.

He stood silently waiting for Tran to respond to the pregnant pause.

Tran's attorney wisely chose to remain a silent witness to the unfolding drama.

Nearly a minute passed before Tran raised his head and glared at Charlie. Slowly, he began to speak in a voice only slightly above a whisper.

"I did not shoot your officer. My friend, Ha Minh, came to the store shortly after midnight to show me a gun. He knew about the robberies I had suffered and wanted to help. He thought I might be interested in getting a gun. Ha knew a man, who could get me one."

"So, you are saying Ha Minh was the one who shot the detective?"

"He didn't have to say I shot the man in the store," Duc Tran whispered, "I wouldn't have betrayed him."

In the observation room, Reese turned to the lieutenant, "I'm on it. We'll have Ha Minh in custody within the hour."

The Dallas police chief, who had watched the exchange in silence, turned to Lieutenant Reynolds, "Is this what you expected me to witness?"

Reynolds grimaced, "Not exactly, but it does explain how the murder weapon happened to be in the store and why we were unable to recover it at the scene. Tran had enough time to get rid of the gun, but there was always a chance someone could walk in on him."

"What happens next?"

"We have two men, both with an equal opportunity, who are pointing at the other as the one who killed Detective Carver. It won't take very long to determine who pulled the trigger, but now we are aware that both suspects were there when he died."

"Which do you think shot him?" the chief asked the lieutenant.

"My opinion or the opinion of my men is not important, chief. We are silent witnesses to what happened in that store. No one will be railroaded by a rush to judgment. In due time, we will have all your questions answered."

"So, it all comes down to a pair of old men, neither likely to live long enough to see justice served," the chief sighed with a note of resignation. "Where does it go from here?"

"I would say with some type of plea bargain," the lieutenant said. "I can't see the district attorney insisting on a capital murder in this case even though it was a policeman killed. My bet is a long term in prison, which, because of their ages, neither will survive."

"Any chance this was an accidental shooting?" the police chief asked.

Reynolds responded, "My detectives reported there was every indication Tran had kept his store open very late for the last several weeks, probably waiting for someone to attempt to rob him. He's ex-military and was said to be an excellent shot. If he wanted revenge for a lifetime of pain and disappointments, the target of his rage was less than ten feet in front of him. Whether he was the one taking the shot is immaterial. I think he chose the bed he's lying in and so has his only friend."

CHAPTER 32

Two weeks later, things were beginning to settle down.

The Police Chief announced that he had accepted the resignation of Captain Andrew James Baldwin and had started an investigation into illegal activities committed by him and four other patrolmen, which could lead to criminal charges. They were suspended from the police force pending the outcome of the Internal Affairs investigation. Charlie and Reese were elated that their names were not among those being scrutinized under the microscope.

Charlie had heard rumors from one of his many sources that the city council was planning an emergency meeting to approve a settlement offer with Kindred James. It was whispered that the city was willing to offer him 17.6 million dollars not to sue the city. That was the sum being bantered about as his potential worth in his first NFL contract, if he had not been shot down.

He had been projected as a three-year All-American for the Oklahoma Sooners prior to the shooting. Apparently willing to fulfill their obligation to their potential superstar, the university offered to retain James on full scholarship in the hopes he would be able to contribute to their program in the future.

When Reese and Charlie went by his hospital room that Monday morning, they found Kindred James asleep. His mother,

Eleanor James, and Paul Godfrey, foreman at the machine shop in Garland, were seated at the side of the bed against the window.

Godfrey rose as the detectives entered the room. He looked down at Mrs. James, who remained seated. "I'll keep in touch, Eleanor, we've all been praying for him."

Eleanor nodded and watched the foreman leave the room.

"At least one of the men Kindred worked with has dropped by every day to check up on us," she said.

From what they had found out about Kindred, Reese was not surprised by the loyalty he had inspired. Several bouquets of flowers rested on a nearby stand and one of the largest was marked as coming from his fellow workers.

"How is he doing today?" Reese asked, shifting his vision from the man in the bed to his mother.

"He still has the nightmares and the headaches still worry me, but the doctors say they will eventually go away. They have him scheduled for another surgery to remove some bone chips near his spine, but they say chances of making a nearly full recovery is still a possibility. I still don't understand why the Lord would allow my boy to suffer so much pain."

Charlie slipped past Reeves and laid claim to the chair recently vacated by Godfrey.

"I'm not sure any of us will ever understand that," he said, reaching out a hand to the woman. "I prefer to believe God saved his life rather than caused the pain."

Kindred's mother bowed her head and shook it slowly side to side.

"Oh, I really don't blame God, but what about the beast that did this to my son?"

Neither Charlie nor Reese had an answer for that question.

Charlie spoke up first.

"We found evidence that he may have intentionally attempted

to kill Kindred out of revenge for the death of his former partner. Whether the Grand Jury will indict him for that crime remains to be determined. The justice system doesn't always work the way we intend, and sometimes the guilty go free, but we know they will eventually have to answer to a higher power, Mrs. James. I don't believe any of us would prefer he face that judgment."

"The doctors said Kindred will probably be in rehab for a year," she said. "That man stole a year out of his life."

"From what I understand, Baldwin was a decent man before this incident," Charlie said slowly, as he appeared to search for the right words. "What he did was wrong and he's going to live with that knowledge for the rest of his life. If he escapes criminal charges, he still knows this will haunt him forever. If you allow it to make you bitter, you will suffer as much as he will. Seek justice, but let the hate go."

"Oh, I don't really hate him," she said, leaning back in her chair. "I just get emotional when I think about what he did. What's going to happen to Mr. Tran? I can't understand why he pointed out Kindred as the shooter."

"We may never know why, Mrs. James. We believe Tran saw a face he was familiar with and could easily describe." Charlie considered the steely eyes of the resigned mother. "There was no reason or justification for what he did although he may not have intended for Kindred to be hurt."

Reese spoke up, "Tran's taking a plea bargain. He's getting twenty to life on a murder charge. Technically, he could eventually go free, but at his age, it's likely a life sentence. Ha Ming has decided to fight his conspiracy charge, but he will not live long enough to see the outside of his jail cell, so technically justice has been served."

"I would have thought they would have executed him for killing a police officer and what he did to my son," she said.

"A part of justice, sometimes, is mercy," Reese said. "What could society hope to gain by executing a confused, paranoid old man?"

ABOUT THE AUTHOR

David Campbell, descended from a true pioneer family, traces his family history in Oklahoma back to the 1890s in Indian territory. Older history reveals a great-great grandfather who was a Texas Ranger and Civil War veteran. Older generations included veterans in the Revolutionary War. These facts contributed to his strong ties to history.

David is a US Navy veteran, serving during the Viet Nam War, a graduate of the University of Oklahoma, an award-winning AP writer, and a former business owner. The father of three daughters, David currently resides in Mesquite, Texas, with his wife, Becky, and two cats, which tolerate him.

Rush to Judgment is his fifth novel and the second of his *Silent Witness Mystery Series*.